Don't Breathe a Word

A Novel

by

Dona McAfee Glasscock

ISBN 978-0-0761012-3-9

In Memory of

Dorrance and Becky

Lifetime companions for 78 years

Don't Breathe a Word

1

Mama tried her best to change me into the girl she thought I should be. But living on the ranch in Fish Lake Valley, Nevada, in 1913 was a bigger obstacle to her success than she could hope to overcome.

The ranch is nestled in the high desert between the Silver Peak Mountains to the east and the White Mountains to the west. That high altitude made for hot, dry summers and frigid winters. We had no electricity or plumbing. Aside from the rich alfalfa fields, there was mostly just dirt and cows and horses and work. Lots of work. But I didn't mind. Cowboys were used to hard work and I fancied myself a cowboy. Not a cow*girl*, a cow*boy*. And that was the problem.

Mama tried her best in spite of these almost insurmountable odds. When one of the local ladies started a ballet class, Mama forced me to attend. I hated wearing the cute little costumes she made for recitals. And I disgraced her with my lack of grace at the performances. Mama was very strict about after school activities. The school was a one-room building about four miles from the ranch. I usually rode one of the horses there and back. But Mama insisted I wear dresses and petticoats to school just the same. After school I was to come directly home. "No fishing or swimming in the creek or playing with the boys."

Except for ballet, I tried hard to make Mama approve of me. I mostly complied with her rules and tried to be enthusiastic about the handiwork she required of me. All those hours sitting and stitching samplers and doilies about drove me mad. But I did it without complaint. I was an exceptional student, always with the highest grades in school. I faithfully did my chores. But I preferred being out with the ranch hands to washing dishes and clothes, ironing, dusting, and sweeping.

There were some chores I *did* like, however. Beating rugs allowed me to improve my baseball swing. Also, Mama and I had worked for years to perfect the soil for our vegetable garden, turning it from dry, sandy, alkaline dirt into rich loam. We added manure and straw each season until we could finally grow the best vegetables and flowers in the valley. We often took home ribbons from county fairs in Tonopah and Bishop.

It seemed like the older I got the stricter Mama was about my comings and goings. It got to be such a burden to me that I began to lie and deceive her just to get away now and then. I remember once I told Mama that Miss Wilson wanted me to stay after school to help her with a special project. Then, after school I went up McAfee Creek to where beavers had dammed it up, making a perfect swimming hole.

In summer, this was the one cool place in the whole valley. The cottonwood trees overhung the clear, cold runoff from the surrounding mountains. If there was any breeze at all, it tended to blow down the creek bed. It was late afternoon on an oppressively hot day the end of May. By the time I got to the stream, the sweat running down my back, beneath my dress, itched so badly I thought I'd cry. I jumped off my horse, undressed down to my birthday suit, and dived into the water. It was heavenly to be immersed to my neck, and it was even more delightful knowing I did it on the sly. I splashed and swam until my lips must have turned blue with the icy cold water. When the sun sank low on the horizon I realized I'd stayed too long. I knew I was probably in for a scolding.

I dressed and rode for home, almost pushing the old horse past his endurance. I sneaked into the kitchen through the back door and began setting the table and acting as if I'd been busy there for quite awhile. Presently Mama came in and started asking me about the project for Miss Wilson. I made up some story about helping to put up a display of student art on the wall of the classroom, all the while working as fast as I could. I brought in a load of wood for the stove and a pail of water for the after-supper dishes, trying to ignore Mama's penetrating looks. Then Mama came up behind me and lifted my long, dark braid from the back of my dress. It was then that I knew I hadn't fooled her at all. My hair was still wet from swimming.

Mama pushed me forward over the dinner table and threw my dress and petticoats up over my head. Then she pulled my bloomers down, exposing my bare bottom, and gave me a few good whacks with the back of the tortoise-shell hairbrush. It didn't hurt so awfully much, but while she was whacking away Uncle Leonard walked in through the back door. The idea of Uncle seeing me with my backside exposed was so humiliating that I ran to bed without supper and cried myself to sleep.

We didn't have a church in Fish Lake, but one of the ranchers hosted a Bible study on Sundays in his parlor. Mama and my uncles weren't much for churchgoing so we didn't usually attend. Occasionally an itinerant preacher would happen through the area and that was cause for a big picnic and revival meeting. We skipped the Saturday revival and Sunday service, but in the afternoon we packed the wagon and went to McAfee Creek for the picnic. Mama insisted that we dress in our best clothes. When we arrived at the creek I knew she had been right because all the girls and women were in their fanciest clothing, busy setting out food or just visiting. Mama told me to sit with the other girls and mind my manners. I didn't think this picnic was going to be much fun.

The preacher and all the men were eating and talking down by the creek. I didn't see any of the boys.

The girls were talking about sewing and boys, and I found the conversation decidedly *un*stimulating. So after a while I wandered upstream. That's where I found the boys. They had made a target on the trunk of a huge cottonwood tree and were throwing their knives at it. They boasted about their perfect aims and teased one another about each poor shot. They were all pretty poor shots if you asked me. After several minutes of observation, I asked if I could throw, too. Of course, the boys knew I could pitch a baseball, but they never saw me throw a knife. So they engaged in some good-natured ribbing at my expense. They laughed and pushed each other and made some disparaging remarks about throwing like a girl. And then they magnanimously invited me to throw, one of them offering me his knife.

I reached into the side of my high-topped shoe and pulled out the 6-inch hunting knife I carried there. With a quick snap of the wrist and a follow-through like a baseball pitch I sent my knife square into the center of the target. The silence was palpable. I loved showing up the boys at their own games, and their silence I took as a sign of respect until I saw them all staring behind me instead of at the target. Not one had seen my expert shot. They were staring at my purple-faced mama. She was horrified that I carried my knife to the picnic and embarrassed her by competing with boys.

Now, Mama knew I had that knife. She hated that I had it. But, so far, she could figure no way to make me give it up. Uncle Leonard had given it to me when one of our dogs got bit by a rattler and died. He said I needed to have it for safety and he showed me how to cut a rattlesnake bite and suck out the poison. But, on many occasions, Mama caught me "wasting my time" carving animals and flowers out of small pieces of wood. I told Mama I was just developing my God-given talents. After all, it was Mama herself who taught me the parable of the talents. She said we shouldn't neglect the talents God gave us, but develop them. She was, at the time, trying to convince me that I needed to stay in ballet

6

because of my God-given talent. Anyway, I think Mama knew that if she took my knife away she wouldn't have a prayer of keeping me in ballet lessons.

It was quite by accident that I learned to throw that knife. I was down by McAfee Creek one spring day, leaned up against the big cottonwood tree, carving some little critter. For some reason I stopped my carving and gazed off into the distance. Then I just flicked the knife at a young tree across the way. I couldn't believe my eyes when I hit it on the first throw. So I figured I had a new God-given talent and began to practice throwing. That was a couple of years ago and now I could even hit a moving target, if the target was moving slowly enough — like a desert tortoise or some such thing. God given talent or not, after this fiasco, I was pretty sure Mama would take that knife away.

But she didn't. And she didn't really say much more about the picnic episode either. But I knew she hadn't forgotten about it. It was soon apparent that Mama was letting several of my infractions slip by. That's when I knew she was gravely ill.

Mama had always worked hard and was always tired, but this was different. She coughed until I thought her insides would come up, and her skin was ash-colored. Then one night she told the family that the doctor wanted her to go to the sanitarium in Bishop for awhile. But Mama said her big concern was what to do with me.

Uncle Frank and Uncle Leonard said I would stay with them as usual. After all, I was old enough to take care of myself and continue to help out on the ranch. But Mama wouldn't have it. She started in about my needing female companionship and influence. She made a pretty good argument in light of the picnic-knife-throwing escapade and my uncles believed she was right. So Uncle Leonard went up the road about three miles the other side of the schoolhouse where the Sisters lived.

Iris and Abigail had a nice little ranch that they managed by themselves. Uncle Leonard asked them if they could board me while my mother was in the sanitarium in

Bishop. The Sisters were thrilled to do it and spent a great deal of effort preparing a bedroom for me from a little storage room at the back of the house.

Uncle Leonard was happy that he had kept me in the Valley, just a few miles from home, where he could see me often. Mama seemed okay with the idea too, until one of the ladies from Bible Study came over for tea. When Mrs. Tanner heard that I would be staying with the Sisters, she took in a deep "Oh-my-Goodness" breath and almost choked on her tea. She looked to make sure I was out of earshot. Actually, I was just across the room reading. Mrs. Tanner lowered her voice so that I wouldn't hear what she had to say. But Mrs. Tanner was a little deaf and always talked louder than she thought. So I heard every word she told Mama.

"Oh, Eva! You can't send Dorrance to live with the Sisters!"

Mama wanted to know why not. So Mrs. Tanner said, "Why they're *sapphists*, you know."

"What?" Mama replied. "Sapphists? What's that? You mean Catholics?"

"No! Sapphists! You know — unnatural."

"Unnatural?" Mama said.

"Yes. You know they sleep in the same bed!" With that, she raised her eyebrows and gave a smug little look and pursed her lips.

I was really confused and so was Mama, at first anyway. I thought the Sisters probably only had one bed and it was probably big enough for two. After all, Mama and I had slept in the same bed for years after Daddy died in the mining accident.

Then Mrs. Tanner went on: "And they're *not* sisters," she hissed. She glanced over to where I sat and lowered her voice just a decibel or two. "They don't have the same last name."

"Well, I don't have the same last name as my sisters. And how do you know all this anyway?" Mama retorted, still skeptical of this new gossip.

8

"Because... because," Mrs. Tanner stammered, "because my Joe went out there to deliver a package. He knocked and called but no one was home. A storm was coming up so he just opened the door to set the box inside the door. Then the lightning started, so Joe stayed in the house a few minutes to avoid getting struck. He just moseyed through the house and saw that they had only the one bed."

"Well, I still don't see how you can make that add up to sapphism," Mama said.

The conversation stopped there. But evidently Mama did make it all add up to sapphism, whatever that was, because the next thing I knew Mama told me I was being sent to California to live with my great-grandmother.

I heard Mama and Uncle Leonard arguing about it a couple of times after that. Uncle Leonard said he didn't care what the Sisters were, that they had always been kind and cheerful, and that they did a darn good job taking care of their place. Mama said that was all well and good but that I had enough strikes against me without having the whole valley gossiping about whether or not I was being indoctrinated by sapphists. So the matter was settled. I was going hundreds of miles from the only home I'd ever known, away from the desert and the creek, away from the horses, cows and chickens, to live in some stuck-up city in California.

2

Uncle Frank and I jostled along on the buggy seat, headed to the train depot in Goldfield. The dust from the horse hooves and wagon wheels rose up in a soft cloud. The elastic that held my hat pinched the tender skin under my chin. Sweat trickled down my back and I felt my stockings grow squishy inside my high-topped shoes. A single tear escape from my eye and I quickly brushed it away. It was disgraceful to cry. Mama always said that tears didn't help and just made other people feel bad. I certainly didn't want Uncle Frank to feel bad.

Mama had reached a "crisis" a few days before and had been rushed to Bishop. Even in her desperate condition she made me promise to wear my best clothes on the train to Great-grandmother's. It would reflect badly on Mama's mothering to have me show up in Bakersfield in anything but my best.

I wondered now if I would ever see Mama alive again. This was her second trip to the sanatorium. The first had been shortly after Daddy died, so I was too young to remember. But this time I felt the loss keenly. Mama and I didn't always see eye-to-eye, especially lately, but I would miss her. More than that, I would miss my uncles and pets and the place I called home. My throat was tight and my eyes stung with unshed tears.

Uncle Frank's voice broke the silence.

"This is quite an adventure you're on, little girl," he quipped. "Bet you'll love the big city. Lots to do, people to meet. And school will be a lot more challenging than the little old schoolhouse you're used to."

I considered Uncle Frank's remarks, but made no reply. So he continued his monologue.

"The train ride will be exciting too. All that beautiful country to see between here and there. Be sure not to talk to strange men. It's okay to talk to women and kids, but stay away from men. Promise me?"

I said "Uh-huh." And we rode along in silence while I struggled to control my emotions. Then I thought my silence was probably hurtful to Uncle Frank, so I tried to participate in the conversation he was working so hard to start.

"What's it like? Bakersfield," I asked.

"I've only been there once. A long time ago. Uncle Sabert tells me there's a trolley system now. There's a library and a couple of theaters. Some nice parks, too. I think you'll like it. And next summer you'll come home."

"Promise?" I asked.

"Only if you want to. By then you'll have so many friends and interests you'll probably want to stay in Bakersfield."

"No, I won't," I assured him. I couldn't imagine not wanting to come home for the summer. Bakersfield could never be *that* good.

I could see Goldfield in the distance as we came up the final grade. A fear rose up in me. I was traveling alone into the unknown. I didn't remember ever meeting Great-grandmother or Uncle Sabert. I had never been west of the Sierra Nevada range.

My voice shook as I asked, "What's Grandmother like?"

11

"Gram?" Uncle Frank smiled. "You'll like her. She's old as the hills and smart as a whip and just eccentric enough to be funny. And she's going to like you, too."

"Are you sure?"

"You're so much like her, she couldn't help it! Let me tell you a little about your great-Gram. First off, she'll want you to call her Gram, not Grandmother. When her husband died, she moved to Los Angeles and worked as a high school teacher to support herself and her kids. There's nothing she doesn't know about math and science. And she's a renegade of sorts. You know, when she married she refused to give up her maiden name. She has always called herself Miss Mary Creel." Uncle Frank chuckled. "She was an early supporter of suffrage for women and always vocal about justice issues. She was even arrested once for leading a demonstration on the Los Angeles City Hall steps. Many people dislike her politics. But she's very persuasive. Eventually, most people come to see things her way."

"Sounds as if she always has to be right," I thought out loud.

"She doesn't have to be. But most folks eventually decide she is," answered Uncle Frank. "But she's a good listener, too. She's not bossy. She prefers to let people make their own mistakes and learn from them. And she'll never say 'I told you so.' You know, I kind of envy you being able to live with her."

Gram didn't sound like the image I had conjured up in my brain. I guessed that was good. But I still regretted having to move. I expected I'd have to wear dresses all the time and stay clean and sit around with girls talking about boys and clothes and dances. All I really wanted to do was dress in my dungarees and run barefoot and ride and fish and swim. And how would I ever realize my lifelong goal of striking it rich? I just knew I would find an undiscovered vein of gold or silver in the mountains east of the ranch. Someone was bound to beat me to it before I came home again next summer.

I let out a long sigh, and Uncle Frank reached over and patted my knee. "You'll be okay," he said with a smile.

Goldfield was a dusty mining town. The school, firehouse, and hotel were built of brick. All the houses were clapboard shacks and the merchant buildings were clapboard buildings with two-story false fronts. The buggy rolled up in front of the depot. Uncle Frank ran in and bought me a one-way ticket.

When he returned to the wagon, he handed me the ticket with his left hand and slipped the knife from its sheath in my shoe with his right.

"I'll just keep this for you until next summer," he said.

"Please let me take it, Uncle Frank."

"I don't reckon there'll be any rattlesnakes in the city."

Then he apologized for rushing off to get to the chores back at the ranch. He would be hard-pressed to get back before dark. He gave me a quick hug. If I hadn't seen the tears in his eyes, I would have been angry about losing my knife to him. But instead of anger I just felt lonely standing beside the tracks waiting for the train to arrive.

The sun beat down on my back. That silly straw hat with its elastic cord was more than I could endure. I lugged my suitcase across the street to the public outhouse. When I emerged I had changed into my farm clothes and boots and tucked my hair up under my farm cap. No way was I going to ride for two days on a train in that uncomfortable dress. I would change back into my good clothes just before the train arrived in Bakersfield.

The shiny, black engine and brightly painted cars hissed and squealed to a stop. Dozens of men disembarked, probably headed to the rapidly depleting gold mines. I lugged my baggage to the platform. The conductor hoisted my suitcase aboard as I struggled with my satchel. Once aboard, I noticed the train was nearly empty.

I chose a seat in the center of the car. It took all my strength as I tried to boost my suitcase onto the rack above my seat. I saw the conductor coming up the aisle and expected him to help me. But when he passed by, he merely tipped his hat and walked on. Perhaps I was too hasty in changing my clothes. Surely he would have helped if I had been a girl. After my case was successfully settled on the rack, I placed my satchel on the seat next to me, hoping no one would sit there. The red plush of the seat belied its hardness. My butt was certain to be calloused by the time I arrived in Bakersfield.

I took a few moments to look over my surroundings. A woman and two small children were sitting across the aisle and a seat behind mine. Two men sat in the seats directly behind me. Many of the windows had been lowered so the hot summer air could circulate. At the end of the car I noticed a water spigot and a tin cup. A sign hung above it indicating there were restrooms around the corner.

My stomach grumbled loudly. I realized it had been hours since breakfast and I was starving. I unwrapped my lunch as the train pulled away from the station. I bit into a fried chicken leg. Then I ate another one and a roll with butter and jam. After that I went to the water dispenser at the end of the car and took a long drink, and then another.

I returned to my seat and listened to the train clack along, swaying gently from side to side, and before long sleep overtook me.

I was awakened by loud voices and hissed curses. The men in the seat behind were engaged in a heated political discussion. The woman across the aisle told them to quiet down and watch their language and "didn't they know women and children were present." One man rudely told the woman to move if she didn't like it. So she did. I thought about changing seats myself, but couldn't face the prospect of moving my suitcase. So I stayed put and listened to the growing argument behind me.

At the first stop the men got off. Another man got on and sat in the same seat behind me. He smelled so bad I thought I'd throw up. Even the breeze created by the open windows didn't dilute the smell of sweat and stale liquor. I saw an empty seat at the end of the car and moved there, taking care to watch my suitcase. Again I placed my satchel on the seat next to me so no one would sit there.

At the next stop many people boarded and I could no longer monopolize the seat beside to me. A man sat down, smiled, and said, "Hi, son."

Remembering my promise to Uncle Frank not to speak to men, I left my seat, satchel, and suitcase and went into the parlor car. I liked it better here because there was no smoking allowed. The fresh air smelled good. I found a seat and gazed out the window until we reached the next stop. Then I hurried to my old seat to check on my bags. The man was gone. My suitcase was still above my first seat, thank goodness. But my satchel with all my food, books, and money was gone. As the train pulled away from the station, I saw that man, my seatmate, walking along the platform with my satchel in his hand.

I ran from car to car looking for the conductor. By the time I found him and reported my satchel stolen, it was too late. The conductor would report the theft, but didn't hold out hope that my bag would be recovered. He said only, "Tough luck, son." I thought that had I been in my dress, I probably would have garnered more sympathy.

I realized just how much had been stolen from me. I had all my books, my two dollars traveling money, food, and other things in my bag. I could do without the food and money, although it would be a long, hungry trip. Also, the sheath that normally held my knife was in that bag.

"Thank goodness Uncle Frank has my knife," I thought.

* * *

I awoke to the conductor shaking my shoulder and saying urgently, "Wake up, young man! This is your stop!"

"Oh, no!" I thought. "And I haven't changed out of my boy clothes yet."

Nothing could be done about it now. I jumped up and pulled my suitcase from the shelf and headed to the door. As soon as I stepped to the depot platform the train began moving out of the station. I knew Uncle Sabert was going to meet me. My stomach growled formidably. It was a wonder I was alive at all with nothing to eat for the last twenty-four hours. The other arrivals greeted their friends and relatives and gradually moved off the platform. Finally, there was only one greeter left, a short, powerfully-built man in a white apron. This had to be Uncle Sabert; he looked just like all the Logan men. I walked up to him and smiled. He gazed past me to the departing train with a look of distress on his face.

"Uncle Sabert?" I ventured.

We made eye contact and he did a sort of double-take. He reached over and removed my hat. My braid tumbled down my back. His face lit up with a broad smile.

"Sorry," he said. "I was expecting my *niece*."

I don't know if it was my hunger, or the heat, or the long trip, or my embarrassment at being caught in my boy's clothes, but tears ran down my face before I could brush them away. Immediately Uncle Sabert's smile vanished and he hugged me close to comfort me. I was nearly as tall as he and that embarrassed me even more——a big girl like me blubbering like a baby. What would Mama say!

"I brought the truck," he said softly. "Let's get you home."

Soon we were gliding along in the grocery delivery truck. My eyes and nose ran and I wiped them on my shirt sleeve. Uncle Sabert pulled a hanky from his pocket and offered it to me. I wiped my face and blew my nose and laid the hanky on the seat between us. Uncle Sabert mopped his sweaty brow and returned the hanky to my knee. I glanced at Uncle's sweat-stained armpits and then at his laugh-wrinkled face. We made a pitiful pair, both using that stinky hanky to mop ourselves up. I smiled at him in spite of myself. He patted my knee, just as Uncle Frank had done on the way to the depot. At once I loved this man, my Uncle Sabert, and felt as if I were home. I rested my head on his shoulder and fell asleep.

3

I lay with my eyes closed and listened to the soft clatter of dishes and smelled bacon frying and biscuits fresh from the oven. My stomach roared in anticipation. A gentle breeze flowed over my body. It smelled like an autumn shower. I opened my eyes to strange surroundings. This must be Gram's house, I thought.

I sat up and wondered briefly how I got here. Uncle Sabert must have carried me inside last night and deposited me on this couch. I still wore my travel-soiled dungarees, but my shoes had been removed and a light afghan had been draped over me. I shook off my sleepiness and sat up, energized and excited to start this new life.

The room in which I found myself was definitely *not* what I expected. I expected an old lady's house to be full of doilies and nick-knacks, floral prints and lace. None of these were present in this plain, cozy room. The furniture was overstuffed and upholstered in heavy, dark fabric. The tables were of dark wood. All the surfaceswere clear of clutter. A braided rug was the only color in the room.

My attention was drawn to an unusual sight. A barrel imbedded in the wall, revolved rapidly, spewing out a fierce wind. It was some kind of fan, but much cooler. I stood in front of it, letting the air blow through my thin shirt. The tendrils of hair that had come loose from my braid whipped around my face. We needed one of these contraptions on the ranch!

I followed my nose to the kitchen. There was Gram. She was taller than Uncle Sabert, or any of the Logans for that matter. You could tell from her salt-and-pepper hair that she once had dark hair, like mine. She had inquisitive brown eyes. She's the reason I look so different from my other relatives, I thought. Gram looked up from the biscuits she was shaking from the cookie sheet.

"Dorrance," she said simply. Then she folded me into her ample figure and hugged me long and warm. I thought she might not release me at all. She put her hands on my shoulders and held me at arms' length and looked straight into my eyes.

"You must be half-starved," she said. "Wash up at the sink and sit down and eat." She heaped up my plate with eggs, bacon, biscuits with butter and honey, and sliced peaches with a dollop of whipped cream. Mama was a good cook, but I'd never eaten such a scrumptious breakfast. Could it taste so wonderful because it had been a day and a half since I last ate? I wolfed down what was on my plate and asked for more biscuits and fruit.

"What an appetite!" Gram exclaimed.

"I'm usually not such a pig," I said, "but I haven't eaten since I got on the train." Then I told Gram about the theft of my satchel.

As I related the story and counted the possessions that were stolen, I began to feel teary. The food I would have eaten by now anyway, so that was no great loss. The two dollars traveling money I might have spent on the train. But my books — seven volumes that had been Christmas and birthday gifts — I would miss terribly. I'd also lost the dresser set that had belonged to Mama's mother. It could never be replaced. Then I thought of Mama's proverb: There's never a great loss without some small gain. It was then I realized that terrible best dress and hat were gone forever.

"It never occurred to me that someone would steal from a child," I said. "I should have been more careful."

"Perhaps, but as for me, I'd rather give people the benefit of the doubt and trust them until they give me a reason not to," said Gram. "It's better than living in constant fear."

"I guess you're right," I said. "Gram, in the dining room, that thing in the wall, blowing air: What is it?"

"It's called a swamp cooler."

"How does it work?"

"It has pads of woven straw around the blower. Water drips on them so the air it blows is cooler. Kind of like when you put a block of ice in front of a fan. I couldn't get along without it.

"If you want to take a walk and see your new surroundings, you best do it early. By dinnertime it'll be too hot. Just about everyone hunkers around their fans in the afternoon trying to keep cool. The bathtub is off the kitchen there. You can take a bath and I'll wash these clothes of yours and get them on the line. They'll be dry in two shakes of a lamb's tail."

I cleared the table while Gram washed the dishes and left them to dry on a towel on the table.

The bathroom was a sight for sore eyes. It had a huge, deep tub that stood on legs. There was a cold water spout that ran directly into it. Gram carried hot water from the stove so my bath wouldn't be too cold. There was also a water closet! No outhouse in the city.

I undressed and left my clothes outside the bathroom door for Gram to wash. I felt guilty about making work for her right away. At home I always did my and Mama's laundry. I promised myself that this was the last time I would trouble Gram. By the time I had a long soak, Gram had found some clothes in my suitcase and handed them to me through the bathroom door.

The thought of wearing a dress and all the underwear that went with it made me cringe. It was just too hot. But I wanted to explore the town right away. So I dressed in bloomers, stockings, chemise, petticoats, and dress, and headed for the front door. I had yet to see my room, but that could wait. I was excited to see my new neighborhood.

"Bye, Gram," I called on my way out the door.

"Don't get lost and be home at noon."

I stood on the front porch and looked east and west along 18th Street. It was already incredibly hot. I looked at the thermometer hanging by the front door. It read eighty-eight in the shade at nine in the morning. Bakersfield was definitely hotter than Fish Lake, probably because it didn't cool down at night. No wonder Gram had the swamp cooler running so early.

I decided to walk east. Just a block and a half from Gram's house there was a two-story brick building with a basement. The sign in front said Franklin School. I supposed this would be the school I would attend in September. The grass around the building was sun-burned brown. I heard shouts coming from behind the school and went to investigate.

I stood in the shade of the building and watched five boys run up and down the basketball court. They were trying to play a game, but had only two boys on one team and three on the other. Mostly they were just dribbling the ball up and down the dirt court. There was a girl standing on the sidelines watching. She kept shouting over and over that the boys should let her play. Finally one of the boys stopped the game and told her to go away because "girls can't play." I didn't understand why. She certainly couldn't be any worse at the game than the boys were. And they could have used another player to even up the sides. I wanted to play too, but didn't want to be humiliated by being told to go away.

I turned quickly and headed for Gram's house. I ran around back and pulled my boy clothes from the line. They were dry except for the seams. I figured the damp seams would help keep me cool. I scrambled up the back steps and into the bathroom to change.

"Is that you, Dorrance?" Gram yelled.

"It's me. I just came to change clothes so I can play basketball with the boys at the school."

"You couldn't play in your dress I suppose. Too cumbersome, huh?" said Gram.

"*That* and the boys said girls can't play."

"I wonder how long you'll be able to pass for a boy? Not long, I expect."

"Long enough to play basketball this morning, though," I said, tucking my hair up into my cap. "I'll be back before dinner." Off I ran toward the playground.

When I arrived at the court, I stood on the sidelines for a few minutes observing the boys. The biggest kid seemed to be the leader. He was a few inches taller than me and probably thirty pounds heavier. There was a kid about my size who had orange hair and freckles all over his face and arms. One of the boys was short and stocky and looked more like a halfback than a basketball player. There were two smaller boys, athletic in build, but much younger than the others.

Pretty soon I hollered to them, "Mind if I play?"

"You know how?" the boy with the ball asked.

"Sure I do," I lied. I'd seen the game played and figured I'd learn as I went along. "It would even up your teams."

"You can play on Red's team," said the biggest boy, indicating the kid with orange hair.

"Why *my* team?" Red asked, defensively.

"'Cause it's *my* ball. *That's* why."

"Okay, kid, c'mon," said Red. "What's your name, anyway?"

"Dorrance," I said.

"What kind of a name is that?" said the biggest boy.

"I was named after somebody's last name. Who are you?" I asked.

"I'm Joe. This is my kid brother, Mike. That's Henry, and Tubby."

"Let's get on with the game," said Red. So that's what we did.

I wasn't sure about the rules, but I knew the object was to get the ball through the hoop. The longer we played the more bored I became. Whoever had the ball bounced it down the court while the rest of the boys stood below the basket waving their arms. Some of them yelled, "Over here, throw it here!" Then, *eventually*, the guy with the ball would toss it at the basket. Invariably it missed. Then someone on the other team took the ball and everyone ran to the other end of the court, where most of us stood below the basket and waved our arms shouting, "Over here, over here!"

Joe had control of the ball all the time his team had it. Red had control most of the time on our team. Nobody else had a chance to dribble or shoot at all. This wasn't the fun game I'd envisioned. These guys were never going to let me have the ball. And they didn't need teams of even numbers, since there was really no game happening here. It was time to pep things up.

Joe had the ball. We all ran to the other end of the court while Joe bounced the ball slowly toward the basket. The boys were all jumping up and down with their arms in the air, about to have heat stroke. Joe was not paying much attention to what he was doing. He didn't need to. The game was played out exactly the same every time the ball changed hands. So, while the ball was on its slow upshot from the ground, I darted forward, grabbed it out of the air, and dribbled it down the court. I jumped and shot. The ball ricocheted off the backboard and into the basket. *Beginners luck*!

"Two points for our team!" I shouted. All the boys stood at the other end of the court stunned into inaction. Not even my teammates cheered my points.

"Hey," Joe yelled. "You can't do that!"

"Why not?" I asked.

"It's against the rules," he said.

"No, it's not!" I shouted.

"It's against *my* rules," Joe said.

"Oh, and you make the rules 'cause it's your ball, right?" I looked at the other boys, hoping for some backup. But they stood silent and non-confrontational. "Don't you guys get tired of *not* playing?" I shouted.

Next thing I knew I was lying in the dirt. Joe had pushed me in the chest *hard* with the palms of his hands. My developing breasts hurt from the impact.

I was back on my feet in an instant.

"Are you always such a bully?" I shouted at Joe.

His answer was another hard push to my chest and I flew backward into the dirt. This time I landed on my elbows, scraping them raw. Now I was angry. I jumped to my feet and before I knew it my right fist had completed a knife-throwing follow-through terminating at Joe's nose.

Joe was holding his bleeding nose, whimpering. No one went to his aid. The other boys stood staring at my hair. Yes, my cap had flown off in the last fall. A *girl* had just decked their big bully friend.

"If you guys ever get a ball or some backbone, look me up. I'd like to play a *real* game of basketball," I said.

I picked up my cap and stalked off the playground. I heard the boys in the background already teasing Joe about having his nose bloodied by a *girl*. My elbows were skinned and stung me. I had really botched my first attempt at making friends. What would it be like when school started and I had to face all those boys again?

By the time I got back to Gram's, blood was running down my left arm. I ran up the back steps and into the kitchen, thinking I could sneak into the bathroom and clean myself up before Gram saw me. But my luck ran out. Gram was in the kitchen preparing dinner.

"What happened to you?" she asked.

"Someone pushed me down. It looks worse than it is."

"How does the other guy look?" she asked.

Then I smiled. "Bloody nose. And he was a lot bigger than me. He started it," I said in my defense.

Gram pulled me into the bathroom. With a soft brush she scrubbed all the dirt out of my cuts. My eyes smarted with unshed tears. Then Gram removed the glass tube from the bottle of iodine and painted my injuries to prevent infection. It stung like a dozen hornet bites.

"We'll leave it uncovered to dry out," she said. "Now, while I get dinner on the table, why don't you go upstairs and unpack your things. It's just one big room up there with three beds. You can choose your favorite. The other beds will be for company, if we ever have any."

The upstairs room was gigantic, as large as the entire house below. The light was dim because all the windows were shaded by huge trees outside. Someone had painted a row of maple leaves around the room mid-way up the walls. There were colorful rugs on the floor.

I chose a bed with a soft, patchwork quilt. The window above it overlooked 18th Street, what you could see of the street through the leaves from a giant sycamore tree. I opened my suitcase and hung my dresses on the pegs beside my bed. There were no closets up here in the attic. My underwear I put into the dresser drawers and my other shoes I slipped under the bed.

Oh, wow! My slingshot. I had forgotten about packing it. I put it beneath my underwear, a nice hiding place. I wasn't sure Gram would approve of it. Having my slingshot took some of the sting out of losing my knife and it was almost as handy as a defensive weapon.

I slid my suitcase under the bed. That didn't take long, I thought. And I ran down the stairs.

We ate a leisurely dinner of egg salad sandwiches and cantaloupe. Gram bragged on the cantaloupe because she grew it herself in the backyard garden. After dinner Gram said she had a surprise for me.

She led me to a sliding door off the entryway. I hadn't noticed it because it looked like part of the wall. Gram slid the door open to reveal a *library*. Yes, floor-to-ceiling bookshelves covered three walls. Two low, overstuffed leather chairs with ottomans sat in the center of the room with a small table between them. There was also a roll-top desk with a chair on wheels. And a shiny cello lay on its side on the floor with a music stand beside it. The rug was hooked in a floral design. If it hadn't been so hot and stuffy, this room would have been paradise.

Gram suggested I choose a book and relax in front of the cooler while she took her afternoon nap. So I spent half-an-hour carefully reading titles on the spines of hundreds of books. Then I chose *Little Men* by Louisa May Alcott and stretched out on the floor in front of the cooler for the afternoon. The cool breeze and the good book drove the morning experience from my mind. I thought I was in heaven here at Gram's.

4

When I opened my eyes the next morning the sun hadn't yet risen. The attic room was filled with soft light filtering through the north and south windows. The wind-up clock Gram had left on the bedside table said five-thirty. Then I remembered that it was Sunday and Gram had told me to sleep in late. Uncle Sabert and Aunt Marilyn and their boys would be here at ten o'clock for breakfast.

I lay in bed for a few more minutes, then slipped on my dungarees and shirt, grabbed my book, and went out to sit on the front porch. I read until I got bored, finally leaving my book on the chair and walking around to the back yard to look at the garden. I was surprised to find such a large vegetable garden behind the carriage house. I wondered if Gram had planted and tended it all by herself. Then I thought that Uncle Sabert or my cousins must have helped. I saw the hoe leaned up against the back wall of the carriage house, so I spent half an hour hoeing weeds. Then I filled a bucket with water and gave the trenches around the plants a good soaking.

It was still only about eight o'clock. I rinsed the dirt off my hands and feet, and beat the dirt off my dungarees with my hands. Now my hands were dirty again, so I rinsed them off *again*. I went back around the house to the front porch, shaking my hands and wiping them on my pants. I sat on the front steps and propped my feet up. My feet were dirty again and my dungarees had damp prints where I'd wiped my hands. My hands were clean, though, so I picked up *Little Men* and was immediately absorbed in the story of Nat and Jo and Mr. Baer. My attention was soon interrupted by the sound of giggling.

When I looked up I saw three girls standing in the front yard near the street. They were all about my age and had on pastel colored dresses with full petticoats, patent leather shoes, and white gloves. They were whispering and tittering. I thought I recognized the girl in the center as the one who was at the playground yesterday.

I looked down at my own dirty boy-clothes and felt embarrassed. These girls certainly had reason to giggle and whisper about me. I made up a story in my head that they were laughing at my appearance. Then I remembered something that happened in Bishop while I was rehearsing my ballet number. A few of the other ballerinas standing off to the side watching me perform whispered and giggled. I thought they were laughing at my performance. I was so angry that I stopped my dance and yelled at them. I later found out that they weren't laughing at me at all. One of them had told a joke and *that's* what they were laughing at. I was embarrassed that I'd lost my temper over nothing. I needed to remember *that* now.

I stood up and looked directly at the girls and smiled.

"Are you Doris?" the familiar girl asked.

"It's Dorrance. How do you know my name?" I asked.

"Red told me you gave Joe Cox a bloody nose," she replied. "Well, I think it was you. He said a girl named Doris who was dressed like a boy bloodied Joe's nose. Are you Doris?"

"It's Dorrance. I am. And I did," I replied shortly. I stood waiting, hoping I had not ruined my chances to be friends with these girls.

"I'm Rebecca Gaines. I want to congratulate you for doing what every kid in town has dreamed of doing for years."

She and the other girls grinned. Then they all came up the steps and shook my hand. They saw the scrapes on my elbows and *oohed* and *ahhed* over my injuries.

"Is Joe always such a bully?" I asked.

"Only to everyone smaller than him," Rebecca replied. "Last June we had an end-of-school picnic at Kern River Beach. The water was deep and swift and icy cold from the snow pack run-off. We'd all been told not to go into the water deeper than our knees. All the kids were playing near the shore, splashing and jumping. Our feet were turning blue it was so cold. Well, anyway, Jeremy Jeffs, a six-year-old, had a little bucket. He filled it with water and threw the water all over Joe. Joe flew into a rage. He grabbed Jeremy by the arm and hauled him into waist-deep water. I'm saying Joe's waist, not Jeremy's. Then Joe picked Jeremy up and threw him into the current. If it hadn't been for the parents and teachers rushing to his rescue, Jeremy certainly would have drowned. That's how really mean Joe is."

"Then why were you asking to play basketball with them yesterday?" I asked Rebecca.

"Because Red invited me to and Joe won't knowingly hurt girls, just boys."

"Well, if Red invited you, why didn't he stand up for you yesterday?"

"Because he's scared of Joe just like all the boys."

"Oh." I had nothing else to say.

Rebecca continued talking. "These are my sisters, Julia and Sarah."

I smiled at all three girls and said, "How do you do?" as Mama had taught me.

"We were just taking a walk before going to church," she added. "Are you just here visiting?"

Julia nudged Rebecca and whispered loud enough for me to hear that she shouldn't be so nosy.

"I'm here to live for awhile. My mother is in the hospital for a long treatment, so I'm staying with my great-grandmother, Gram," I replied.

"How long will you be here? Are you going to attend Franklin School? What grade are you in? Do you like to swim?" Rebecca was an endless fountain of questions. Julia kept jabbing her in the ribs and saying, "Shhh."

"I'm not sure how long I'll be here. Probably at least one semester. I was in 8th grade at home, but I don't think I'll be that far along here. I *love* to swim." Then I smiled again.

Julia spoke next. "We're going swimming at Kern River tomorrow morning. Would you like to come?"

"I'd love to!"

"We'll stop for you at about ten o'clock. Bring your lunch and a blanket to lie on. We'll stay until it gets too hot," instructed Julia.

"Okay! I'll be ready. Bye."

"Bye," they all shouted as they walked away.

I was feeling really good about making three new friends who were girls. On the ranch I didn't have any girl friends. All the girls at school were quite a bit younger than I. And I liked competing with the boys anyway. It felt good to have hit it off with these three sisters. I especially liked Rebecca.

Gram was up and in the kitchen when I went back into the house. I told her that I'd met the Gaines girls and they had invited me to go swimming tomorrow. Gram said they were nice girls and that I could go swimming. Then she spent about half-an-hour warning me about the dangers of the Kern River. By the time Uncle Sabert's truck rolled to a stop in front of the house, Gram and I had breakfast on the table.

Uncle Sabert and Aunt Marilyn stepped out of the front seat. My cousins, Jack and Andrew, hopped out of the back of the delivery truck. Uncle paused by the front fender to give the 1913 Model T Pie Wagon an affectionate pat and a swipe with his hanky. I wondered if that was the same hanky we had used on Friday night. The truck was certainly a "looker." The white paint gleamed in the sunlight and the black and gold lettering on the side proclaimed boldly "Logan Grocery" and "Free Delivery." I hoped I would have another opportunity to go for a ride before long. I vowed to stay awake next time.

Evidently, breakfast on Sunday with the Logans was traditional. Neither Gram nor Uncle's family attended Sunday services at a church. This meal together substituted for church. Immediately after breakfast Uncle, Jack, and Andrew left to make Sunday deliveries in the truck. Gram, Aunt Marilyn, and I did up the dishes and cleaned the house. This was the routine.

Aunt Marilyn showed me where all the cleaning implements were stored. She showed me the "proper" way to do the dozen chores that needed weekly attention. Auntie didn't say so, but I assumed these chores would now fall to me. I was happy to see that I could be of service to Gram, but I really would rather have helped with the grocery deliveries. So that's the way Sunday passed. And before I knew it, it was Monday morning.

5

At nine o'clock Monday morning I was on the porch watching for the Gaines girls. I could hardly wait to go swimming. I didn't have a swim suit, but Gram insisted it would be fine for me to swim in my bloomers and chemise. Gram had packed me a generous lunch, large enough to feed all us girls. So I sat on the porch in my dress, sweating in the ninety-degree heat, watching the ice man make deliveries, and wondering when Rebecca, Sarah, and Julia would arrive. To kill time, I opened *Little Men* and began to read. I was soon caught up in the story.

"Hi, Doris," shouted Rebecca from the street. All the girls were in their stylish swim suits. The bottoms were tailored and came to just below the knee and the tops had puffed short sleeves. All the suits were the same except in color. Rebecca's was blue, Sarah's pink, and Julia's brown. The girls had towels tucked under their left arms and were waving to me with their right hands. Julia also carried a picnic basket and Sarah had a quilt draped over her head and shoulders. How could she stand it in this heat?

I joined the girls and we hopped and skipped down the street toward the anticipated cold water of the Kern River. But we soon slowed as the oppressive summer heat sapped our energy.

"By the way," I said, "my name is Dorrance, not Doris."

"But it's such an unusual name, I just can't seem to remember it," apologized Rebecca.

"Then I'll tell you how I got the name. Maybe that will help you remember. The name Dorrance was the last name of the doctor who saved my aunt's life when she was born. He also saved my grandmother's life when she gave birth. So my grandmother named my aunt Dorrance, after Dr. Dorrance, and I was named after my aunt."

"Oh, yes, that makes more sense, I guess," said Rebecca. "But I still think it's confusing. I'll need to practice your name more."

"Don't feel bad about the confusion," I said. "Dr. Dorrance's son and I attended school together. Everyone was confused about my first name and his last name being the same. The boys always called John by his last name. So every time somebody yelled 'Dorrance' we both turned around." The girls chuckled at the thought of that.

When we got to Oak Street we walked north to 21st Street. From there we cut across a field and down to the river. The other girls carefully spread their quilt on the ground and removed their shoes. But I really could *not* wait to hit the water. I dropped my bundle of stuff on the ground and quickly pulled off my shoes and dress. Then I looked around to see where the other picnickers and swimmers were. Everyone seemed to be on the other side of the river several hundred yards upstream.

"Are we the only ones swimming here?" I asked.

"No one ever comes here," said Rebecca. "The sandy beach is upstream. We always swim here and no one ever bothers us. Plus it's so much closer to home here, not so far to walk when we get tired."

Back at the ranch, I was used to swimming naked and saw no reason to change my habit as long as we were here alone. So I quickly stripped off my chemise and bloomers and jumped into the river.

My new friends stared at the pile of clothes on the shore and then at me splashing about in the cold water. They quietly began to discuss their options.

Julia said, "Will you look at that. She looks so cool and free. And she won't have to walk home with wet clothes chafing her every step of the way."

Sarah said, "These swim suits are like swimming fully-clothed. So uncomfortable."

Then mischievous Rebecca said, "Maybe we should hide her clothes and make her walk home naked."

Then all three girls looked up and down the river bank. Seeing no one, they took my lead and stripped off their swim suits and leaped into the water. For the next few hours we all splashed and swam and laughed and talked. It was absolutely glorious.

When we tired of swimming or got too cold, we lay on a sand bar about ten feet from shore. The bar protected our swimming hole from the swift river current. It lay just below the surface of the water, so we could rest on it and warm up without exposing all of our naked bodies.

Sometime after noon Sarah mentioned being hungry. Then Julia reminded us of the cookies in the basket on the shore. Then I remembered the plums from Gram's tree in my dinner bag. So we all climbed up the river bank and wrapped ourselves in towels. But as we ate and began to dry we discovered a painful problem. We were all sunburned from forehead to heels. Even my head was burned where my hair was parted.

Soon we were in so much pain that we lost our appetites and decided to head for home. We dressed in our hot, confining clothing, trudged across the field and up the many blocks home, lugging our belongings. We were quiet and subdued, concentrating on our burning backs and shoulders.

Suddenly Julia said, "It's your fault we got burned, Dorrance."

Then Sarah said, "If you hadn't gone into the water naked, the rest of us would have left our suits on."

Then Rebecca said, "Leave her alone. We decided to swim naked. It's our own faults we got burned."

I felt terribly guilty. But Rebecca's little speech made me feel some better. I gave her a shy smile and she smiled back at me. Something about the twinkle in her eyes let me know that she really liked me. I really liked her too. I felt a fluttering in my chest and a blush come to my cheeks. If I hadn't been so sunburned, Rebecca may have noticed my embarrassment.

Gram saw my red face and arms as soon as I came in the house. She told me to soak in a cold bath to keep from burning further. When I got out of the tub and dried off, Gram handed a dish of cool gel through the cracked bathroom door. I spread it on my arms and face. It felt so good that I asked Gram to put it on my back too. That's when she saw how *really* sunburned I was. She carefully smoothed the gel on my back. Then she handed the bowl back with instructions to cover my chest and legs also.

Gram laid a sheet on the floor in front of the cooler and placed a pillow there for my head. She told me to lie down bare naked with my book and rest and stay cool.

"How do the other girls look?" she asked. "They had swim suits on, right?"

"They did when they got to the beach," I said. "But they took them off to swim."

"Oh, dear," Gram said.

Next I heard Gram on the telephone in the hallway talking to Mrs. Gaines. Of course, I could hear only Gram's side of the conversation. She gave detailed instructions for making a batch of the sunburn remedy and its use. Then she listened for quite awhile. I assumed Mrs. Gaines was giving Gram the tongue-lashing that should have been mine for getting her daughters sunburned.

I lay on the sheet in front of the cooler, worrying about the final outcome of the swimming escapade. I hoped that I would still be allowed to play with the Gaines girls, especially Rebecca. Then I read myself to sleep.

6

A few days later, I awoke with a biting homesickness. Monday's sunburn was turning to tan and the scrapes on my arms from the schoolyard fight were scabbed over. The excitement of the train ride and finding new friends had worn off. I missed Mama and my uncles and the animals. I even missed my chores. Although I had new, different chores here to replace them, it just wasn't the same. I regretted anew the loss of my possessions on the train. And I regretted my decision to swim naked with the Gaines girls. I was sure they'd been forbidden to see me again. I was too uncouth for such nice girls. I was sure their mother hated me. It seemed I was never good enough.

I sat on the edge of the bed and felt sorry for myself. I had been gone from home nearly a week and hadn't yet received a letter. They were probably glad to be rid of me at home.

When I arrived at the table, Gram was already there with breakfast made. Here I was creating more work for Gram. She would probably be happy to be rid of me too. She couldn't be happy about me creating a rift with her friend Mrs. Gaines. As I sat down woefully, quietly, remorsefully, I noticed a pile of mail beside Gram's plate.

"No hello this morning?" Gram asked cheerfully.

A tear slipped from my eye and I quickly brushed it away.

"A bit homesick today, huh?" she added. "Well, it was bound to happen. Most natural thing in the world. Excitement wears off and the routine of daily living sets in. Fortunately, it won't last long. The homesickness, that is. Routine is always with us."

I dredged up a wan smile and dished up my plate. Gram began to slowly sort through the mail, carefully opening and reading each piece. I shoveled food into my mouth, keeping one eye out for a letter. When Gram lifted the next letter off the stack, I smiled in spite of myself. For there, underneath, was an envelope with familiar handwriting. I waited patiently for Gram to hand it to me. But she merely turned it over and opened it with the silver letter opener. Gram raised her eyes and saw the look of disappointment and outrage on my face.

"Oh, I'm sorry, Dear. This letter from your mother is addressed to me."

"There must be something inside for me," I answered.

"Well, let's see…" said Gram as she quickly read the note. "As a matter of fact, there *is* something here for you. Eva has sent some money for you to buy what you need for school."

"But surely she sent a note for me, too."

"No. Just that and your final report card," said Gram as she passed me the five-dollar bill. "Perhaps tomorrow another letter will come. In the meantime you need to decide how this five dollars might best be spent."

"Doesn't Mama say how she's feeling or hello or anything?"

Gram turned the envelope over and looked at the postmark. Then she looked at the date on the letter. "Oh, my," she said. "This was mailed the day you left Fish Lake to come here and the letter was written before that. I guess she hardly had time to miss you before you left."

Then there was a knock on the front door. When I opened it, Sarah stood there, smiling from a very tanned face.

"Hi, Sarah. It looks like your sunburn is already turning to tan. Mine, too." I wondered where Rebecca and Julia were. It seemed like the girls always traveled in a pack.

Sarah laughed and said her sunburn had turned to tan overnight and her back was already peeling. Then she stepped forward to whisper in my ear, "Poor Rebecca got the worst of it."

I was overcome with remorse. My eyes filled with tears.

Then Sarah added quickly, "But she's feeling better today."

Thank goodness. I hope she's not angry with me today like her sisters were Monday, I thought.

Sarah continued, "We're going downtown to shop for school clothes and supplies today. Would you like to go, too? My mother will be going with us, if you don't mind."

"I guess she won't trust you alone with me again after I got you all sunburned," I said. Then I laughed a little chortle to try to make light of the situation. "My mother just sent me some money to shop for school. Come in and I'll ask Gram if I can go with you."

Gram told me to go ahead and go.

"I was planning to have Aunt Marilyn take you, but Mrs. Gaines is probably more qualified because she has three girls in school," commented Gram.

So I put on a dress with all the hot, confining underwear and walked home with Sarah.

The Gaines household was *so* much busier than Gram's house or my house in Fish Lake Valley. It was also smaller than Gram's. The entire house was located on the ground floor and had only two bedrooms. There was also a living room, dining room, and bath. The kitchen was huge, much like Gram's. Mrs. Gaines was scrubbing the sink out with Ajax and a rag.

"Hello, Mrs. Gaines," I said. "Thank you for inviting me to go shopping with you. I haven't been downtown yet."

"We'll be happy to have you along," she replied.

I left her to her chore and followed Sarah into the living room. It was cozy, with a fireplace at one end and a piano at the other. There was a small floral settee and several comfortable, mismatched armchairs. One electrical outlet accommodated a lamp in the front window. There were also gas lamps on the wall above the piano.

"Who plays the piano?" I asked Sarah.

"We all play a little bit," she replied, "but Julia plays the best. Rebecca plays the violin and I'm learning the oboe. We usually practice after supper. Do you play an instrument?"

I thought about the beautiful cello lying on the library floor.

"Not yet," I replied, "but Gram has a cello. I've been thinking of asking for lessons."

"Oh, I hope you do take lessons. Then we could all practice together. We would practically be an orchestra."

"Where are Julia and Rebecca?" I asked, gazing around.

"They're still sorting clothes in the bedroom. C'mon."

We walked through the dining room on the way to the girls' bedroom. Besides the large pedestal dining table, a long, high buffet stood against one wall. A six-inch mirror ran along the entire back, reflecting a plethora of small ceramic and wooden salt and pepper shakers. I'd loved the word plethora ever since I read it in a book.

Sarah led me down a hallway and into the bedroom all the girls shared. It was a large room in the rear of the house and it had a small add-on room behind it that had windows on all sides. I think it was once a porch that had been enclosed. Julia slept in the add-on, her compensation for being the eldest. Sarah and Rebecca shared the larger room. Mrs. Gaines kept her treadle sewing machine in the girls' room. There was a walk-in closet with a small, high window on the outside wall. Even in the closet with the door shut, there was enough light to see.

Rebecca and Julia were busy sorting through their clothes, deciding what could be handed down or made over, and what should go in the rag bag to be made into quilts and rugs.

I was astonished at the great piles of dresses. I had three and considered that an ample supply. I *would* like to have a couple more pairs of dungarees, though.

Soon Mrs. Gaines called us into the living room. "We're going to take the buggy downtown, because we'll have lots of parcels to bring home. You girls may squeeze in as best you can for the trip down, but you may have to walk back if we run out of room."

The buggy was built to seat two and had a place behind the seat for cargo. Mrs. Gaines climbed aboard behind the horses; Julia sat beside her with Sarah on her lap; Rebecca and I sat on the cargo bench, facing the rear with our feet dangling down. Off we went toward Sears, Roebuck, & Company on the corner of 19th and K Streets.

"Mother says you're a bad influence," blurted Rebecca, "but she says your grandmother will refine you soon." I gave Rebecca an uncomfortable look because I didn't know what to say. Then she added, "I hope she doesn't refine you too much. It's very exciting to be bad sometimes, isn't it?" And with that said, Rebecca reached over and squeezed my hand.

I had a warm rush of feelings. Rebecca's hand was soft, yet strong and comforting. She was a year younger than I, but was already looking womanly, while I still had a boy's figure, tall and flat. I had mixed feelings about that. I liked the lack of problems my late development caused. But I didn't want to be treated like the little girl I appeared to be. I was thinking about how much I would like to be more womanly so that Rebecca might find me more attractive. The very thought made me blush. I chastised myself for these feelings and hoped Rebecca wouldn't notice my flaming neck and ears. What kind of girl wants to be loved by another girl?

The arrival of the buggy downtown shook my mind from my feelings for Rebecca. The street was paved with bricks and the buggy wheels bounced over the bumpy surface. I watched the bright red trolley cars rumble along the length of Chester Avenue as far as I could see. The buggy had to cross two sets of tracks. One crossing nearly pitched Rebecca and me into the street. But the ultimate sight of the three-story Sears, Roebuck & Company building was worth the hazardous crossing.

I had never been inside a department store. There were none in Bishop, just a general store and a few specialty shops. I trailed the others through the three-story building. Everywhere I looked there were displays of the most wonderful innovations. Housewares were located on the ground floor, including washing machines, gas stoves, electric irons and candlestick telephones, and even an electric food mixer. Several models of gramophones and hundreds of records took my breath away. The second floor held racks and shelves of men's and boys' clothing and shoes. The third floor was devoted to clothing for women, girls, and babies. Sears also sold toys, books, linens, and school and office supplies. Anything that wasn't stocked in the store could be ordered from the catalog department in the basement.

We traveled to the top floor on an elevator. I had never ridden in one before. It felt like my stomach was still on the ground floor as we rose quickly upward. The elevator operator expertly pulled open the door to let us off. I decided I would take the stairs when it was time to leave. Being shut up in a little box hurtling downward was not my idea of a good time.

I walked and watched and waited while Julia, Sarah, and Rebecca shopped for undergarments, shoes, yard goods, lace and buttons, and stockings. Mrs. Gaines encouraged me to shop for clothes, but I thought my three dresses would be enough. I didn't want to waste my five dollars on clothing. At one point I sat on the floor and leant up against a wall to rest. Finally, the Sears shopping was completed. Mrs. Gaines, Sarah, and Julia rode the elevator to the ground floor, but Rebecca and I took the stairs. Then we all walked across the street to the Kress dime store.

It was at Kress that the Gaines girls purchased their school supplies and where I decided to part with some of my precious five dollars. Linoleum-covered stairs led to the main entrance on the second floor and to the lower entrance just below street-level. The floors inside were wood and rang with the steps of the many shoppers. We entered the lower level because that's where the school supplies and toys were sold. I walked around gazing at the variety of merchandise, frequently handling something that caught my eye. Then a rude voice interrupted my concentration.

"May I help you find something in particular?" asked the floor-walker. But the voice *really* said, "Do you have money or are you just looking for something to steal?"

I quickly pulled the five-dollar bill from my pocket and waved it in the clerk's face.

"I can take my business elsewhere, if you prefer," I quipped.

"Oh, I'm terribly sorry," stumbled the clerk as he left me to my shopping.

When I turned away from the floor-walker I saw Mrs. Gaines' astonished expression. "My," she said, "I guess I don't need to worry about you taking care of yourself, do I?" I didn't know how to answer, so I just stood there trying to come up with a reply that would satisfy her. Then Mrs. Gaines added, "I like that kind of spunk in a young woman."

I was relieved not to have again disappointed Mrs. Gaines. I decided it was time to make my final selections. I purchased a pen and nibs, a bottle of black ink, a tablet of good quality paper, a wooden pencil box, a blotter, three pencils, a sharpener, and a new book entitled *The Wind in the Willows*. I had more than three dollars in change.

All the parcels were loaded into the buggy, except mine, and we girls began the walk home. I was glad to be moving again. I had never been on such a long shopping trip. When I shopped with Mama or my uncles we were in and out of the store quick as a flash. *Get what you need and get going*. That's what Mama always said.

The Gaines girls took on the responsibility of narrating the trip home, pointing out various important sites along the way. The clock tower in the center of the intersection at Chester Avenue and 17th Street said three-thirty. Along Chester Avenue I saw a theater, drug store, candy store, market, and several specialty shops and restaurants. The town was easy to navigate because all the streets ran north and south or east and west. The north-south streets were lettered. The east-west streets were numbered. It was easy to figure out how far you had to walk by adding up the letters and numbers to your final destination. It was fourteen blocks to Gram's house from Sears, Roebuck & Company. On that hot afternoon, my bag of school supplies became heavier with every block. Sweat ran down my back and dust from the street rose up with each step. I thought that if the trolley ran past Gram's house, I'd gladly part with some of my remaining three dollars to pay the fare home.

But, aside from the heat, I felt better than I had all day. I still had my friends and I still had hope of receiving a letter from Mama tomorrow.

7

By my second week in Bakersfield, Gram and I had settled into a daily routine. I found it hard to stay in bed past five-thirty. At home I would need to already be up and busy with chores. Things were so much easier in the city.

Take milk, for instance. On the ranch I needed to begin the day by milking the cow. I carried the milk inside and filtered it through cheesecloth into another bucket. Then I poured the filtered milk into large, shallow pans. I carried the pans to the cellar to allow them to cool. The cream rose to the top and we skimmed it off and churned butter from it. Then the skimmed milk was poured into scalded glass jars, sealed and put down in the cellar.

In the city, there was a milkman. The milkman came twice a week and left bottles of milk on the porch. He also left butter, cottage cheese, and other dairy products if we ordered them on a slip of paper stuffed into the top of one of the emptied bottles. It was important to put the milk into the ice box at once, so it didn't sit on the porch and spoil.

Here in the city there was an ice man who came two or three times every week. He carried large blocks of ice into the kitchen and put them in the ice box. In Fish Lake we harvested ice in the winter when the lakes froze over. We cut blocks of ice with saws and hauled them home in the wagon.

We stored the ice blocks in the cellar, packed carefully with sawdust so they wouldn't melt.

Another wonderful thing was the mailman, who came twice a day to deliver letters to the box on the porch. In Fish Lake we had to drive miles in the buckboard to pick up the mail once a week at the post office.

So, every morning I got up way before Gram and made my own breakfast. I usually ate leftover biscuits with butter and honey or preserves. I also drank a glass of milk and one of juice. Then I washed up my dishes and put them away in the cupboard. About every three days I took a bath. On the days I didn't bathe, I took a cooling afternoon soak in the claw-foot tub. I always made my bed and kept the house tidied up. And I worked in the garden while it was cool outside. Once those things were done, I retired to the library to read and browse among the books on the shelves. I didn't touch the cello, nor did anyone else.

Gram got up about nine and made dinner by noon. Then I washed the dishes. Gram always baked cookies or some other delightful treat for a late afternoon snack. I cleaned up the baking things. Then Gram cooked a delicious supper and I washed the dishes. This system of Gram cooking and my cleaning up worked out well. You see, Gram loved to cook but made a huge mess. And I loved to eat and didn't mind cleaning up a huge mess in order to do so. And we enjoyed each other's company.

One day Gram said, "I'm so glad you came to live with me. I haven't felt so young in years. And I love what you've done with the garden!"

"I like being here, too," I said. "I'm not as homesick as I was. You were right. It doesn't last forever." But it definitely still comes and goes, I thought.

Each morning and afternoon I met the postman in hopes of receiving a letter from Mama. Finally, one Saturday, my anxiously-awaited letter arrived. I handed the stack of mail to Gram and she at once placed the letter in my hand. I sat at the kitchen table, caressing the envelope and treasuring the sight of Mama's fancy handwriting. Then I opened the envelope, gently sliding my finger along under the flap. The paper inside was covered with script from top to bottom. Then the paper had been turned sideways and covered again from top to bottom. The affect was that the paper had a sort of plaid appearance. I began reading it, but before long I had to ask Gram's help. All the lovely curlicues and flourishes were hard enough to read when there was only one layer of writing. With these lines written atop each other, it was impossible for me to read. But with Gram's more experienced eye, she had no trouble deciphering the letter.

Mama said she was settled in the sanatorium and confined to bed rest for now. Little by little she would be allowed more activity as her condition improved. She said she slept eighteen to twenty hours a day. She said she missed me and promised to get well as quickly as possible. She said she hoped I wasn't too lonely and that I would make friends and like school. And she reminded me to "help Gram all you can. You know she's no longer a spring chicken." As soon as Gram finished reading the letter, and now that I had Mama's address, I began writing the first of what would be daily letters to Mama.

About two o'clock Sarah knocked on the front door.

"Hi, Doris," she said when I opened the door.

"Dorrance," I replied.

"Dorrance," said Sarah. "You want to go over to the train tracks?"

"Why?" I asked.

"Just to see what the rail tramps left," said Sarah. "I'm not allowed, but Mother and Julia and Rebecca shooed me out of the house. They're sewing and I just complain. Anyway, you want to go?"

"Sure. Just give me a couple of minutes to change clothes." I changed into my dungarees, shirt, and boots. I tucked my braid into my cap and stuck my slingshot in my back pocket. Gram was resting in her room, so I called a soft goodbye and left the house.

Sarah and I trudged south on A Street toward the railroad tracks, suffering in the afternoon heat. At 16th Street we turned west for half a block and cut across a field of tumbleweeds toward the Round Table, which we could see on the far side of the tracks. The Round Table was a large, semi-circular house in which the engines could be turned to face the opposite direction. Just before we reached the tracks we saw a large circle of logs with a cold campfire in the center. This was obviously a resting place for tramps. I had never seen a tramp, but Sarah seemed to know a lot about them. She cautioned me about their evil appearance and behavior. There were various discarded possessions scattered about the campfire circle: spoons; cans; long, sharpened sticks; and a kerchief. There really wasn't anything else to see and we considered going to Jastro Park next.

But then I had a brilliant idea! "Let's set these old tin cans on the logs and shoot them off with my slingshot."

"I never used a slingshot before," Sarah said.

"Oh, there's really nothing to it. I'll teach you."

I gathered half a dozen empty cans and set them along the biggest log. I set Sarah to work finding some penny-sized pebbles. We stood about fifteen feet away. I showed Sarah how to place a pebble into the slingshot pocket and pull the rubber strap back to her ear, sighting along the strap to aim the shot. Sarah released the strap and the pebble launched forward and hit the dirt in front of the log. She tried another shot. It hit even further away than the first one. She handed me the slingshot.

I loaded a pebble and launched it at the first can. *Thwack!* A direct hit. The can bounced into the dirt on the other side of the log. I loaded another pebble and aimed at the second can. A near miss. I tried again and knocked the can a few feet with a resounding clink.

I handed the slingshot back to Sarah so she could try again. She shot four pebbles, all of them falling short. I showed Sarah how to raise the trajectory a bit. Her fifth pebble nicked the middle can. She was ecstatic. "Wow, did you see *that*?" she shouted.

"What in tarnation are you young'ns doin'?" came a gruff voice from the back side of the log across the circle. "I'm tryin' to take a nap here."

The long-haired, bearded man stood up. His skin was tanned brown as a walnut and he had deep wrinkles in his forehead and the corners of his eyes. His pants were stained and had fox tails imbedded in the cuffs. He stepped over the log and sat down. He pulled the pair of worn-out boots in his hand onto his bare, calloused feet. I was glad I had socks inside my boots.

I glanced at Sarah. She stood frozen and trembling beside me. I felt bad about invading the tramp's privacy. "I'm sorry. I was shooting pebbles at cans and I didn't see you sleeping behind that log."

"Well, maybe you shoulda looked harder, boy. This is my home for now. I sleep back there because it's the only shady spot," said the tramp.

Sarah and I just stood there looking stupid. It never occurred to either of us that someone could consider a log in a clearing his home. I began apologizing all over again. The tramp sat patiently waiting for me to finish.

Then he said, "Now, young'n, seems to me any halfway bright boy would know better than to bring his sister over by these here tracks. Some of the men who live here ain't as nice as I am. Now you get along home and don't let me catch you here again."

"Yes sir," we said in unison. We headed for home. When we reached 18th Street, Sarah ran east the half block to her house. I walked slowly west the block and a half to Gram's. We had only been gone for about an hour and Gram was still sleeping when I got there. I lay down on the floor in front of the cooler and pondered the tramp. I hadn't even asked his name.

I wondered what had led him to ride the rails. He didn't seem to meet the profile Sarah had described. Yes, he was dirty and ragged, but he wasn't mean and violent. Was he just off on an adventure? Or maybe he had a family somewhere. Maybe he worked when he could find a job and then sent money home to his wife and children. Or maybe he was a sort of missionary. Maybe he told stories and jokes to make the other tramps laugh. After all, I had seen the laugh lines at the corners of his eyes. Perhaps his purpose was to give hope to the hopeless. It made me sad that I hadn't asked him some questions. I felt that I'd missed a once-in-a-lifetime opportunity. I almost got up and went back to the tracks to talk to him. But his warning not to come back kept me away.

The next day Sarah told me that she had told Julia and Rebecca about our adventure. "They laughed when I told them the tramp thought you were my brother."

Somehow Mrs. Gaines heard about the incident and gave Sarah a stern talking-to. Sarah said her mother was relieved that I was along, and said, "Lord knows what would have happened to you if you hadn't had your *brother* there for protection."

8

The next morning, I once again thought about the tramp. I was feeling a strong pull to go back to the railroad tracks. Somehow I felt the tramp needed help. I knew he had to be hungry, but it was more than that. I had the feeling that he was injured, or hurting. I worried about him. After Gram lay down for her afternoon nap and I cleaned up the dinner dishes, I made my decision. I would go to see the tramp.

I packed up a kerchief with leftover food from dinner: some biscuits, fruit, and a jar of milk. Then I set out in the afternoon heat. I walked a different route today, going through Jastro Park, across Railroad Avenue, and directly through the field to the fire circle. I slowed my pace considerably the closer I got. I scanned the clearing for the tramp. I worried he might be taking his afternoon nap behind the log. I was secretly hoping he had hopped a train and was gone. That way I could tell myself I had tried to help and still not put myself in a dangerous situation.

There was no one at the circle. I crept across the clearing to look behind the log. When I saw what was there I jumped back a little in surprise. The tramp *was* gone. But in his place lay a very matted little dog with a tin can stuck on his nose. He was so quiet I thought he might be dead. I cleared my throat. The dog raised its head and peered at me through soft brown eyes. He whined. I sat down and patted his head. He drew back a little and softly growled, then whimpered again. I cautiously reached out and stroked his back. He sat up. He whimpered and tried to paw the can away from his nose. This little dog was in a real pickle.

He had evidently been trying to lick some food from the can when his nose became lodged inside. Good thing there were holes in both ends or he would have smothered. I thought I could pull the can from his muzzle. But then I realized that doing so would cut his nose, since the can had jagged edges at both ends. What would I do?

I patted the dog again to be sure he was not going to turn vicious. He was very sad, but seemed to trust me. I took a couple of steps back and called to him, "Here, puppy." He just lay there looking at me with those milky, brown eyes. I knew I would have to get him help. So I decided to take him to Gram's. I gently reached down to pick him up. He wasn't crazy about that. He made a sort of growly, whimpery noise. But I took courage and, speaking soothingly to him, I hoisted him into my arms, being careful not to touch the can or his head. He was lighter than I expected. He seemed to be all hair and very little else. I left the snacks on the log because my hands were full of dog. As we walked, he relaxed in my arms and rested quietly on the entire walk to Gram's.

Gram was still sleeping, but I knew I had to wake her. I carefully lay the dog on the kitchen floor and peaked into Gram's room.

"Gram, *Gram,*" I called to her.

"What? What?" she said back to me.

"I need your help."

Gram jumped up like a jack-in-the-box. "What's wrong? Are you hurt?"

"Not me, but someone else. Please, hurry." And she did.

Gram followed me into the kitchen. As soon as she saw the forlorn little dog, a look of distress came across her face.

"Oh, my! Poor little thing!" she exclaimed. She asked the dog, "How did you get in such a fix?" And then she said to me, "Quick, get my kitchen shears."

I handed Gram the shears and she began trying to cut away the tin can. The little dog struggled and whined. I could not get him to hold still, small as he was. The shears were having a hard time cutting through the can. They were designed for cutting meat, not tin.

"Wait here," Gram said. I comforted the dog while Gram rushed to the phone. I heard her talking to Uncle Sabert, telling him to come right away and to bring tin snips.

Uncle Sabert's grocery was only about four blocks away, so he was there lickety-split. Without demanding a word of explanation, he went to work on the can. Gram and I held the dog's head while he worked. Snip, snip, snip and the can was cut open. Uncle deftly spread the sides apart and lifted the can from the dog's muzzle. The little dog shook his head and jumped up to lick my face. He licked and licked and licked he was so happy.

Gram put some ground meat on a saucer and offered it to the dog. He wolfed it down without even tasting it. Gram gave him some water in a bowl. He lapped it up in great gulps. Then he jumped in my lap and licked my face over and over again. Uncle just sat there laughing, his blue eyes twinkling.

Then he said, "That's the ugliest dog I've ever seen." And he laughed some more.

And Gram asked me, "What do you intend to do with him now?"

"I think he needs a home," I said, hoping they would both take the hint that I wanted to keep him.

"Well, I can't argue with that," said Gram. "I've never seen a more disreputable looking animal."

"That's the ugliest dog I've ever seen," repeated Uncle.

"He won't be ugly once he's cleaned up," I argued.

"He'll take a *lot* of cleaning up," Gram stated.

"I can do it," I pleaded.

"Well, you'd better get busy then," said Gram. "Start by clipping all the mats off him. Then give him a good bath with lye soap. When he's dry we'll sprinkle him with boric acid to try to kill his fleas. And whatever you do, don't let him into the rest of the house until he's absolutely flea-free."

Uncle Sabert turned to Gram and asked, "You don't intend to keep that stray, do you?"

"I guess that depends on how well he cleans up," Gram said, and she laughed.

"Now that the can's off his face it's hard to tell which is the front and which is the back," Uncle said.

"Well," said Gram, "I think it's the front that's in Dorrance's face."

"I should hope so," said Uncle.

Uncle went back to work and Gram told me to follow her out the back door and around to the front porch. There we sat on the wicker chairs and began the clean-up project on the dog. I held him and comforted him. Gram began snipping away at the mats. We worked on the little dog for over an hour. There wasn't much dog left when we finished clipping his mats. But there was a huge pile of hair on the porch. Gram told me to put it in the barrel so the fleas wouldn't infest the yard. She said Uncle Sabert would come by later to burn it.

Then I carried the dog into the bathroom and ran water into the claw foot tub. Gram poured heated water from the stove to warm up the bath. The dog liked it and was content to lap up water and soap suds as I scrubbed him. Gram kept saying he would get sick licking up the lye soap, but he never did. After I soaped and rinsed him three times, he seemed pretty clean and free of fleas. But Gram spotted one on his belly as we rubbed him with an old towel. So she ordered me to sit on the front porch with him in my lap until he was completely dry. Then she came out with a box of boric acid powder and sprinkled it liberally all over his head, neck, back, tummy, and legs. She rubbed it in well. She said I was to leave it on for about an hour and then rinse him with warm water. So that's what I did. After his final bath, I brushed him briskly with an old hairbrush Gram found in the bathroom cupboard. The little dog didn't look half bad. I asked Gram if I could keep him.

She said, "Let's see what Uncle Sabert thinks when he comes back."

Uncle came up the front steps shortly after six o'clock. The little dog had found a comfy spot on the rug in front of the cooler and fallen asleep. He was still groggy from his nap when Uncle knelt down to pet him. The dog licked Uncle's hand and gazed up at him with eyes of love.

"Looks like this dog has himself a new home, huh?" he asked Gram.

"Looks like it," Gram replied.

Uncle Sabert handed me a package wrapped in butcher paper and smiled. I gave him a *huge* hug.

"Better give Gram her hug, too," he said. "She's the one who has to live with the ugliest dog in the world."

I gave Gram a *huge* hug, too. Then I carried the package of meat scraps into the kitchen to prepare the dog's dinner. Uncle carried the dog in and set him on the floor in front of his dish.

"What's his name?" he asked.

"Button," I said. "Short for Button Brown Eyes."

"Certainly his best feature," said Uncle. He turned to Gram and said, "I guess I'd better add dog meat to your weekly grocery order." And then he laughed.

The next day Sarah and Rebecca stopped by the house. When I opened the door, Button jumped all over them, licking and wagging his whole back end. I had to throw a stick across the yard to distract him from his "love attack" on the girls. While he ran to fetch the stick, Rebecca presented me with a soft package tied with string.

"My mother sent this for you," said Rebecca simply, shrugging her shoulders.

"What is it?"

"Open it."

So I did. Inside was a blue and white gingham dress, a simple style with no lace or bows or other frills. I liked it.

"My mother says being as school starts Monday, you'll need another dress. We made it yesterday. All except Sarah, anyway. She stood around and complained," stated Rebecca.

Sarah and I exchanged a sly smile. I thought we had more fun at the tracks than Rebecca and her mother had sewing.

"Please thank your mother for me," I said. "Tell her I love it."

Later I wrote and posted a thank you note to Mrs. Gaines. It was my chance to prove I was not as uncouth as she might think.

9

On the eighth of September, I met Rebecca and Sarah on the front steps of Franklin School as planned. Julia was in high school this year. Sarah and I were in 8th grade. Rebecca was in 7th.

"Hi, Doris," piped Rebecca enthusiastically.

"Dorrance," I answered. I smiled at Rebecca. This was a game we played now, her calling me Doris and me correcting her.

"Dorrance," repeated Rebecca. She smiled back at me.

We entered the building together. The school was unusual and familiar at the same time. It was huge compared to the one-room school house I was used to, but it smelled of chalk and books just as I knew it would. Rebecca offered to go to the office with me while I registered.

Sarah rushed off to the 8th-grade classroom to see who the new teacher would be. Last year's teacher, Mrs. Cook, left in June, as she had married and was expecting a baby.

Rebecca knew her teacher would be Miss Harris. She also knew that everyone in 7th-grade last year loved the kind-hearted and humorous young teacher. Rebecca was extremely happy to be back in school as she loved book work and socializing. I guessed she probably liked hearing the gossip even though she never passed it along.

Miss Scott in the office registered me for school. She wrote down the information from my last year's report card. Then she sent me to Room 8. Rebecca walked along with me before crossing the wide hallway to Room 7. Most students were in their seats even though it was still a few minutes before eight o'clock. The desks were of dark wood and metal scroll work, and rested on wood rails. Each desk had a seat mounted on its front. So if the student sitting in front bounced or wiggled, it jiggled the writing surface of the student behind.

A teacher's desk stood on a platform at the front of the class. A tall-backed mahogany chair on casters was behind the desk. Blackboards ran along two walls, one at the front and one on the wall next to the inner hallway. The outside wall held five large sash windows. A stove was at the back of the room. We were lucky to have a building that had only been open for a few years. The lighting and heat were adequate and the classroom was spacious.

I took the seat behind Sarah and in front of a girl who said her name was Winifred. The girls sat in the two rows next to the windows. The boys sat in the two rows next to the hallway. After I had taken my seat a familiar boy took the seat across the aisle from me. It was Red. He smiled at me and I smiled back. I looked around the room for the bully, Joe. I didn't see him.

"Where's Joe?" I asked Red.

"Not here. He's in high school this year. Lucky us!"

The students were noisily greeting one another after the long summer holiday, when all at once the room grew silent. An imposing figure had entered the classroom. He wasn't a tall or large man, but the way he carried himself intimidated us. He stood at the front tapping a ruler against his palm. He had the attention of even the most boisterous boys. He looked at each student individually, all the time tap-tap-tapping the ruler on his palm. Red had gone completely white with the exception of his brown freckles. He looked as if he might die of fright, or at least faint. I guessed Red's timidity with Joe had not been an act after all.

I became conscious of my own appearance as the teacher's gaze came closer to my seat. But I didn't dare move to see if my long dark braid hung straight down my back or if my bangs were combed. I was wearing the new blue gingham dress, new stockings, and new shoes. I was fairly confident the teacher would find me acceptable. Then his gaze fell upon my face. My mouth went dry and my cheeks began to burn. I was so nervous that I grinned. What am I doing? I thought. And then I noticed, ever so faintly, a twinkle in the teacher's eye and one side of his mouth twitched as if he would smile. Then quickly his gaze moved to the next student, Winifred, and on around the class. He tap-tap-tapped the ruler on his palm until he had terrified each and every student.

Then he gave his palm three sharp whacks for attention. I figured he slapped the ruler too hard, because he rubbed his hand vigorously on his pants. Then he spoke for the first time.

"In unison, spell SILK," he commanded.

"S-I-L-K," recited the class.

"Again!" commanded the teacher.

"S-I-L-K," recited the class.

"Again!" the teacher shouted.

The class continued to spell SILK again and again until every student began to wonder how they were spelling it wrong.

Then the teacher said, "What do cows drink?"

Without a thought the entire class chanted in unison, "MILK!"

"Ha, ha, ha!" roared the teacher's laughter, scaring us almost as much as the tap-tap-tapping of the ruler. And with that joke the teacher attempted to change from tyrant to playmate. But I knew this man could be dangerous, striving to keep us off-balance, never knowing what to expect. It was a hideous tactic to control us with fear.

Then he said, "My name is Mr. Griffin. My expectations for each of you are high. Meet my expectations, or better yet, exceed them, and you will delight in your academic growth. Fail to work to your potential and you will grieve lost opportunities and suffer the wrath of the ruler." With that said, he slammed the ruler on his desk with a sharp crack.

What Mr. Griffin failed to tell us is what his expectations were. My sense of it was that if he liked you, you would meet his expectations. If he didn't like you, you would suffer his abuse. I did *not* like him and I expected he would *not* like me.

Mr. Griffin lost no time in beginning instruction. Until ten o'clock he drilled the class in spelling, math, and history. At precisely ten he excused the class for recess. We students left the room in an orderly manner until we hit the hallway. Then we ran for the great outdoors.

The girls collected around the front of the school building on the grass, talking and giggling. I was soon bored and became interested in what the boys were doing. I saw several games going on, from baseball to kick ball to kick the can. I didn't see any reason to sit out recess with these prissy girls, so I joined the boys.

After recess, as the students re-entered the classroom, a primly-dressed girl, with her hair in ringlets and bows, leaned over to me and spat, "Tomboy!" in my ear.

Then she walked quickly to the front seat by the window. Two more hours of drills and reading passed. Then it was dinnertime. Sarah, Rebecca, Winifred, and I sat on the front lawn enjoying our sandwiches and fruit. Rebecca talked on and on about the virtues of Miss Harris. It was wonderful to see her so excited and happy. After dinner I again went to join in the boys' games. I was already gaining a certain respect among them for my skill at kicking, throwing, catching, and running. I was equally skilled at all the games. Of course, I'm sure my reputation preceded me. It seemed as if everyone in the school had heard about Joe's bloody nose.

When I returned to the classroom after dinner, my hair had begun to come out of its braid and hung in damp tendrils down the sides of my face and over my ears. I took my seat in time to hear the nasty words in my ear: "Tomboy. Sapphist." The prim girl walked on to her front corner seat followed by a second girl who sat immediately behind her. I considered the insults. "Sapphist" is what the church lady had called the sisters in Fish Lake. I wondered what it meant. "Tomboy" I knew and didn't particularly mind, depending on who said it and in what tone of voice. I did *not* like this girl's tone.

That afternoon each student was assigned a reading group. I was in the most advanced group, Sarah in the least advanced. The prim girl was also in Sarah's group, as was Winifred. I quickly became absorbed in the assignment, but occasionally overheard the prim girl making rude remarks to Winifred.

At one point I heard the prim girl whinny like a horse. I glanced at Mr. Griffin who evidently hadn't heard the noise as he worked individually with someone at his desk. I wondered what made the prim girl so hateful. Then I put the thoughts aside and went back to my assignment.

Soon the first day of school was over. Students headed for home or stood around outside talking about their day. Rebecca, Sarah, Winifred, and I stood near the front steps making plans to study together. Then the prim girl walked by with her friend and said, "Well, who have we here? It's the Tomboy and her Horse!" The prim girl and her friend laughed and walked on with their heads held high.

"They are so rude!" exclaimed Rebecca.

"Never mind," said Winifred. "I'm used to it. They've called me Whinny since the fourth grade."

"Just the same," said Rebecca, "she shouldn't get away with it."

"She reminds me of Joe, except she's sneakier," I said. "She'll get what's coming to her someday."

Rebecca threw me a look that said, And you're just the one to give it to her.

But I was thinking that I had made enough of a statement with Joe to last me the rest of my life. I didn't intend to get into anything with the prim girl.

10

When I got home from school, Gram was waiting on the porch. "Tell me all about school," she said.

We sat in the wicker chairs and I gave Gram an edited version of my day, leaving out all the negative stuff. I described Mr. Griffin's entrance and told her he had a southern accent. I described my new friend, Winifred, and my plan to help her and Sarah with reading and history, which is, after all, mostly reading. Gram and I decided I'd continue to carry my dinner to school until the weather turned cold and damp. Then I'd walk home for a hot lunch. At that point we retired to the kitchen for a snack of applesauce and frosted oatmeal cookies.

After snack and more conversation, I did my homework and wrote my daily letter to Mama. Button lay with his head on my foot the whole time. I felt content but the experience with the prim girl continued to annoy me. I went to the library and opened the unabridged dictionary. I looked for S-A-F-I-S-T. There were no listings for anything close to that. So I began looking at all the words starting with S-A-F. There were lots of words, but none that I could imagine as an insult. My curiosity was so great that I decided to ask Gram. She was reading in the parlor

.

I sat on the ottoman facing Gram and Button flopped down at my feet. His chin rested on my shoe and his long, silky ears stretched out on either side of his head like wings. Gram looked up and removed her spectacles.

"You look as if something's bothering you," she said.

"Well, I do have a question, Gram," I answered. "What's a sapphist?" I hadn't really intended to just blurt it out like that. What if it was a cuss word? I knew not to use language like that, and Gram would not be happy about my cussing.

"A sapphist," repeated Gram. "Where in the world did you hear that word?" Gram looked a little shocked, and a lot thoughtful, like she was trying to figure out how to tell me something she didn't want me to know.

"I heard it at school." I sat very still, studying Gram's facial expression. It was something bad.

"In what context was the word used?" said Gram.

"Someone called someone else a sapphist."

"Well," she said with a long pause. "Did you look it up in the dictionary?"

"I tried, but it wasn't there."

"And how did you spell it?"

I told her, "S-A-F-I-S-T."

"Try spelling it S-A-P-P-H-I-C," said Gram.

I thanked Gram for her help and went back to the library with Button at my heels.

"C'mon, Button. Let's try again," I said.

I leafed through the 1913 Webster's Unabridged Dictionary until I found *sapphic*. The dictionary listing read:

sap' phic
1. Of or pertaining to Sappho, the Grecian poetess; as, Sapphic odes, Sapphic verse.
2. (Pros.) Belonging to, or in the manner of, Sappho; said of a certain kind of verse reputed to have been invented by Sappho, consisting of five feet, of which the first, fourth,

and fifth are trochees, the second is a spondee, and the third a dactyl.
3. (Pros.) A Sapphic verse

"Well, that's no more help than before," I said to Button. "C'mon, let's go for a walk."

* * *

At school the next day, after the flag salute, Mr. Griffin had everyone remain standing to sing *Dixie*. Most of the students didn't know the words, but Mr. Griffin sang loud enough for everyone. I enjoyed singing and remembered hearing this song once at a political rally in Bishop. So I sang lustily: *I wish I was in the land of cotton. Old times there are not forgotten. Look away, look away, look away, Dixieland.*

Once the song was over, Mr. Griffin announced that everyone should learn the words, as the class would be singing *Dixie* every day after the flag salute. Some of us students looked at one another, wondering if perhaps the *Star Spangled Banner* had been replaced by *Dixie* as the national anthem.

On the playground, the prim girl continued her name-calling, always being careful no teachers were around to hear her. Sarah, Rebecca, Winifred, and I ate dinner on the lawn. Then I went off to play with the boys when the conversation turned to clothes, parties, dancing, and what not.

When class resumed after dinner, the students were shocked when Mr. Griffin called forward two boys who had neglected to complete their homework. Tommy and Jesse stood before the class while Mr. Griffin slapped their palms three strokes each with his ruler. The boys smiled and chuckled on the way back to their seats, attempting to make light of the punishment, but I saw tears in their eyes.

After that, I had a hard time concentrating on my studies. The world had become a hostile place. Mr. Griffin was hard to figure out. One minute he was funny and almost likeable, and the next he was just plain mean. I didn't trust him at all.

Then I began to wonder about the prim girl. Was she just spoiled? Was she threatened by my easy relationships with the boys? Or was her behavior because of insecurity? Only time would tell. But I found myself thinking I didn't want to take the time to find out. My emotions were raw and my heart hurt. I couldn't understand why people were so cruel to one another. A deep sadness welled up in me and it was all I could do not to cry.

In spite of Gram's kindness and the Gaines girls' friendship, in spite of Uncle Sabert and Aunt Marilyn's nurturing, in spite of Button's wet kisses and loyalty, I just wanted to go home to Bishop and Mama. I quickly wiped away a tear that slid down my cheek, hoping none of the students noticed.

After school, my arms full of books, I hurried down the steps. Suddenly I tripped and almost fell. I caught myself on the railing but all my books tumbled to the ground. I looked around to see what I had tripped over.

"*SO* sorry," the prim girl said, sarcastically.

Rebecca had seen the prim girl stick her foot out to trip me, and as the prim girl passed her, Rebecca grabbed her sleeve.

"Leave her alone, Frances! She's not hurting you," Rebecca said angrily.

"Be quiet, Little Girl," returned Frances. "And get your cootie fingers off my arm."

With that Frances turned to me and said, "So you have to have little girls fight your battles, do you, Tomboy? Everyone says you're such a tough one. Huh! I'll believe that when I see it." Then she walked off laughing with her friend.

Rebecca helped me gather my spilled books. Then she looked into my eyes and I saw the watery softness of her tears. Much as I wanted to go home to Fish Lake Valley only an hour ago, I knew I could never leave this girl behind.

11

As I entered the kitchen for my after-school snack, I saw a fat envelope with Mama's handwriting propped against a glass of milk. I eagerly tore the envelope open and was relieved to find a letter written in only one direction. I could read this letter without Gram's help. I carefully returned the pages to the envelope.

"I'm going to save this letter to read after supper tonight," I told Gram. "It will be my dessert."

So after supper, dishwashing, homework, and my customary game of fetch with Button, I went into the library, closed the sliding doors, and settled into the overstuffed chair to be alone with Mama.

Mama wrote in her curlicue script and her usual cheerful manner, but this letter was newsier than the others I'd received. Mama was feeling better each day, but the doctor said she wouldn't be out of the hospital by Christmas. Mama asked me to think about what I wanted to do for the holidays. I could stay in Bakersfield or come to Bishop. If I came to Bishop I wouldn't be able to see her, but I could enjoy the snow. Of course, the trip would be hard, mostly by train but also a long wagon or sleigh trip from the depot to Fish Lake Valley. I would stay with Uncle Leonard and Uncle Frank at the ranch. However, I would make the overland trip with

Uncle Harry who had offered to pick me up and transport me to the ranch and back to the train again after Christmas.

Uncle Harry was not my *real* uncle. He and Mama had been friends since I could remember, so calling him Uncle seemed natural. I loved spending time with Uncle Harry. He was educated and had a good sense of humor. He had been the town dentist when Mama and I lived in Virginia City. After Daddy died Mama had already begun her coughing spells and she couldn't keep up with the rigors of cooking for all those miners. So we moved to Bishop to be close to family in Fish Lake Valley, where Mama had grown up. I guess Uncle Harry missed us, because a few years later he followed us to Bishop. He had saved some money and borrowed a good deal more from the bank and bought *The Bishop Herald* newspaper, where he was now editor.

Unfortunately, Mama and I had not been able to spend much time with Uncle Harry after that. Mama's health worsened and we moved to Fish Lake Valley so Uncle Frank and Uncle Leonard could watch her closely. Uncle Harry stayed in Bishop working day and night and weekends, too, to keep the newspaper going and increase readership enough to pay the note on his loan.

Mama said that she had received several letters from Uncle Harry. He seemed to communicate better in writing, Mama said. I guess that's why he became a newspaper editor.

I leaned my head against the cushioned back of the chair and shut my eyes. I imagined past Christmases. The smells of roasting turkey, spiced apples and yams, fragrant pies and breads, pine boughs, tallow candles, and wood oil seemed right in this room at summer's end. I could hear the snapping fire, the squirrels chattering at the feeder box, and the bells on a passing sleigh. I felt the warmth of the fireplace, the softness of the crocheted afghan, and the coziness of my deerskin slippers lined with lamb's wool. Through my closed eyes, I pictured reflections of ornaments in the window glass, outdoor bonfires with colorfully-clad children warming mittened-hands while singing carols, fluffy snowflakes settling gently on bushes and walkways, icicles coating bare branches of trees that had been covered with red and yellow leaves only a month before.

Tears slipped from the corners of my eyes as I remembered. Then Button slurped up the tears with his soft tongue and gazed into my face with a look of empathy. I took Button's face in my hands and said in a gentle voice, "Don't worry. I won't go away and leave you. I'll always take good care of you. I promise." Button laid his head on my shoulder, and then settled down on my lap to nap.

Before bed I jotted a letter to Mama.

Dearest Mama,

I miss you so and I miss the old Christmases, too. But I think I'll stay in Bakersfield this holiday to be with Gram and Button. Perhaps next year we will all be together once more. Please give my kindest regards to Uncle Harry and please thank Uncle Leonard and Uncle Frank for the invitation. I love you, Mama, and will hold all our best memories close to my heart.

Your loving daughter, Dorrance

12

It was finally Friday of the first week of school. I again wore my blue gingham dress. I had it all figured out. With four dresses I could wear a different dress each day, except Friday when I would wear Monday's dress. By rotating my dresses in the same order I would wear each dress five times a month. I realized that I was luckier than many of the students, both boys and girls, who wore the same clothes every day, or who alternated between only two outfits.

On this particular Friday I was regretting having mailed the note to Mama. I was feeling as if I couldn't possibly cope with another day of teasing by Frances. I was fearful of making a mistake in class that would draw the wrath of Mr. Griffin on the palm of my hand. My stomach ached and churned. I had thought of telling Gram that I was too ill to go to school. Not only did I feel it was cowardly to stay home to avoid these two warped and hurtful people, but I remembered Gram's rule about school attendance. If I was too sick to go to school on Friday, I would have to stay in all weekend to be sure I was well for school on Monday. I guess it was a pretty sensible rule. Without it I may have taken a three-day weekend every week. Besides, Rebecca and Sarah and I were in the process of making plans for Saturday.

I dilly-dallied all the way to school, hoping to arrive just as classes began. But I still arrived early. Sarah and Rebecca were on the steps waiting for me.

"Hi, Doris," Rebecca said with a grin.

"Dorrance," I said and gave Rebecca a wink.

"Dorrance," repeated Rebecca. "Want to go crawdadding tomorrow? Daddy said he'll take us girls to the canals."

That was an exciting prospect!

"Your daddy takes you crawdadding?"

"He loves it but he doesn't like to go alone. Sometimes we girls have to play like sons to keep him happy," replied Rebecca.

"We always take a picnic and come home with a mess of crawdads," chimed in Sarah. "Of course, Daddy does most of the catching. Personally, crawdads give me the willies unless they're already chopped up in stew."

I couldn't think of a better way to spend Saturday.

And then that nasty Frances passed me, bumping my elbow and knocking my books to the ground *again*. I stooped to pick them up and thought of giving her a bloody nose when I stood up. But I decided not to make trouble on a Friday. It might cost me my crawdadding trip.

Frances gave me a startled look, pretending to see me for the first time.

"Well, if it isn't the sapphist in her tacky gingham dress." Frances began primping, smoothing her fashionable skirt and blouse with tiny pearl buttons. Her clothing certainly was up-to-date and more grown-up than the other girls wore. That didn't take the sting out of her words, though. I loved my dress. And I knew Frances's words hurt Sarah and Rebecca, too. They knew how hard their mother worked to make it.

Rebecca was still angry over Wednesday's incident, but she kept quiet. She didn't want me to be teased any more about letting a "little girl" defend me. Sarah and I rolled our eyes and walked to Room 8, taking our seats.

As Mr. Griffin entered, the class stood at attention for the *Pledge of Allegiance* and the singing of *Dixie*. After roll call Mr. Griffin announced there would be a spelling bee a week from Friday. The boards had been covered with lists of words. He instructed the students to copy all the words correctly and begin studying for the spelling bee.

Then Mr. Griffin sat in his chair on casters and tipped way back, his hands clasped over his stomach, and his eyes barely open. The students worked diligently for about twenty minutes. Then Tommy, thinking Mr. Griffin was sleeping, began whispering to Jesse and Jesse laughed out loud before clapping his hand over his mouth. His eyes opened so wide I could see the whites all around his pupils. Then Mr. Griffin was on his feet, wide awake. His eyes flashed. I couldn't decide if he was angry or happy about the infraction. I thought he looked forward to meting out punishment. Mr. Griffin ordered Tommy and Jesse to the front of the class. Evidently creating a disturbance was a greater infraction than not completing homework, because each boy received five whacks with the ruler. Neither boy made small of the punishment today. Tears slid down their cheeks as they walked back to their seats. They could barely hold their pencils because their right hands were so red and swollen.

Mr. Griffin had made his point. The classroom was dead silent. Mr. Griffin returned to his position, tipped back in his chair with his eyes barely open. My hand was trembling as I tried to copy words from the board onto my tablet. I wondered how many I had misspelled. I saw Frances waving her arm in the air trying to get Mr. Griffin's attention. He made eye contact with Frances and signaled her with a flick of his wrist to come forward.

I continued to copy words and tried to remain undistracted by the quiet conversation between Frances and Mr. Griffin. But Frances was leaning over Mr. Griffin in his tipped-back chair and was blocking the words on the front board. Then in a split second the most extraordinary thing happened. *Gravity took over.*

The tall, mahogany chair began to tip over backward. It looked as if one of the casters had rolled off the rear of the platform. Mr. Griffin reached out to grab something, anything, to prevent his backward fall. What he grabbed was Frances's beautiful blouse with the pearl buttons. There was a clatter of those buttons across the wood platform that caught the attention of all the students just in time to see *THE FALL*. Mr. Griffin lay on his back with his legs in the air. Frances lay on top of, and perpendicular to, his torso, her blouse over her head and her camisole the only thing between her birthday suit and thirty pairs of eyes.

The class was stunned into silence for a fraction of a second. Then stifled laughter overcame even the most self-controlled.

"Class dismissed for recess," Mr. Griffin coughed as he tried to right himself.

Frances screamed in hysteria, obviously uninjured as far as her vocal chords were concerned. Thirty students scrambled for the door. Merry laughter and rude guffaws erupted as soon as each one crossed the threshold. On the playground it was agreed that the "unfortunate accident" couldn't have happened to two more deserving people.

I thought I finally understood the biblical proverb Mama often quoted: *Pride goeth before THE FALL.*

When we came back from recess, Frances was gone, presumably to change her dress. The platform on which Mr. Griffin's desk and chair stood was pushed into the front left corner of the classroom, flush with the two walls. There was no danger of a caster slipping off the dais in the future. But Mr. Griffin was taking no chances. He sat on the corner of his desk from that day forward, usually tapping his ruler on the palm of his hand.

When we were all seated, Mr. Griffin assigned us two chapters to read in our history books. There was still some muffled chuckling from the boys' side of the room, but most of us set to our assignment in earnest. No one wanted to face Mr. Griffin's ruler while he was still feeling humiliated.

Then Sarah raised her hand.

"What is it?" asked Mr. Griffin.

Sarah stooped down and picked a tiny something up off the floor. She carried it to the front of the class and laid it gingerly on the desk. As soon as she released it, it rolled off the edge and bounced across the floor.

Sarah gasped and said, "Oh, I'm sorry!"

She chased the elusive object across the front of the classroom and finally retrieved it under a window. Rather than risk its fall a second time, she gently laid it in the pencil trough on Frances's desk. It was a pearl button.

Sarah scrambled back to her seat and resumed reading without making eye contact with Mr. Griffin.

I heard a snort from one of the boys. The rest of the class was hiding behind books with broad smiles on their faces. I glanced up at Mr. Griffin for a split second and saw the beginnings of a lopsided smile play across his lips. He must have realized it was only a matter of time until he lost control of the class, because he quickly stood and dismissed us for dinner half an hour early.

When we reconvened after lunch there were seven pearl buttons in Frances's pencil trough.

By the time Frances returned to school the next day, she had a nickname. Forever after she would be known as Buttons. Everyone called her that but me. I refused to insult my dog by calling her anything but Frances to her face.

13

Saturday morning I got up early, ate breakfast, cleaned up my mess in the kitchen, fed Button, and dressed in my dungarees, shirt, and boots. I gave Button a parting scratch behind the ears and assured him I'd be home soon. I grabbed the sack dinner that Gram had packed for me last night and headed for the Gaines house.

Rebecca and Sarah were already in their father's four-passenger carriage. Julia was tying the picnic basket to the "trunk"; then she climbed into the front seat. I sat on the trunk with the basket, my feet hanging down into mid-air. Rebecca and Sarah had a stack of blankets and towels, and two buckets on the back seat with them. Mr. Gaines got in and took up the reins.

"Everybody ready?" he shouted.

"Yes!" we all shouted back.

"Giddy-up!"

The carriage rolled south on A Street, east on Railroad Avenue, and south on H Street to the edge of town. Then we saw the canals. They were actually irrigation ditches, wide though, with slimy banks of mud and algae. As soon as we stopped, I pulled off my boots, rolled up my dungarees, and ran to dip my feet in the cool water. The seat of my pants was already muddy when Mr. Gaines handed me a bucket and showed me how to catch crawdads.

"Mr. Gaines, do the pinchers hurt?"

"Just call me Daddy," he replied. "Mr. Gaines was my father." Then he laughed and the corners of his eyes showed deep wrinkles, just like Uncle Sabert's.

"Pick them up like this," demonstrated Daddy Gaines with a small critter on the bank. "Then drop them in the bucket of water. That way they won't pinch you and they'll stay fresh until we get home. And watch your bare toes. Those crawdads will think they're a tasty snack."

I looked around for the girls. They had spread the blanket under a large sycamore tree and were eating already. Daddy Gaines followed my gaze.

"Don't worry," he said. "They won't eat it all. They just come along because they think I need company. I'm glad *you* like crawdadding, at least."

All morning long Daddy Gaines and I combed the canal banks, catching crawdads and dropping them into the pails of water. By dinnertime my arms were muddy to my elbows and so was the front of my shirt and dungarees. Daddy Gaines had managed to stay quite a bit cleaner.

"Why don't you take a quick dip in the canal and clean up for dinner," he told me. So I did.

In the canal, up to my chest in murky water, I scrubbed the front of my dungarees and shirt until most of the mud was rinsed off. I dried quickly in the late summer heat. Then we all sat in the shade enjoying fried chicken, boiled eggs with salt, and cookies. I ignored my sack dinner in favor of the food the Gaineses had brought. The lemonade was warm, but it was wet and sweet and the perfect finish to a yummy dinner.

Daddy Gaines and I decided to gather crawdads for another hour while the girls packed up the picnic basket. Daddy Gaines crossed the canal and worked the other side while I worked the near side. I dropped another crawdad in my bucket just as Rebecca shrieked. I turned to see Sarah and

Julia slapping at some flying insects, while Rebecca sat on the ground holding her neck and howling in pain.

I dug a large fistful of mud from the bank and ran for Rebecca. Her neck had a large red spot and was already beginning to swell. I checked for a stinger, but there was none. So I figured she had been stung by a wasp, not a bee. I smoothed the handful of mud on her neck, knowing it would probably not help. I was right. Rebecca continued to cry.

"Poor Becky," I lamented. "Too bad we don't have any vinegar."

"Oh, but we do," Julia said. She flipped open the lid of the picnic basket. Handing a cruet of vinegar and oil dressing to me, she said, "We ate all the lettuce and tomatoes before dinner, so I didn't put this out."

I scraped the mud from Rebecca's neck and applied a liberal dose of salad dressing. She stopped crying almost immediately.

"That's the best treatment for wasp and yellow-jacket stings," I said. "Mud is okay for bees, but baking soda is better."

Daddy Gaines had now splashed across the canal and was comforting Rebecca.

"That's the second time you've saved one of my girls," he said, reminding me of the incident with the railroad tramp. "How about we go home and make some ice cream? That should help us all feel better."

"Okay!" we all yelled.

Sarah sat on the carriage trunk on the way home and I sat beside Rebecca on the back seat.

"Poor Becky," I said, as I examined her swollen neck.

Then Becky took my hand.

"By the way, Doris," she said, "my name is Rebecca, but you may call me Becky." She looked at me expectantly.

"Thanks, Becky," I said. "You may *still* call me Dorrance."

14

Sunday was a day I looked forward to all week. As soon as Uncle Sabert's truck pulled up in front of the house, I ran to greet him and Auntie and the cousins. Then I helped carry the week's grocery order inside. When we were all seated at the table, Uncle Sabert said grace and we dished up our plates.

Today, Gram and I had prepared a breakfast of bacon, eggs, potatoes, pancakes with maple syrup, and applesauce. The maple syrup was ordered special from the state of Vermont. It came in a square gallon can with a metal handle for easy carrying. Gram poured a generous portion in a ceramic pitcher and heated it in a pan of water on the back of the stove. I slathered my pancakes with butter and soaked them in syrup. It seemed like eating dessert first. I wolfed down the cakes, then ate my eggs, bacon, and potatoes lukewarm. I finished my meal with a dish of Gram's homemade chunky applesauce sprinkled with cinnamon. Mmmm!

Button sat under the table eagerly awaiting spilled food and smuggled scraps. But Sunday breakfast was slim pickin's for hungry dogs. This morning he had to be satisfied with potato peels and some egg scraps.

After breakfast, Auntie and I usually cleaned house. So when everyone looked as if they were through eating, I began clearing the table. But Uncle Sabert told me to sit down again, saying he had something important to discuss with me.

He said, "Jack and Andrew help me with deliveries to my poor and elderly customers on Sunday. But I'm considering making a change in that routine. Gram noticed you eyeing that old cello in the library. And she told me the Gaines girls have been encouraging you to take up an instrument. Well, I wondered if you'd like to take lessons from me in exchange for your help with the deliveries."

"Really?" I blurted.

"Really, if you want to."

"Of course, I want to!" I smiled and wiggled in my chair from excitement.

Uncle finished explaining his plan. From now on Jack and Andrew would pull the groceries at the store, pack the boxes, and load the truck. I would help with deliveries and unload the empty wooden boxes from the truck at the end of the day. Jack and Andrew were glad to have more time to themselves on Sunday, since they worked at the store every day after school and all day on Saturday. I was overjoyed to be spending time with Uncle Sabert and earning my once-a-week lesson.

I got up and gave Uncle Sabert a huge hug. Then I hugged my cousins and thanked them all for this opportunity. I promised to do a good job. Then, as an afterthought, I turned to Gram and asked her permission. She answered with a wide smile.

So the plan was ratified and I would work next Sunday. The week went rapidly by as I looked forward to the first day of my new job. Frances, aka Buttons, continued to plague me daily with her taunts, but I was getting used to it, just as Winifred had. And Frances was getting her share of teasing from the boys. They didn't let a day go by without reminding her they had seen her underclothes.

Sunday morning I was trembling with excitement as I started my new job. The truck bounced along the streets making its putt-putt noise and turning the heads of people out for their Sunday strolls. As the truck pulled up in front of each house, I announced our arrival by squeezing the black ball on the back of a long, golden horn.

The customers I met were all friendly and cordial, greeting Uncle with comments like, "I see you have a new helper." And "What'sa matter? Those boys of yours can't handle the job anymore?" One old gentleman said, "Looks like Marilyn converted you. I never thought you'd hire a girl to do a boy's work. But I guess a man's gotta do what he's gotta do to keep the peace at home." Uncle chuckled, smiling at the old gentleman, and giving me a wink.

I remembered the names and addresses of each customer and marked the deliveries in a record book. Each customer had told Uncle to add the delivery to their account. And each customer told Uncle they had not received a bill in awhile. As I entered the amounts of deliveries I noticed that everyone's account balance was zero.

Uncle took a good long time visiting with each customer. He also took quite a bit of good-natured ribbing from the men on his route. While Uncle visited, I was plied with homemade delicacies such as cookies, candies, and fruit punches. All the women were interested in the who's, why's, what's, when's, and wherefores of my "temporary" move to Bakersfield. I smiled so much my cheeks hurt and answered so many questions that my brain was more exhausted than my back at the end of the day.

On the return trip to Gram's house, my curiosity about the accounts book got the better of me.

"Uncle, I noticed in the account book that all those customers have a zero balance." I waited for a response, but got none.

"Uncle?" I repeated.

"Yes, that's right," said Uncle. "Zero balances. All good customers."

I sat quietly trying to understand the hidden meaning behind Uncle's reply. I wondered how he could stay in business by giving away his inventory.

"Uncle?" I asked.

"Yes?"

"What did that gentleman mean when he said Aunt Marilyn had converted you?"

Again there was such a long pause that I wondered if I had asked too personal a question. But I was serious about learning as much as I could about my customers. And I also worried about the amount of ribbing Uncle had so gracefully endured, in light of the teasing I was taking from Frances at school.

"Well," Uncle said as if weighing his words before saying them. "Aunt Marilyn is quite outspoken in her feelings about women having equal rights. You know she worked very hard for women's right to vote in California. In 1911, when we became a suffrage state, I thought the war was won. But Marilyn thought it was just the first battle. In fact, she also thinks women should have the opportunity to do any job for which they are qualified and with equal pay. And I agree with her. We both worked equally hard to establish our business. And, in addition to that, she has carried the lion's share of the work at home. Oops! I guess I should say "lioness's share" since it's the female who does the hunting in the pride. So, here I come with a girl box boy. Guess Mr. Clark couldn't help but tease me about being 'hen pecked.'"

"But, Uncle, you didn't say anything to defend yourself."

"Everyone's entitled to his own opinion. My job as a grocer is to feed people. Besides," said Uncle, "don't you think I said more with my actions than I could have with words?

"And you, my dear, said all the rest. My customers got better service today than they ever did before, because you were there to talk to the women. After all, they do the ordering."

I realized that Uncle had not only given me the opportunity for cello lessons, but he had given me a valuable lesson in customer service. Certainly Uncle Sabert exemplified, and may have invented, the saying: *The customer is always right.*

At my first cello lesson, Uncle Sabert taught me how to tighten the bow and rosin the hairs. He also taught me to tune the strings. That was the hardest part for me because I didn't have much of an ear for notes. Then I learned to change the notes the strings played by pressing them down at certain precise positions.

Finally, Uncle said, "I think that's enough for the first day."

After Uncle left for home, I went to discuss my day with Gram. I filled her in on the pleasures of riding in a motorized delivery truck and on some of the gossip I heard from the customers.

When I became thoughtful, she noticed and asked me if anything was wrong. Was I too tired?

"No," I replied to her questioning. "I was just wondering something."

"Well, I'll answer your question if I can," she said.

"Gram, I noticed when I was entering orders in Uncle's account book that all those people had a zero balance. But they had all told Uncle to charge the order and bill them. And they reminded him that he had not billed them recently. Gram, I think Uncle is giving all those groceries away. I'm worried that he will go out of business doing that."

Gram thought about my question for a full minute. Then she said, "Let's just say that Sabert's deliveries are his form of Sunday worship. The groceries he gives away on Sundays are his tithing."

"What's tithing?"

"Tithing is the ten percent the Bible says we should give back to God."

"Why doesn't he just go to church and put the ten percent in the collection basket. Isn't that what everyone else does?"

Gram explained, "You see, Sabert doesn't attend church because he feels there's too much politics preached, and not *his* politics. He also feels that some people are excluded from church and the gospel message. So instead of attending and donating to a church, Sabert uses Sunday to practice his own form of worship. He donates a full tithe of food and time on Sunday to those he sees as disenfranchised by society: the elderly, women and girls, the sick, and others."

As I later climbed the stairs to my room with Button at my heels, I pledged to fix this day in my memory forever and to try to practice what I'd learned about customer service, tithing, and being a good example.

15

Monday morning I excitedly told Rebecca and Sarah about my job and my first cello lesson. Rebecca invited me to begin practicing at their house as soon as I knew enough to play songs. We also made plans to study after school every day this week, homework first, then spelling words for the competition on Friday. Sarah was very nervous about the spelling bee because parents were invited. She felt sure she would be the first one disqualified and embarrass her parents.

I was confident about spelling, but some of the words on the list were new to me. And I had my heart set on winning. Gram and Aunt Marilyn were planning to attend and I wanted to make them proud.

At noontime, when we were dismissed for dinner, Mr. Griffin asked the boys to remain in class. I soon finished eating and was ready to play, but the boys were still in class. So Sarah and Winifred and I quizzed each other on words from the spelling list. Many of the words were common and short and easy, but many others were long, obscure, and difficult to spell.

We were pretty engrossed in our studying when a loud voice interrupted us.

"Studying for the spelling bee?" Frances asked.

"Yes," I said. "You want to join us?"

All the girls turned to gape at me. Then they looked at Frances to see what her reply would be.

"Huh!" she snipped. "My best subject is spelling. What could I possibly learn from a tomboy and her band of reading retards?" And she whooshed off with her two friends trailing behind.

"What in the world did you invite her for?" Sarah said.

"Force of habit, I guess. Mama always says 'hope springs eternal.' Guess I still hope she'll change."

"I wonder if she realizes that she just insulted herself," said Winifred. "She's in the same reading group with Sarah and me."

Then we all laughed. Soon noon hour was over and we all returned to class. Nothing was said about why the boys had to stay in at dinner recess. My curiosity ate at me all afternoon. So as soon as class was dismissed for the day I ran to catch up with Red.

"Wait," I called.

He stopped and smiled at me.

"What were you doing all dinner hour?" I asked. "I waited to play ball and none of the eighth graders were out!"

"That dumb Mr. Griffin spent the whole hour telling us how we needed to study hard so we can win the spelling bee. Well, that and showing us how to remember the spellings of certain words," said Red. "See? My dinner is still in its bag and I'm so hungry."

"He'll probably do the same thing to the girls tomorrow," I said. "It's probably just his way of creating a competitive spirit."

"Yeah, maybe," he replied doubtfully. "See you tomorrow, Dorrance." And Red ran to catch up with his friends.

Later in the afternoon, Sarah, Winifred, Rebecca, and I sat around the Gaines's dining room table doing homework. When we began studying spelling words, Rebecca excused herself to help her mother prepare supper. I told Sarah and Winifred what Red had said.

"We'd better eat an extra-big breakfast tomorrow in case we have to miss dinner," suggested Sarah.

We studied the easy words first, then tackled the harder ones. Each of us girls took a list of words to look up in the dictionary after supper. Tomorrow we would devise tricks to help us remember spellings based on origins. Then Winifred and I left for home.

I entered the quiet house and walked to the kitchen where Gram was taking cookies off a sheet.

"Hi," I said cheerfully.

The cookie sheet clattered to the floor when Gram threw her hands in the air.

"Oh, my word," she exclaimed. "You scared my liver!"

I roared with laughter.

"Oh, I'm sorry. I really didn't mean to startle you. But, Gram, you are so funny!"

Regaining some of her composure, Gram said with a stifled chuckle and a twinkle in her eye, "Yes, well, be that as it may, my poor liver may never recover. Now help me get all these crumbs off the floor."

"It looks as if Button is already taking care of that."

Gram and I enjoyed supper with applesauce and *no* cookies for dessert. I told Gram about my day at school and the study group for the spelling bee. I also asked if there had been any word from Mama. There had not. After the dishes were washed and put away, I practiced the cello for half an hour, looked up origins in the dictionary, and went to bed. I studied spelling words by lamp light until after ten o'clock.

School on Tuesday morning went by rapidly. At dinnertime Mr. Griffin announced dismissal and told the boys to remain in the classroom. An audible groan went up from the left side of the room as we girls rose and went outside for dinner.

The main topic of conversation on the front lawn was why Mr. Griffin was tutoring the boys and not the girls.

"I think he thinks boys are better than girls. He thinks

he's wasting his time educating girls who will just grow up to be wives and mothers," Sarah said.

Winifred said, "Well, he's right. I don't see why we have to learn all this spelling and math. I know how to clean and cook and sew."

"Is that all you want from life?" I asked her.

"Well, what else is there, really? I don't want to teach school or be a secretary," announced Winifred.

"Girls should be able to do anything boys can," I said.

"That will never happen," Sarah said. "Sure, women can vote in California, but the American government won't let us. As long as men vote, men make the rules. Men are never going to vote for equal rights for women."

"My Uncle Sabert says women need to keep trying. He says things will change, just as they're changing in California. He hired me to do a boy's job. There must be other men like him."

"Well, there probably *are* somewhere," said Winifred, "but Mr. Griffin's not one of them."

"Then we need to prove him wrong. We need to win that competition in spite of him," I said.

"Let's do it!" chimed Sarah and Winifred.

So we all took out our word lists and began studying. We studied together after school every day and at home until late at night. We were committed to winning, no matter what.

Friday morning we girls dressed in our best clothes and reported to school confident that we would make an excellent showing. Parents and friends arrived at nine o'clock to witness the spelling bee. The boys stood next to the wall on the left side of the class. The girls stood in front of the windows on the right. Parents squeezed into the students' desks, except those too big to fit. They sat on top of desks or stood in the back of the room.

I watched as Aunt Marilyn and Gram entered the room. A man gave his seat to Gram while Auntie stood against the wall. I waved to them. I watched the other students wave as their parents arrived for the bee.

Frances stood second in the girls' line, dressed in her beautiful dress with the tiny pearl buttons. Evidently she had recovered them all from the classroom floor and pencil trough and sewn them back on. I could see her craning her neck looking for someone. But I never saw her wave a greeting.

Mr. Griffin entered, introduced himself, and welcomed everyone in his rich southern drawl. Then he introduced the boys' team and, finally, the members of the girls' team. He announced the rules. A word would be read, used in a sentence, and read again. The speller would be disqualified if he missed and the word would go to the next team. The last team with members remaining would win the bee. With that said, the contest began.

The first word, BRIEF, went to the boys' team. Jesse spelled it correctly.

The second word, AMBIDEXTROUS, went to the girls' team. Winifred spelled it correctly.

Word three was SCOUT. The boys got it right.

Word four was LOQUACIOUS. Frances was disqualified—the first one eliminated. Most of the students smiled. Frances stomped down the center aisle and left the room, slamming the classroom door behind her. Some of the boys jabbed each other in the ribs and snickered at her display of poor sportsmanship.

Buttons' word went to the boys' team. They missed it also. Several of the girls covered their mouths to hide their mirth. Now it was the girls' turn. A girl named Cynthia finally spelled the word correctly.

Word five was RIDDLE. The boys' team got it right.

Word six was BILATERAL. The girls' team spelled it correctly.

The next word to the boys was SPARKLE. Tommy spelled it with an E-L and was disqualified.

The contest went on until there were four girls and two boys remaining. Then Mr. Griffin announced a change in the rules. Each speller would get a word. The word would not be passed along to the next speller when it was missed.

The next word went to the girls' team. It was my turn. I spelled CONSEQUENTLY correctly.

The boys' word was SKATE. They got it right.

The girls' word was LUDICROUS. Sarah spelled it correctly.

The boys' word was ANGEL. A boy named Herbert spelled ANGLE and was disqualified.

The girls' word was APTITUDE. The sentence Mr. Griffin gave was: One must have a good aptitude to succeed in school. Cynthia spelled ATTITUDE and was disqualified.

Those students remaining were Jake on the boys' team and Sarah, Winifred, and I on the girls' team.

Mr. Griffin gave Jake the word ANGLE. Jake spelled ANGEL. The classroom erupted in cheers for the girls' team. Mr. Morris, head of the PTA, hurried to the front of the room, shook Mr. Griffin's hand, and announced the prize. The three winning girls would be treated to silent films at the Regal Vaudeville and Moving Picture Theater. Mr. Morris, who was also the owner of the Regal, presented each girl with a ticket for tomorrow's matinee.

Then he called Cynthia to the front of the room and presented her with a ticket also. "Young lady, you also deserve a prize, considering the ambiguity of the sentence Mr. Griffin gave you and the difficulty I had in deciphering his accent. If it were entirely up to me, I would reward nearly all the girls since the contest was so obviously skewed in the boys' favor."

Mr. Griffin scowled when Mr. Morris usurped his authority. But we girls tasted revenge--and it was sweet.

16

I could hardly sleep Friday night. I just knew Saturday would be the most exciting day of my life so far. I had never been to a picture show. Mr. Morris was to drive us girls in his motorcar. So I had to be ready to go by eleven o'clock and walk to Sarah's house where all four of us were to meet. I hurried with my household and garden chores and took Button for a walk. Then I took a bath, dressed in my blue gingham, said goodbye to Gram, and was out the door at ten-thirty. When I arrived at the Gaines's early, I was surprised to find the others already waiting for me. We were all so antsy we couldn't stand still. We hopped and chattered with each other as we looked up and down the street for Mr. Morris's car.

Cynthia had not been to a picture show either. She wore her school dress, the one she always wore. Cynthia had no one at the spelling bee to see her win, but she said her mother was very proud of her. She said her little sisters were jealous of her prize.

It seemed like hours before Mr. Morris arrived in his long, black motorcar. The paint was waxed to a spotless, glossy shine. The seats were tufted red leather with the interior so spacious that all four of us girls fit across the back seat comfortably. Mr. Morris chauffeured us to the theater at the corner of 21st and H Streets.

I had never seen anything as splendid as the Regal's lobby. Red carpet covered the floors and the wide staircase to the balcony. The wallpaper was flocked with ornate designs. Crystal chandeliers hung from the ceiling, casting a soft glow to the walls and making circles of light on the carpet below. On the right, four sets of double doors opened into the theater. Ushers dressed in red wool jackets and shiny black shoes stood at each door ready to show patrons to their seats.

On the left side of the lobby was a concession stand. Behind the counter six smartly-dressed young men filled the patrons' orders. The smell of fresh popcorn made my mouth water. Mr. Morris led us to the concession area and ordered popcorn, lemonade, and candy for each of us. I chose rock candy, Sarah selected peppermints, Winifred ordered horehound drops, and Cynthia asked for black licorice sticks. She carefully wrapped the four sticks in a paper napkin and put them in her dress pocket to take home to her little sisters.

An usher escorted us to our seats in the center front row of the balcony. Five hundred seats spread out below us. I felt like an angel gazing down on the lowly inhabitants of earth.   The folding seats were covered with velveteen upholstery and looked more comfortable than they were. We all set our drinks on the balcony ledge and kept our feet on the floor so we wouldn't knock them off onto the heads of the spectators below.

We slowly munched popcorn hoping to make it last through the double feature. But by the end of the opening newsreel all the popcorn was gone, so we started on our candy. I shared my rock candy with Cynthia. The lemonade was especially sour now that our tongues had pure sugar with which to compare it.

We all sat spellbound through *Bunny Buys A Baby*, carefully reading the captions. The organist in the orchestra pit played music to accompany the silent film. During intermission, an usher brought us more popcorn and lemonade. We went to the lavatory two at a time while the other two protected our refreshments. We chatted about talk we had overheard in the lobby. Sarah heard two people saying the movies would soon talk and there would be no need for the organist and subtitles. That was exciting news indeed. I could hardly wait to see my first talking movie.

Soon another newsreel played and then *The Drummer of the Eighth*. Before we were ready for the day to end, the second feature was over and Mr. Morris was leading us to the car. I asked Mr. Morris about talking movies on the way home. He was as excited as we girls, saying that when "talkies" were released he'd be ready. Mr. Morris said, "Everyone will want to see them," and congratulated himself on his forethought in having built such a large theater. Of course, Sarah and Winifred knew that the Regal had been used for vaudeville shows for several years before movies were invented.

In a short ten minutes we were standing on the sidewalk in front of Sarah's house. We profusely thanked Mr. Morris for the wonderful day. Then we shouted "Thank you" and waved as he drove away.

It was after two o'clock and Cynthia said she needed to hurry home. So I walked part way with her, chatting about the story lines of the movies along the way. When I arrived at my house, I asked Cynthia how much farther she needed to walk.

"Not far," she answered as she waved and ran west on 18th Street.

I hurried up the steps and ran to the kitchen. I told Gram about both movies and about the "talkies" that would soon be showing everywhere.

*   *   *

Sunday morning I was up early. I did my chores and practiced the cello with Button asleep on my foot. Promptly at ten the truck and buggy drew up at the curb. Uncle Sabert limped into the house with the rest of the family trailing behind him. He reluctantly explained that he had twisted his ankle while loading groceries. We all ate our traditional Sunday breakfast. Then I put on the white apron Uncle Sabert had provided and sat in the front seat. Uncle cranked the delivery truck to start it and climbed into the driver's seat. Aunt Marilyn and the boys would return home in the buggy.

"I hope you're feeling extra strong today," said Uncle Sabert. "With my hurt ankle, it's all I can do to drive this ol' truck. I'm afraid you'll have to do all the loading and unloading yourself. Are you up to it?"

"Oh, yes, no problem with that. I'm really quite strong," I replied. "I expect it's all the football with the boys at recess."

The route was exactly the same as last week. I efficiently delivered groceries, visiting with the women as I unloaded their orders, and listening to the good-natured ribbing from the men. But there was one change I noticed right away. All the men insisted that I take a nickel tip.

After the first tip was offered, I asked Uncle if it was appropriate for me to accept it.

Uncle said, "You need to understand men. They have a hard time expressing affection and gratitude. So they do two things. They tease and they tip. You took the teasing with a smile, so you also need to take the tip. It makes the customer feel good. And, I dare say, it probably makes you feel good, too!"

I smiled in spite of myself each time I added another nickel to my apron pocket.

At the day's last stop there were still several boxes of groceries in the back of the truck. Uncle said they had a new delivery and he told me the story of how it came to be:

"A woman came to the store last Monday pulling a homemade wagon consisting of a two foot by four foot piece of wood mounted on odd wheels, two small rubber ones in the front and two large wooden ones in back. The handle was an old belt. The woman had a baby tied to her back and two tiny girls hanging off her skirt. All their clothing was clean but so old I thought it might just disintegrate any minute.

"The woman was extremely careful with her purchases, often looking into a small change purse, and sometimes putting a selection back on the shelf. The little girls never whimpered when things they would especially like were not purchased.

"As it turned out, the woman bought mostly staples, like flour, brown sugar, molasses, oatmeal, eggs, and saltines. When I totaled her purchases she was six cents short, so I offered to open an account for her. She thanked me but put the saltines back rather than take credit.

"Thinking the woman could use a job, I mentioned to her that I was looking for someone to help with stocking the shelves. Then she paid me and left, pulling the groceries and the little girls on the cart.

"Well, on Tuesday afternoon this wisp of a girl comes into the store, introduces herself, and says I told her mother I was looking for a stocker and she was here to apply for the job. So I hired her. She's come every day for three hours after school and done a bang-up job. That's who the groceries in the back are for.

"Think you can handle this delivery with appropriate sensitivity?" Uncle asked.

"I'll sure try," I said.

The truck pulled up in front of a gray, clapboard shanty next to the railroad tracks at 16th and Oak Streets. I jumped down, took a box containing oranges, cherries, nuts, and white sugar, and knocked on the door. I heard a thunder of little feet and giggles, and then the door swung open to reveal — Cynthia and a whole gaggle of little ones.

"Uh, hi, Cynthia," I greeted her, almost at a loss for words.

"Hi, Dorrance." Then looking past me to the truck she asked, "Do you work at Logan's Grocery, too?"

"Just on Sundays making deliveries," I said. "I have the rest of your order in the truck. I'll bring it in."

"But, Dorrance, I don't think Mama ordered anything."

I shrugged and said, "Mr. Logan said to deliver these to you. He delivers to all his employees on Sunday. He'll take it off your account." And I turned to get another box from the truck. By the time I returned, the little girls were shrieking with delight over the fruit and dancing around Cynthia for earning such good food. Soon the five boxes were unloaded on the dining table and I carried the empties back to the truck.

"See you at school," I called with a wave of my hand.

With a look of disbelief and relief, Cynthia waved back.

On the way home Uncle Sabert asked, "How many brothers and sisters does Cynthia have? There was at least one child I haven't seen before."

"Looked like three sisters. I think the baby is a boy."

"Oh, my!" said Uncle.

At home I counted the tips in my pocket. Thirty cents. "Ten percent of that," I thought, "is three cents. But I have no pennies, so I'll round up." I placed the coins in three separate stacks on top of my dresser. I put a nickel in the tithing stack to save for when I found a good cause. Then I put five cents in the next stack for my own savings, never to be spent. The twenty cents that remained I put in the final stack and gave myself permission to spend it.

17

Before long it was Halloween time and the weather had finally cooled off. The leaves were turning color, mostly brown, but some yellow and red. I added another chore to my list. Twice a week I raked the yard and put as many leaves as would fit into the incinerator barrel. This was a tall, wide, steel can with a grate on top. When it was full, I raked the rest of the leaves into piles nearby. On Sundays Uncle Sabert burned the leaves. Then on Tuesdays when all the ash was perfectly cool, I spread it in the garden and threw a little dirt over it to keep it from blowing away. In spring, before planting, it would be my job to turn all the soil so the ashes would be well mixed in.

Gram swore by this gardening method, saying it gave her the plumpest tomatoes and the largest, most flavorful squash in town. Gram also swore by fall cleaning (as well as spring cleaning). She calculated the exact date of this project by the state of the weather. It needed to be cool enough to work hard but dry enough to be able to beat rugs, hang bedding to air, and open all the windows to let fresh air remove the musty, dusty smell of summer. For now, though, I was looking forward to Halloween.

Gram was not a big fan of Halloween. She disliked getting up and down to answer the door and hand out treats.

Last year she said she sat on the porch all evening handing out pumpkin-shaped frosted cookies. This year Gram decided to make candied apples on sticks. Uncle delivered a bushel of green apples, a box of wooden skewers, and a huge bag of cinnamon candies. Gram would spend all Halloween day dipping apples and all evening sitting on the porch giving them away.

I, however, was energized by the anticipation of Halloween in the city. In Bishop, and especially in Fish Lake Valley, Halloween had to be celebrated at school and home. Houses were too spread out to trick-or-treat. Here in Bakersfield there was to be a Halloween party right after school and Gram had told me I could go trick-or-treating with my friends. She reminded me that next year I'd be too old.

Costumes were not allowed at school, but I was working on one for the evening — the Statue of Liberty. Gram gave me an old ball gown. I fashioned a headpiece from cardboard and a piece of gold satin. I looked elegant but told Gram the Statue of Liberty just wasn't the same without a torch. Gram argued that if I carried a torch, I wouldn't be able to carry a candy bag and lift my gown to go up and down steps.

I conceded that could be a problem. So I gave it some creative thought. I hoped I'd come up with a solution before Halloween.

By Halloween morning I'd thought of several solutions, none of which were satisfactory. I figured I could carry a torch and have Rebecca or Sarah carry my treat bag, but that would create a hardship for them. Or I could carry a paper torch in my treat bag and pull it out at each house. Or I could eliminate the torch. I tried making a fake arm holding a torch, attaching it to the gown. But try as I may, the arm kept going limp and dragging the gown off my shoulder. Needless to say, most of the school day my mind was on torches.

I plodded through my studies until dinnertime, when I joined my friends on the grass to eat. After dinner I played a game of basketball with the boys. The physical activity helped me focus. I made basket after basket and the boys on my team slapped me on the back when we won the game. Then it was time to go back to class. At two-thirty classes were dismissed for the party.

We all went into the auditorium in the basement. Miss Scott, the office secretary, and Miss Williams, the first grade teacher, had decorated the room with all sorts of scary pictures. Dry ice was used to simulate smoke in a cauldron with a hairy hand and arm sticking out. Someone had donated a collection of cow skulls. I'd seen many of these in the desert, but the other students exclaimed "Yuck!" and "Ew!" at the sight of them.

In the center of the room was a wash tub full of apples. Most of the upper-grade students lined up to bob for them. It was sure to get their school clothes wet, but they couldn't wait to compete. The first one in line was Red. He got on his knees, hands behind his back, and leaned forward, mouth open, to try to catch an apple. He trapped an apple next to the side of the tub and came up with it in his mouth, water streaming from his face and curly red hair. A monitor handed him a towel to dry off. But Red waved it away, his soggy shirt and hair a sign of his victory. Several other boys tried for an apple, some successfully and some not.

I was the first girl to try. It was a bit harder to get an apple now that fewer were in the tub. The apples floated more freely and it was more difficult to trap one at the side. Then I managed to find one with my mouth and followed it all the way to the bottom of the tub. I came up with the red fruit in my mouth but I was wet down to my waist. I gladly accepted the towel and dried my hair and dress.

As I walked away to the congratulations of many, I heard Frances's cutting remark:

"Tomboy, tomboy, does anything the boys do. Why don't you act like a girl sometime?"

My happy victory was turned upside-down by this unpleasant, critical sour puss. I threw her a look of disdain and walked off to the refreshment table. I soon heard the words "I dare you," coming from some of the boys. Then I

96

heard "I double dare you," and "I triple dare you." I looked around to see who was being dared. It was Frances.

"Fine," she said, "I can do anything that disgusting Tomboy can do." She daintily arranged her dress around her and pulled her ringlet curls back from her face with one hand. The other hand she placed on the edge of the tub for balance.

Someone called, "Hey! Buttons is cheating!" The crowd taunted Frances until she put her hands behind her back. She cautiously opened her mouth hoping to snag an apple while remaining completely dry.

"C'mon, hurry up," the boys, and now the girls, chanted. Frances leaned forward a little more, now putting most of her weight over the tub. Then, suddenly, she was in the water, feet in the air. One of the boys had grabbed her ankles and lifted her head-first into the tub. She came up sputtering and coughing. Most of the kids stood around laughing. One of the teachers ran over to see what had happened. Buttons was now recovered from the dousing and was screaming about "stupid boys" and "mean kids" as she dried off as best she could with a damp towel.

I was stunned that Frances had been retaliated against in such a cruel way, not that she didn't deserve it. It just seemed as if the other students had stooped to her level. I watched her run from the party and I followed.

"Frances, wait," I shouted.

She turned around, tears streaming down her face. "Get away from me," she shouted viciously.

"I just wanted to make sure you're okay."

"Do I look like I'm okay, Tomboy?" she shouted angrily. "This is all your fault anyway."

I was angry myself now. "Just how is it my fault?"

"I'm not going to talk to you. I wouldn't waste my breath."

"You certainly waste enough breath calling me names," I said. "Maybe if you spent some time getting to know me, you could save both your breath and your embarrassment."

"I don't associate with sapphists," said Frances as she stalked away.

"Good riddance," I muttered. I returned to the party and thoroughly enjoyed myself. At four o'clock we all drifted home to prepare for trick-or-treating.

As I walked home, thinking about my costume, I saw a small boy about six years old. He appeared sad as he looked at the note hanging from a string around his neck. I thought, Poor kid, in trouble at school on Halloween. I could imagine the fate likely awaiting him at home. Probably a whipping and loss of his trick-or-treat privileges. Among these thoughts another trickled into my awareness. Why not hang my trick-or-treat bag around my neck? That way I'd have both hands free, one for the torch and one to lift my skirts. I felt only a twinge of guilt taking the idea from the boy with the note from his teacher.

After supper Gram took her seat on the porch with a tray of candied apples beside her. I took great pains to assemble my costume just right. Then I piled my hair up on my head, pinned it in place, and added my crown. I grabbed my special torch and candy bag and went to be inspected by Gram. She smiled wide and sent me on my way.

My costume was a hit everywhere I went, especially because the candle-stick-and-squat-candle torch looked real until the flame blew out. Without a match to relight it, it was of no further use. So I took the treat bag from around my neck, dropped the torch inside, and continued my rounds much less encumbered.

The girls and I trick-or-treated until well after eight o'clock. Then we went home to search our loot. My pillowcase bag was half-filled with homemade candy, lollipops, peppermint sticks, licorice, and fruit. I removed the torch and emptied the goodies on the kitchen table.

My only real disappointment in trick-or-treating was when I discovered all the cookies crumbled to nothing but crumbs in the bottom of my bag.

18

Gram always hired a lady to help with fall cleaning. On Saturday, November 8, Nadine arrived at seven o'clock to begin. I was ready and waiting. The day couldn't have been better — clear blue sky and cool temperatures. Nadine and I rolled up rugs and dragged them outside. We hoisted the heavy rugs over the strong clothesline wires. I beat them with a tool that looked a little like a tennis racket, watching the dust clouds rise and drift away in the light breeze. While I beat rugs, Nadine dusted the floors. Then the rugs were re-rolled, carried into the house, and unrolled on clean floors. After that I carried all the winter bedding to the line and hung it to air.

I washed the sheets and rang them out as best I could, put clean sheets on all the beds and brought the aired quilts and comforters from the line and spread them on the beds. Then I hung the clean, wet sheets on the line to dry.

Nadine had already washed the outsides of the first-floor windows with vinegar and water. I worked on the inside windows and polished until they had not a speck of lint or a streak. I also washed the insides of the upstairs windows. Gram had a friend with a long ladder who would do the outsides next week

.

Then it was time to break for dinner. Gram had made a delicious meal of sandwiches, vegetable soup, and cherry pie. We all drank cold milk since the milkman delivered on Saturday and Tuesday. It was wonderful to relax and talk for awhile before resuming our work.

After dinner it was time to polish the furniture. I was assigned the library. I polished the chairs and tables, and dusted lamps and bric-a-brac first. Then I dusted the books and polished the book shelves. Last I rubbed the oak music stand and the beloved cello to a glossy shine. When I was finished with the library, I worked on the attic room.

By mid-afternoon the sheets on the line were dry. So I folded them and put them in the linen closet. Then I washed my clothes and hung them out to dry.

Gram spent most of the day with a bottle of silver polish working on the flatware and the silver tea set. I was glad. There's nothing I hate worse than polishing silver.

When suppertime finally came I was ready for bed. The house smelled of pine, ammonia, and soap. Every surface sparkled and shined. I was so tired I barely talked during supper. After the meal Nadine went home. I walked Button and played fetch with him, then went to bed. Tomorrow was another work day with Uncle Sabert.

I woke up Sunday morning refreshed from a good night's sleep. By the time breakfast was eaten, I was eager to go on our deliveries. Uncle's ankle was good as new after the slight sprain last week. When we arrived at the Clark house, Uncle engaged Mr. Clark in conversation while I unloaded and unpacked the groceries. When I was done, Mrs. Clark signaled for me to follow her. She opened the closet in the front hallway and took down a good-sized cardboard box. She opened the lid to reveal hundreds of greeting cards and colorful postcards, Valentines, and Christmas cards.

As she handed the box to me she said, "I thought you might like to have these to cut scraps. Then you could make decorated boxes and such for your family for Christmas."

"Oh, Mrs. Clark," I said, "What a good idea. But are you sure you want to part with all these memories?" Secretly

I wondered what I would do with all these cards. I was not at all artistic. I figured the box would sit up in my room collecting dust until spring cleaning when I'd toss it out. But Mrs. Clark seemed so happy to be handing down these mementos.

"My, yes," she replied. "The memories are here." And she patted her chest over her heart. "Please take these and use them. It will make me happy."

So I accepted the box and gave Mrs. Clark a hug of appreciation. On the way to the truck, Mr. Clark patted me on the shoulder and pressed a nickel into my hand. I thought I saw a tear in his eye. In the truck Uncle Sabert related some of the conversation he'd had with Mr. Clark.

"I want to talk to you about something, Dorrance." He sounded serious.

"What is it, Uncle? Have I done something wrong?"

"Oh, no! You've done a great job. In fact, the Clarks have grown very fond of you over the weeks. That's why this is going to be hard to tell you."

I sat quietly waiting for Uncle to find the words he wanted and imagining the worst.

"Well, I guess there's no easy way to say it," said Uncle finally. "Mr. Clark told me that his wife is very ill. This will probably be her last Christmas."

I couldn't control my tears and they fell on the cardboard box I held on my lap. Uncle let me cry until I was down to the dry sobs. He even pulled off the road to allow me some time to compose myself before the next delivery.

"I shouldn't have told you this until our day was done," apologized Uncle Sabert.

"I'm glad you told me, Uncle. It's just that Mrs. Clark gave me these today." I lifted the lid to show Uncle what lay inside. "She should have given these to her children or someone more important. They're all her memories."

"Dorrance, she wanted you to have them. She discussed it with Mr. Clark and they decided together. They both thought you were the one to appreciate them. You've made Mrs. Clark very happy. Most of her friends have deserted her since she's been unable to get out much. You always give her your time and love."

Tears still leaked from the corners of my eyes.

"I'll remember her whenever I cut one of the scraps. I'll use them well."

Uncle patted my knee and we went on with the delivery schedule. Our last stop was again Cynthia's house. Cynthia and I carried the groceries in and unpacked them on the table amid squeals from Cynthia's three little sisters. The baby sat on the rug chewing on a rattle.

A wood stove stood in the corner, unlit on this warm, fair day. A clothes rack sat folded against the wall beside it. Two daybeds were arranged along adjacent walls in the front room, a pillow at each end. Through the one bedroom door, I could see a bed and a crib.

The house was cluttered but clean. The children were clean also, and wearing the same clothes they wore every day. They wore only socks on their feet, *probably to save their shoes*, I thought.

"I haven't met your mother yet," I said to Cynthia.

"She works every Saturday and Sunday keeping house for some people. She has to work weekends so she can be here to tend the little ones while I'm at school."

"Oh, well. Maybe I can come over some evening and meet her."

"Maybe," replied Cynthia. "Thanks for the food. Have Mr. Logan take it off my account."

"Okay," I said. I had the feeling Cynthia was done talking. "See you at school tomorrow."

"Bye," returned Cynthia and waved at me and Uncle as we drove away.

That night, as I lay in bed, I played the day over in my head, saying a silent prayer for the Clarks and for Cynthia's family. Then I dropped off to sleep.

19

Monday morning I woke up anticipating an answer to my Sunday night prayer. But nothing brilliant came to mind about how to help Cynthia or Mrs. Clark. At school I tried to focus on my work, but often became distracted by Cynthia's appearance. She looked as if she had gained a little weight because her dress was beginning to look too small. Her eyes were dull with dark circles underneath. I thought she was probably suffering from too much responsibility. Aside from the movie trip in September I figured Cynthia had done nothing but work, study, clean house, and babysit.

I thought again about my box of cards. I wanted to share them with my friends. I thought it would be fun to spend a Saturday with all my girl friends cutting pictures from the cards (this was called cutting scrap) and visiting. I was sure Sarah, Rebecca, and Winifred could do it, but I knew Cynthia would be stuck at home with her little sisters and brother. I thought perhaps Sarah's sister, Julia, would be willing to babysit, but I couldn't ask her without breaking Cynthia's confidence.

I thought I could bring the box to school and cut with my friends at dinner time. But it was getting too cold to sit out on the lawn. Gram had told me this would be my last week of bag dinners. Next week I'd need to come home for dinner hour. Gram would have a hot soup or casserole ready.

I thought perhaps the other girls and I could cut the scraps and just give some to Cynthia. But that was no fun. The fun was in the togetherness. Besides, Cynthia would never accept a gift. She didn't want to appear needy or irresponsible. I knew she would go without food rather than ask for help. And I had promised to tell no one about her situation.

I sighed and thought, "Lord, what am I going to do?"

"Ask Gram," said a still, small voice in my heart.

"What?" I whispered. But the small voice was silent.

I looked around to see if anyone else had heard the voice or my whispered question. Evidently not. The only activities in class were reading and writing at the moment, not even quiet gossip or note-passing. Mr. Griffin sat on his desk, eyes almost closed and ruler in hand. I lowered my head and went back to work.

That night after supper, I found Gram in the parlor.

"Oh, Dorrance, could you do old Gram a favor?"

"I'll try," I replied.

"I surely would like a fire in the fireplace tonight. Do you think you can light one?"

"Of course."

I loved lighting fires. I carefully laid the tinder and kindling on the grate, and placed a small log atop, then struck a match and lit the tinder. Before long a warm, homey fire was burning.

"That's so nice, Dear," Gram said. "I can sure feel winter coming on in these old bones of mine."

"Gram, I need to ask your advice."

"I'll do my best."

"Well, it's kind of complicated to explain."

Gram waited while I collected my thoughts.

"Um..." I stalled. "Remember the box of cards I got from Mrs. Clark yesterday?"

"Yes."

"Well, I want to share them with my friends, so we can all cut scrap to make Christmas gifts."

"That doesn't sound so terribly complicated," said Gram.

"Yes, well, the problem is that I have a friend who can't get together with us after school or on weekends. I really want her to be part of the fun." *There. I said it without violating Cynthia's confidence.*

Gram sat and thought a few minutes.

"Why don't you invite the girls to come here for dinner each day? I can have a pot of soup and some hot cider or cocoa ready. If your friends prefer to bring their own dinners, that's fine, too. Then you can all eat quickly and cut scrap until it's time to go back to school."

I jumped up and hugged Gram and kissed her cheek.

"You're an absolute genius, Gram! Are you sure it won't be too much trouble? Or too noisy? Or too messy?"

"It will be fine, Dorrance. It'll get me into the spirit of the holidays early. One thing, though. May I help cut?"

I answered her with another hug.

On Tuesday recess I invited the girls. Everyone was excited to get started. Rebecca said her mother had a box of little scraps of ribbon, buttons, broken pins, chains and such that she called "findings" that we could use to make our gifts. Each of us made a list of gift rcipents.

So beginning Wednesday, we spent every dinner at my house making Christmas gifts. I looked forward to Sunday deliveries so I could tell Mrs. Clark how her cards were being used.

After supper each night, Gram prepared a pot of vegetables, broth, and meat and set it on the stove to make a hearty soup. I sat at the table preparing my list. It was quite long. The relatives were listed first, then the customers on my delivery route, and finally Cynthia's family and my other friends. Gram heard my sigh and looked over my shoulder at the list.

"Don't worry, Dear," she said. "It will all be done by Christmas."

20

Just before Thanksgiving the weather turned cold. I received a parcel in the mail from Uncle Harry containing a new winter coat. Even with the red wool coat I found the mornings chilly. Some days the fog refused to lift all day long. The noontime scrap party seemed the only bright spot in the long, dark, cold days. Gram confided to me that the winter fog and cold had always made her "blue." But she said that the daily dinner preparation and scrap party kept her mood more elevated. But I had a concern about continuing the parties. Cynthia had no winter coat. She walked back and forth from home to school, then to Logan's Grocery, in a thin cotton jacket. Mr. Griffin, in one of his more compassionate moments, privately offered Cynthia a warm coat that had been abandoned at school last year. But Cynthia had turned away, saying she was warm-blooded. She said the jacket she had was fine and that she had a warmer coat at home but didn't wear it because it was too hot. Cynthia told me about Mr. Griffin's offer with a note of anger in her voice. She even called him a "do-gooder." I listened attentively without comment. Yet every day I watched Cynthia's teeth chatter on the way to the scrap party.

I wondered if the noon gatherings would be one trip too many in the winter weather. I worried about Cynthia taking cold. That would be very hard on her family, knowing how much Cynthia's income was needed.

Rebecca also noticed Cynthia's discomfort with the cold. Mrs. Gaines told Rebecca that she had a coat she could make over for Cynthia. I advised against offering it, knowing how Cynthia felt about "charity."

Gram was so concerned that she called the Presbyterian Church for help. The lady at the church asked if Cynthia's family attended services regularly. When Gram told the lady "no," the lady said they couldn't help.

"*Wouldn't* help, more likely," fumed Gram before launching into a long monologue about Jesus serving the gentiles as well as the Jews. I listened to Gram's tirade. And I spent a good deal more time mulling over possible solutions. Then one very cold and damp afternoon, over a snack of hot cocoa and toast with jam, I asked Gram some theological questions.

"Gram, why did Jesus want us to do impossible things?"

"Like what?" asked Gram.

"Well, like wanting us to do helpful things for people who don't want help?"

"I don't remember Jesus specifically asking us to do that."

"But you told me the story in the Bible where Jesus said if we help sick, poor, and imprisoned people it's like helping him."

"Yes, I did. Now let me ask you a question. When you help someone, how does it make you feel?"

"It makes me happy. It makes me feel grateful for what I have. But most of all, I feel happy."

"So do you think Jesus told us to be helpful because of how it makes *others* feel?"

"I always thought so before," I answered. "But now, I guess it's for the giver as well as the receiver."

Then I thought about this concept for several minutes.

"Gram," I finally said, "if everyone felt too proud to receive help, no one would get the happy feelings of being able to help."

Gram just smiled.

As I did my homework I kept being distracted by my conversation with Gram. I thought of the many times people had helped me and how it made me feel. I had given little thought before this as to how the giver felt. I remembered when Gram let Button come to live with us permanently. I remembered how glad I was to have the good little companion for my very own. Then I remembered Gram's face when she said Button could live with me. I saw her kind smile and the unshed tears in her eyes. And I could almost feel how Gram's heart must have grown snug in her chest when I hugged her tight.

I remembered my first day of work for Logan's Grocery. I thought about all I had learned, the excitement of helping the customers, and the warm feeling of getting to know Uncle better. Then I remembered Uncle telling me his feelings about women's rights. I tried to imagine how hiring me gave Uncle joy. Then I imagined Aunt Marilyn's joy to have her husband give a girl a chance where only boys had opportunities before.

It was very exciting for me to think about how things came together for everyone's good. But the question I still pondered was: how could I help Cynthia understand this circle of joy that can grow out of showing both your strength and your weakness. Then I remembered one more piece of advice from Gram. "People may be where they are for a reason," she had once said.

*   *   *

We girls finished our clipping and snipping and began to make gifts the day after Thanksgiving. Cynthia was able to stay all day with us because of school vacation. Uncle gave me all the cigar boxes from the store. He brought enough so that each of us had three, with three left over.

Gram donated small pieces of cardboard she had been saving for years. Rebecca brought the bag of "findings" from her mother's sewing supplies. Cynthia brought a spool of wire, pine boughs, pine cones, and dried flower petals. Before the weekend was over, we had made wreaths, napkin rings, wall calendars, decorated trinket boxes, bookmarks, sachets, calling cards, and greeting cards with envelopes. Cynthia made paper dolls for her little sisters and a mobile to hang over the baby's crib. All the gifts were decorated with scraps from Mrs. Clark's beloved box of cards. Gram took pictures of each of us, surrounded by our gifts. She also took some pictures of the five of us together. Then she took the film from the Brownie camera and sent me to have it developed at Booth's Photography on H Street.

School let out for Christmas vacation and there were still many unused scraps in the box. I invited Cynthia over to make a Christmas wreath for Mrs. Clark. Cynthia was talented at attaching the pine boughs to a ring of wire. I tied scraps to the pine boughs with red bows. Then Gram affixed painted clothespins to the center of the wreath. To these clothespins she clipped pictures of us girls. On the back of each photo we wrote short biographies of ourselves and Christmas wishes for Mr. and Mrs. Clark. The wreath was to be delivered the Sunday before Christmas.

As Cynthia was preparing to leave for work she mentioned to me that her mother had next Sunday off. I said excitedly, "Oh, good. Then I can finally meet her!" Then I added, "Better yet, would you like to help with deliveries that day?"

Cynthia accepted but added, "I won't expect any wages. But I'd really like to meet the Clarks."

I called Uncle Sabert to make sure the plan was okay.

On the Sunday before Christmas, the first stop was at Cynthia's. I carried boxes in and left them for Cynthia's mother to unpack. I would pick the empty boxes up on the return trip. The little house was warm, with a fire in the stove and a tiny Christmas tree on a table in the corner of the room.

Cynthia's mother, who wanted to be called Mutter, said, "Please wear my coat, Cynthia. I'll not need it today."

Cynthia and I piled into the truck and began our rounds. In addition to the usual groceries, Uncle had added wrapped gifts and a box of chocolate candy for each customer. Cynthia's enthusiasm for the truck ride reminded me of my own first ride. She was a very observant. She watched how the customers graciously accepted the extras on their orders, saying a simple, but heartfelt, thank you to Uncle. She also watched the nickel tips drop into my pocket. She saw the easy give and take of conversation between me and the women. And she watched Uncle banter with the men. Cynthia's expression lost its seriousness as the afternoon progressed.

"This is the Clark's," I said as we pulled up in front of the house. I handed the wreath to Cynthia and I carried a box of groceries to the door. Mr. Clark answered. His eyes were rimmed in red and a worry line was visible between his eyes. He smiled at me and shook Cynthia's free hand.

"Missus is in bed," he said.

Uncle engaged Mr. Clark in conversation while I unpacked the groceries and put them away in the pantry and ice box. Cynthia stood awkwardly in the kitchen holding the wreath. I heard a sniffling sound and turned to see Cynthia wiping her red, runny nose on the hem of her dress. It seemed her mother's coat had not prevented her catching a cold.

I said to her, "Mrs. Clark is very ill. But she's always been up before when we deliver on Sunday. The scraps were a gift of her memories. I thought it was real important to let her know how they were used."

Cynthia wiped her nose again. Then she followed me into the parlor.

"The Missus would like to say hello," Mr. Clark said to me, with a nod toward the bedroom. Cynthia and I entered the room on tiptoes. Mrs. Clark was propped up in bed on several pillows. She wore a flannel nightgown with a crocheted bed jacket over it. The bed was softly piled with comforters and a variety of medicine bottles stood on the

110

bedside table. I gave Mrs. Clark a soft hug and introduced Cynthia. Cynthia timidly stepped forward, handing Mrs. Clark the wreath. Mrs. Clark's face lit up when she recognized the scraps decorating the wreath. She removed the photographs one at a time and examined them closely, spectacles perched on her nose.

"Why, Cynthia," she said, "here you are. What lovely gifts you made!" She slowly read the biography on the back of the picture. Mrs. Clark smiled and nodded, evidently pleased with what she saw or thought she saw in Cynthia's handwritten message.

Mrs. Clark asked me to describe the other girls and the scrap parties. Then she thanked us for the visit. Just as we were leaving the room, Mrs. Clark called Cynthia back. "I notice you have a nice, warm coat, but I wonder if you'd do me a favor," she said. She didn't give Cynthia time to answer. "In the armoire, hanging on the door, is a very nice coat. I would be so pleased if you could find a good use for it." Then she smiled and closed her eyes.

Cynthia gently opened the armoire door and took down a beautiful blue coat of soft cashmere. She turned to tell Mrs. Clark thank you, that she could indeed find someone who needed a coat. But Mrs. Clark was sleeping.

"Thank you," whispered Cynthia.

On Monday morning I knocked on Cynthia's door. When she opened it I took a deep breath and said very quickly:

"I need to tell you something. Mrs. Clark died yesterday, right after we left." Cynthia and I cried together. Then Cynthia put on the blue coat and she and I took a walk.

I imagined the great joy Mrs. Clark felt as she departed this life. Cynthia allowed her that joy by being a willing receiver. I also knew the valuable gift she had left with Cynthia and me: The ability to give and receive with dignity.

21

     The day before Christmas Eve, I went over my mental TO DO list. I had mailed handmade cards to my family and friends in Fish Lake and Bishop. I had enclosed bookmarks in Mama's and Uncle Harry's cards. Gram gave me a roll of colorful paper and I wrapped my gifts for the people I knew in Bakersfield. I had managed to make gifts for Rebecca, Sarah, Winifred, and Cynthia without their knowledge. Each would receive a picture frame with a picture of the five of us.

     I also helped Gram decorate the house. Gram had not decorated in years and had, in fact, given her tree ornaments away long ago. So we decided not to put up a tree. Instead, we hung a wreath beside the front door and decorated the mantel with pine boughs, cones, and pyracantha berries. In the middle of the dining room table I arranged a centerpiece of red and white candles surrounded by fluffy cotton batting that looked like snow. The house had a scent of pine and reminded me of home on the ranch, except there would be no snow on the ground.

     Tomorrow I'd deliver my gifts to the girls, before Gram and I left to spend Christmas Eve and Day with Uncle Sabert, Aunt Marilyn, Jack, and Andrew at their house. I looked forward to having a scrumptious Christmas Eve supper and singing carols until midnight.

Gram had been cooking all week in preparation. She baked four pies and several pans of dinner rolls. She had also prepared her special 24-hour fruit salad, no small trick finding the necessary fruit this time of the year. Fortunately Gram had bottled cherries, plums, berries, apricots, peaches, and grapes last summer.

On Christmas morning everyone would rise early to exchange gifts and see what Santa had left in the stockings. Gram had knitted a bright red one for me with my name across the top.

There was just one more thing I wanted to do to prepare for Christmas.

"Gram," I called, "may I walk downtown to see the decorations?"

"It's so cold, Dorrance. Are you sure you can brave it?"

"I really want to go, Gram. I promise to dress warmly."

"Wear that muffler hanging on the hall tree, and a hat and gloves," she replied with a sigh. Gram probably thought I'd come home frozen. I bundled up, took the money left from my weekly tips, and headed downtown. I felt a little sneaky telling Gram the trip was to look at decorations, when I really planned to do a little shopping. I was warmed up nicely by the time I arrived at Kresses. I untied my muffler and shoved my hat and gloves into my coat pocket. Then I began to look carefully at all the merchandise. Finally, I made several selections. Then I went downstairs to where the toys and Christmas decorations were displayed. I chose a white Christmas stocking with poinsettias knitted into the pattern and a white cuff at the top. I walked slowly through the toy department. I especially admired the boys' toys like the trains and the Erector sets. I looked at the slingshots and decided my own was superior. Uncle Leonard had made it for me for my tenth birthday. The dolls were attractive, but what could a person do with them? Sit them on a shelf so the porcelain heads and hands wouldn't break. Not much fun there. The baseball gloves were tempting and I tried on several. Then I walked to the clerk and paid for my purchases.

When I left the store I realized I'd spent more time there than I'd planned. I put on my hat and gloves and tied my muffler and hurried home.

After supper I pretended to be overtired. I told Gram I was going to bed. Once in my room, I took the stocking from its hiding place and gathered my needle and embroidery floss. I sat on the bed close to the lamp and cross-stitched a name on the stocking cuff. It took me about two hours, less time than I thought it would take, considering how much I hated any kind of needle work and how truly unskilled I was. Then I carefully wrapped each of my purchases and stuffed them into the stocking. I pulled a lap robe from the closet and wrapped the stocking inside, then laid the blanket on the trunk beside all my wrapped gifts for tomorrow's deliveries. At eleven o'clock I turned off the lamp and went to sleep. Wednesday morning I got up early and made my breakfast. I packed my gifts into two cloth bags and, at nine o'clock, I started on my Christmas Eve rounds. My first stop was the Gaines house because I could drop off five gifts at once, giving me that much less to carry. I wondered if Santa planned his deliveries that way, largest families first. After the Gaines's, I stopped at Winifred's, then Cynthia's, then the customers on my Sunday delivery route, saving Mr. Clark for last.

I worked especially hard on the card for Mr. Clark. I'd finished it before Mrs. Clark died, so it was frillier than if I'd prepared it for only him. I had also written the sentiment inside early last week, addressed to both Mr. *and* Mrs. Clark. Now I worried about causing Mr. Clark additional pain by reminding him of his recent loss. I rapped on the door loud enough to be heard if Mr. Clark wanted to answer, but not so loud as to be obnoxious. The door soon opened. There stood Mr. Clark dressed in his usual tidy manner, hair combed and mustache trimmed. His face broke into a smile when he saw me.

"Please come in, Little Lady," he said, "and enjoy a cup of tea with me."

So I did. I spent a good hour with Mr. Clark, listening to him reminisce about his wife and past Christmases. He stopped often to control his quavering voice. He said he thought he and his wife would have this one last Christmas together. A tear slid out of the corner of his eye.

"Will you be alone, then, this Christmas?" I asked.

"No," he replied, "I have an invitation to Christmas dinner."

I pulled the handmade card from my pocket and handed it to Mr. Clark, saying, "I hope Christmas helps relieve some of your grief. Your wife was very good to me and my friend Cynthia. We both miss her, too."

Mr. Clark read the card and carefully admired the workmanship. Then he smiled at me and said, "I hope you'll be my box girl forever. You're the only one who knows where the groceries go."

I stood up and gave Mr. Clark a hug.

"Merry Christmas," I said.

"Merry Christmas, Little Lady. See you Sunday?"

"Yes, of course." I smiled, let myself out, and walked home.

Uncle Sabert's carriage pulled up just as I arrived home. Uncle hopped down and gave me a hug. We quickly loaded presents, food, overnight case, and Button into the carriage. Gram sat up front with Uncle and I rode in back with the rolled-up blanket, concealing Gram's Christmas stocking, on my lap. Uncle said "giddy up" and we were across town greeting Aunt Marilyn and Jack and Andrew before we knew it.

The Logans had a huge, decorated tree in their spacious parlor. Four stockings hung from the mantel and there were hooks available for several more. Gram took my stocking from among the gifts and hung it on a hook. Then she and Auntie went to the kitchen to attend to Christmas Eve supper. I took the overnight case to the guest room and unpacked the contents into the dresser. Gram and I would share this room tonight. Then I went back to the parlor to place my gifts under the tree. Button nosed among the packages and tree ornaments until Jack and I shooed him away. Then I hung the stocking I had embroidered, with Gram's name facing the bricks. I wanted it to be a surprise in the morning.

Jack and Andrew and I were excited about the gifts under the tree. We began trying to guess the contents. We all laughed and talked while eating homemade candies from a plate on the parlor table. Button got more and more rambunctious as we fed him bites of taffy. We watched him try to lick the sticky goo from the roof of his mouth. He continued to beg and bounce until Jack began playing the piano. When he finally calmed down, he lay with his head on my shoe while we sang carols. Soon Auntie, Uncle, and Gram were singing along.

After quite some time, Jack stopped playing and said he was hungry. When would supper be? Auntie replied that we were waiting for another guest to arrive.

Sure enough, the table was set for seven. Jack played Jingle Bells and we all sang again. At about six o'clock the doorbell rang.

"Dorrance," asked Auntie, "will you please answer the door?"

Everyone seemed to be watching me, so I jumped up and ran to the door. As I opened it, I saw only a pair of arms loaded with wrapped boxes. I stepped forward and removed the topmost packages. Behind them was the smiling face of Uncle Harry!

"Merry Christmas, Dark Eyes," wished Uncle Harry. Then someone took the packages from us, and we hugged each other warm and long. We soon found ourselves in the parlor, everyone talking at once.

Gram and Auntie knew about Uncle Harry coming for Christmas, but everyone else was completely surprised. I had received the warm, red coat from him in November, but I never imagined he would come all this way to spend Christmas with me. After all, he was Mama's good friend, not mine.

"Mama wanted to be here, too, but since she couldn't come, she sent her manservant to represent her." Uncle Harry laughed. "Not really," he teased, "her gifts were late getting finished, so I volunteered to play postman."

"It's so good to see you," I sighed.

"Mama misses you so much she aches," Uncle Harry told me. "We're hoping she'll be able to leave the sanatorium by springtime. She's so bored and lonely that her moods run from very low to slightly higher. But she's getting the rest she needs and the coughing spells are much less frequent."

Gram interrupted saying, "Supper's ready. Please come to the table."

Jack and Andrew rushed to the dining room. I sat between Gram and Uncle Harry and across the table from Uncle and Auntie. I felt completely surrounded by love.

After supper and clean-up, everyone adjourned to the parlor once again. It was a Christmas Eve tradition for each person to open one gift. The grown-ups chose which gift the children would open. Gram suggested I open the gift from Mama. So I did. Inside the large box was a hand-crocheted afghan made with shades of blue and purple. It was very much like the one I missed from home in Fish Lake Valley.

Button nosed the wrapping paper and rolled on his back to play with it. Then he bounded toward the tree to investigate the other gifts. I jumped in his path just in time. I was so afraid he would upset the tree or destroy the unwrapped gifts.

I gazed around the room, fixing this Christmas in my memory: the tree, the crackling fire, the happy faces, the brightly-wrapped gifts, and the ornaments, wreaths, and candles. I shut my eyes and listened to the sounds of cheerful talking and tearing paper as the boys opened their presents. I smelled the remnants of dinner and pumpkin pie cooling in the kitchen. I felt sublimely content.

At about seven o'clock the next morning I heard voices downstairs. I looked beside me and Gram was not there. I jumped up and pulled on my robe, then danced down the stairs in anticipation of gifts and breakfast. The grown-ups were talking and laughing and drinking coffee in the kitchen. It was apparent they had been up for some time. I sneaked into the parlor and turned Gram's stocking on the mantel around so her name would show. Then I joined the grown-ups in the kitchen.

"Where are Jack and Andrew?" I asked.

"Sleeping!" replied Uncle. "Guess they didn't beat everyone to the gifts as promised."

I tromped upstairs and banged on the boys' door. "Get up! Get up, Sleepyheads!" I immediately heard the boys' heavy footsteps as they ran around putting on robes and slippers. Andrew opened the door and all three of us ran to the tree to snoop among the gifts. Button was beside himself with excitement. He jumped and yipped and licked until I put a stop to it with a firm word. The grown-ups, hearing the commotion, soon gathered around the tree.

Uncle Sabert handed stockings to us kids and to Gram. Gram admired the cross-stitch that read GRAM in block letters. She began opening the tiny packages inside, all from Kress: a handkerchief with embroidered blue forget-me-nots, a package of hair pins, a scarf of soft blue silk, and a tiny pin with small multi-colored flowers. In the toe of the stocking was a bag of peppermints. I enjoyed watching Gram as much as I enjoyed opening my own gifts.

Uncle Harry handed me his present to open first. An Erector Set!

"Oh, I love it," I cried. And then I remembered that Uncle Harry would have nothing to open.

But just then he pulled an envelope from his coat pocket. It was the gift I had mailed him. Uncle Harry opened it to reveal the handmade card and bookmark.

"Just what I need," he said. Then he sat admiring my handiwork for some time.

Auntie opened the hair receiver I had made for her. She was saving her hair for a switch. Uncle had a trinket box to hold his cuff links and tie tacks. Andrew and Jack also got bookmarks. Gram got a picture frame with a snapshot of me and the girls.

I opened the rest of my gifts: a red cap and mittens knitted by Gram, a work apron with loops for tools and a hammer from Auntie, a baseball from Andrew and Jack, a ball glove from Uncle, and two new books from Uncle Frank and Uncle Leonard. It was the best Christmas I could imagine. I was especially grateful that I didn't receive the customary "girl" gifts. *I really got things I wanted!*

After breakfast, while Auntie and Gram began supper preparations, Uncle Sabert, Uncle Harry, the boys, and I had a rousing game of five-way catch in the street in front of the house. Then Andrew, Jack, and I played on the parlor floor with The Erector set. We all pulled pieces from the box and began screwing them together trying to build something. We soon gave up because we were in such a hurry to build, not one of us had read the directions on the box lid.

At about two o'clock Uncle Sabert and Uncle Harry left in the carriage. When they came back, Mr. Clark was with them. Soon we were all seated at the dining room table, eating turkey, dressing, mashed potatoes, candied yams, green beans, candied carrots, cranberry sauce, Gram's fruit salad, zucchini and banana bread with cream cheese, olives, and pickles. For dessert there were four kinds of pie: pumpkin, pecan, apple, and mincemeat.

I chose mincemeat because it smelled good and I had never tried it before. After the first bite I was sure I'd never try it again. I passed it to Jack, who wolfed it down and asked for more. I wanted to try the pecan pie, because it was new to me also. But after being disappointed with the mincemeat, I decided to play it safe and ate a piece of apple and a piece of pumpkin.

Aunt Marilyn sighed with satisfaction, deep in thought.

"Penny for your thoughts," said Uncle.

"Oh, I was just thinking how worried I was about Christmas being perfect. And it is," she said, grinning.

At that moment Button came streaking from the parlor as if his tail were on fire. Immediately there was a huge crash punctuated by shattering glass. I jumped up to look.

"Oh, no! He's knocked the tree right over!" I shouted.

"Well, that's just perfect," said Uncle. And everyone burst out laughing.

22

After dinner Uncle Sabert took a carriage-full of revelers home. Mr. Clark was dropped off first. Then Gram, Uncle Harry, and I were taken home. Uncle Harry was staying in a sleeping bag on the library floor. He didn't think it was appropriate to share the attic with me. That night he built a fire in the parlor fireplace and we all spent the evening chatting.

Uncle Harry told some funny stories about the happenings in Bishop and Fish Lake Valley. I told Uncle Harry about school, my job, and my friends. Gram told him what a help it was having me living with her. Then later, Gram took out her Bible and read the Christmas story from the Book of Luke.

Before bedtime, Uncle Harry invited me to play catch with him after breakfast tomorrow. Then he turned to Gram and suggested we all go to the Southern Hotel for breakfast.

"Normally I would like that," Gram answered, "but I'm all in from Christmas. I was really looking forward to sleeping late tomorrow. Why don't you and Dorrance go, though?"

So we did. We arose early on Saturday morning and walked to the hotel. Uncle Harry seemed nervous on the walk — and preoccupied, too — like he had something to say and couldn't find the words. When we were seated in the hotel dining room and had placed our order, I questioned Uncle Harry's quietness.

"I do have something on my mind, Dorrance," he said. "I even wrote down everything I wanted to say, and practiced. But somehow I don't know how to get started now that the time has come."

I sat quietly fearing the worst — bad news about Mama. My eyes began to tear up. Uncle Harry noticed and reassured me saying, "Oh, my, I didn't mean to frighten you and I sure hope what I have to say won't make you cry!"

Uncle Harry continued on. "I'll get right to the point. I came to ask your permission to propose marriage to your mama. And I also hope you'll let me adopt you as my own daughter. That is if your mama says yes."

"Oh, Uncle Harry, I never imagined such a thing! Oh, it's just a wonderful idea! Oh, I'd love it so much!" I jumped up and threw my arms around his neck.

"So I take that to mean you have no objections?" he asked.

"None! None at all!" I replied with an uncustomary giggle. "When? Where?"

"I need to actually propose to your mama first. But, if she says yes, then I'd like to get married in the spring. I hope she'll be out of the hospital by then."

"I'm so excited I don't think I'll be able to eat!" I cried.

"There's a favor I want to ask," said Uncle Harry.

"Anything," I said, and giggled again.

"Do you think we can arrive at a suitable new name for me? Uncle Harry doesn't sound quite right, since hopefully I'll soon be your father. I don't expect you to call me Father right now, or ever, if you don't want to."

"It may sound a little disrespectful," I said, "but could I drop the *Uncle* and just call you Harry for now?"

"I'd be delighted to be called Harry," he said and then he kissed me gently on the cheek just as the waitress brought our breakfast.

After eating, Harry and I went home to share the news with Gram. Gram said to Harry, "I wondered how long it would take you to settle down with a good woman. Congratulations!"

"Thank you. But it might be a tad early. Eva hasn't accepted my proposal yet," answered Harry.

"There's no question of that happening," said Gram. "She's been in love with you for a good long time."

"I have another surprise. I bought a house in Independence," said Harry.

"What about the newspaper?" asked Gram. "How will you manage such a long-distance business?"

"I sold the Bishop paper and bought one in Independence," Harry continued. "I got enough for the Bishop paper to pay off the note on it and buy the house in Independence outright. Then I borrowed from the bank to buy the *Independent*. Financially, we'll be in better shape now."

"It seems you've put some good thought into all this. I'm very happy for you," said Gram.

"There's one problem, though," Harry went on. "There's no schooling past eighth grade in Independence."

I gasped, but sat quietly listening to what solution the grown-ups would work out for me.

"Of course, I know Eva would like to have Dorrance at home. But the high school in Bishop is too far away and has no student housing. Dorrance will have to get her schooling elsewhere. I'm hoping she can stay here, coming home for summers and vacations."

"What do you think about all this, Dorrance?" he asked.

I now had permission to speak. But I was so confused. Ever since coming to Bakersfield I had viewed my stay as only temporary. My daydreams were full of Mama and me together again.

"I don't know," I stammered. "I like it here but I was hoping to live with Mama and you."

"I understand," said Harry. "I don't expect you to give me and Gram an answer today. But as you decide, please do two things. Keep an open mind so you can see all possible solutions. And do what's going to be best for you in the long run. This is one of the most important decisions you'll ever make."

To Gram he said, "I'm sorry to ask you to assume this extra responsibility. You'll need to think it over carefully, as well. These are your 'golden years.' Remember, there are always alternatives. Now I'm going to take a walk and give you two an opportunity to talk all this over in private."

Gram and I sat staring out the window watching Harry walk away. Anger seethed in my heart. I felt manipulated. Two hours ago I was so happy, picturing a life in Bishop with a "real family"---a mama and a papa. I had unconditionally given my permission and approval without question. Now I looked at a stranger walking away. I felt as if I were given a father and been abandoned by him the same day. Not only that, but I felt abandoned by Mama as well. If they were going to move anyway, why couldn't they move somewhere with a high school---like Bakersfield?

Suddenly I was overcome with an all-consuming grief. I began sobbing and hiccupping from deep in my soul. My heart ached as though a chunk had been torn from it. Then I felt Gram's arms around me, holding me close and stroking my hair.

Gram was also feeling angry. I knew she loved me. She loved having me here. But she also felt Eva and Harry had made decisions that deeply affected her and me without giving our feelings much thought. And Harry had walked away leaving her to deal with my emotional trauma. "Just like a man," she said under her breath.

"I have a hard time believing Eva had much input to these decisions, but she's in love and love sometimes makes people do foolish things," Gram said.

Then she said no more while I cried and cried.

I woke up with my head on Gram's shoulder. I was a little disoriented at first. When I was fully awake I sighed and closed my eyes again. Gram coaxed me to open my eyes and talk about my feelings and my options. I was quiet, thinking. Then with tears in my voice I said, "I'll quit school and go home."

"And then what?" asked Gram.

"I'll get a job."

"Doing what?"

"What I do here. Deliveries and such."

"And how long will you do that?"

I pondered Gram's question for several minutes. Then I said, "That won't work. No one but Uncle will hire a girl for a boy's job."

"Let's say they did. Let's say you got a job in a grocery store, or even in your mama's deli. How long could you do that six days a week before you got bored?" asked Gram.

"Oh, I like my job a lot," I replied quickly.

"You're thirteen years old. Is that what you want to do for the rest of your life?"

I remained silent with tears welling in my eyes.

Gram began asking more questions for me to ponder. "How long would you be living with Mama, anyway? Until you're eighteen? Until you marry? When you leave your parents' home what will you do? Cook? Clean? Have babies? Do you want more from life than being dependent on your husband?

"Dorrance, I know you're very hurt right now. But I don't think Mama and Harry made these decisions to hurt you. I think they looked into the future to see what might be best for you. Your mama and I have often talked about how intelligent and capable you are. Eva always wanted you to go to the university so you can learn a profession. You know how hard your mama's life has been since your father died, especially since she took ill. She doesn't want you to face the same hardships."

My head whirled with so much to consider. Finally, I said I wanted to think alone. Gram excused herself and told

125

me she'd be in the library when I was ready to talk some more.

"Gram," I said, "I think I want to go walking."

"That's fine," she answered. "Dress warmly."

I pulled on my coat, hat, and gloves and headed for Cynthia's house. I figured if anyone would understand my pain it would be Cynthia. On the way to her house I thought about Cynthia's mother. She was alone with five children. She had no education beyond grammar school. She had to clean other people's houses for a living. It must hurt her terribly to have to send her daughter out to help support the family. I knew of other women in similar situations. I certainly didn't want to end up like Cynthia's mother, living a life of constant worry and poverty.

I was soon on Cynthia's doorstep, knocking loud enough to be heard over the noise inside. Cynthia's little sister, Gwen, opened the door. I looked past her into the house. Bedlam ensued within.

"Where are Cynthia and your mom?" I asked seven-year-old Gwen.

"They had to work," replied Gwen.

"So you're here alone?" I asked, semi-horrified.

"Only until five-thirty when Cynthia gets home," stated Gwen matter-of-factly.

"Would you like some company for awhile?" I asked. "I could help you with the little ones."

"No, thanks," answered Gwen. "Mutter wouldn't like that."

"Well, could I just come in and rest awhile before I go home?" I asked.

"I guess that would be okay."

So I entered the busy house. Gwen seemed absolutely starved for attention and talked non-stop about everything from the weather to private family matters.

"We was hoping Patter would come home for Christmas," she said. "But he didn't. We thought he'd bring toys and candy, but he didn't. Mutter is sad because she doesn't know where he is. He left last summer to find work in the oil fields.

"Cynthia is very sad because she always liked Patter the best. Cynthia and Mutter argued all day Christmas. I was so sad. Now I'm the babysitter. Mutter and Cynthia are working to save money so we can move to Los Angeles and live with Granna and Gramps."

I stayed until dusk and then went home. I was very tired from listening and chasing after babies all afternoon. But the experience put my own dilemma into perspective. I arrived home feeling less self-pity.

I checked in with Gram, who was cooking supper. I told her about my afternoon with an infant, two toddlers, and a second grader. I said I was feeling a little better but that I hadn't yet made a decision. Gram said she had been giving the situation some thought as well.

I wondered if she had decided anything so I asked, "Gram, if I wanted to stay here, could I?"

She smiled her warm smile and said, "I'd love to keep you with me permanently, if that's what you decide is best."

Harry arrived in time for supper. The meal was as pleasant as it could be under the circumstances. Harry smelled funny and he didn't talk any more about the impending marriage and adoption. I didn't bring the topic up either.

After supper Gram invited Harry to the library and shut the door. I thought Gram was probably reprimanding Harry for coming home smelling of alcohol.

I retired to my bedroom and began making a list of all the things I would like to be when I grew up. WIFE and MOTHER did not appear on the list. Then I went through the list again and put a check mark by everything requiring a high school diploma. Then I placed an X by everything needing a college education. I then knew I needed to continue my education. I needed to challenge the status quo---the way things had always been. I wanted to learn the ways of people in foreign lands. I wanted the same opportunities and privileges men had. As much as I felt abandoned right now, I knew in my heart that this experience would make me strong, if I could survive it.

I turned my paper over and made a second list — Survival Tactics. I listed: summer with Mama, good friends in Bakersfield, work at Logan's Grocery, school, writing letters, phone calls (talk Mama into getting a telephone), athletics, music, Button, Gram, Uncle and Auntie, saving money, taking photos with the Brownie to exchange with Mama, invite Mama to visit at Christmas holiday. Then I ran out of thoughts. But my list was pretty long.

I realized I had been fairly happy here with Gram. Yes, I knew I could do this thing that had been thrust upon me.

At breakfast next morning I told Harry I would stay here with Gram. I made him promise I could spend summers in Independence. I asked him to get a telephone so I could call Mama. Harry promised to pay my expenses through college. So it was done.

23

Christmas vacation was soon over, Harry was gone, and I returned to school. I had seen little of my school friends over the holiday. The Gaineses had taken a trip to the snow between Christmas and New Year's Day. Cynthia had been working every day. Winifred had out-of-town guests. All the other girls enjoyed their holiday. The visit from Harry had ruined mine, but I said nothing to my friends. We were glad to see each other and get back to the routine of school.

Mr. Griffin had evidently had a much-needed rest. He returned to the classroom in a good-natured mood. I knew he would soon flip-flop between jovial and sadistic. But I had also learned a lot of academics from him. Because I was studious and well-behaved, I knew I need not fear his ruler any longer. Besides, Mr. Griffin seemed to have already singled out the few students he would use as his scapegoats.

Mr. Griffin also had a couple of "pets." Frances was one of them. She often boasted about Mr. Griffin having dinner at her house. Speculation among the girl students was that he was looking for a wife. Frances's mother was divorced. I had heard the boys on the playground say Mr. Griffin was not looking for a wife at all — just a "roll in the hay." I wasn't really sure what that was, but it didn't sound very nice. I began to wonder if that's all Harry wanted with

Mama. I decided it wasn't. I believed Harry actually loved Mama. It was time Mama had someone to love her. She deserved it. I hoped I could trust Harry not to hurt her, as they both had hurt me.

When I walked home for dinner I missed having Sarah, Becky, Winifred, and Cynthia to visit and scrap with. When I returned to school, the girls told me they missed it too and asked if they could eat dinner at my house until spring. That night I asked Gram who said, "Of course." So the second week in January we began the dinner routine again.

Instead of cutting scrap, we often put records on the gramophone and danced. I had never liked dancing. I disliked waiting for a sweaty-palmed boy to choose me as a dance partner, like one would choose a ripe melon or a fresh loaf of bread. I disliked having my feet trod by boots. I disliked pretending to have enjoyed the dance. It made me feel phony, dishonest. Much as I hated ballet, I preferred it to dancing with boys. After a few country dances in Fish Lake Valley, I had given it up. I would not accompany Mama to the dances, preferring instead to read or clean house.

I discovered I liked dancing with the girls, though. They had a good sense of rhythm and didn't hold me too tight. They also didn't try to squeeze my developing body when the chaperones had their backs turned. There were no expectations beyond the dancing. No need to worry about some boy monopolizing my dinner break or wanting to hold my hand or telling lewd lies about me to the other boys. The only really bothersome thing about dancing with the girls is that I felt like a substitute for a boy my partner was secretly thinking of. Sarah and Winifred talked about boys way too much for my taste. Cynthia usually chose to dance alone or to just watch. Becky was the only one who made me feel *cherished.* I thought that was probably because Becky was young enough not to be boy crazy yet. I again wondered why I wasn't boy-crazy.

I still played sports with the boys whenever I could — usually basketball after school these days. I liked boys as friends. The boys thought of me as one of their own. I doubted any boy would consider me girlfriend-material. The feeling was certainly mutual. I thought over Frances's "tomboy" chants. I had heard grown-ups refer to me as a "late bloomer" when they thought I wasn't listening. For now, I was glad I wasn't interested in boys. Girls seemed to lose all their common sense when a boyfriend was involved.

But I wondered more and more often if there was something wrong with me. I obsessed over the idea that my *tom-boyishness* had a lot to do with Mama's and Harry's decision to have me stay in Bakersfield. I wondered if I was an embarrassment to Mama. Certainly the church lady in Fish Lake must have thought so. These thoughts and feelings began to plague me that second half of my eighth grade year.

The second week in January Mr. Griffin assigned the class to write a research paper. He gave specific instructions on how this was to be accomplished. Most of the class moaned and groaned over the assignment. But I was excited about the prospect. I could select my own geography topic and research for the paper at the recently completed Beale Memorial Library. The assignment presented a challenge that would take my mind off the turmoil of recent events and feelings.

Another exciting event was also being planned. There was to be a basketball tournament. I knew my playground team could easily beat any other team at Franklin School. Red was to turn in the list of teammates on Friday. The tournament would take place during dinner recesses for five days the last week of January. The winning team would receive a trophy to be displayed in the Franklin School office along with a picture of the team.

I decided to write my research paper on the Amazon River Valley in South America. I spent most of Saturday at the library with Becky, who was also researching a paper. I did not have much experience with libraries, so Becky showed me how to use the card catalog. We both spent the day pouring over encyclopedias and magazines, taking notes on small note cards. Then we walked home, chatting about all sorts of things and reminiscing about last summer's skinny dipping adventure.

Sunday was occupied with deliveries, my cello lesson, laundry, and chores that had been neglected on Saturday. Then it was Monday again. When I arrived at school I went to the office to view the posted teams for the basketball tournament. There was Red's name, captain of the team. But my name was missing. There were only four names posted — not enough for a full team. I entered the office to report the mistake and found Red already there, talking with the principal, Mr. Owens.

"I'm sorry," Mr. Owens was saying, "girls can't play basketball."

"But Dorrance is our forward. She makes more baskets than anyone. She can even make half-court shots," argued Red.

"I'm sorry. Girls have never played basketball, especially on boys' teams. If you want to play in the tournament, you'll need to replace Dorrance with a boy," stated Mr. Owens unequivocally. Then he turned and went into his office, shutting the door.

Red turned to face me and shrugged his shoulders. "I guess you can't play," said Red.

"But that's not fair," I cried. "I've practiced all year with the team. I shouldn't be excluded just because I'm a girl."

"I guess you're right, but what am I supposed to do about it?" asked Red lamely.

"Ask the team what they want to do, I guess," I said. But to myself I thought, "Of course you don't know what to do. You've never been prevented from doing things because you're a boy." And then I said to Red, "When you go home today, ask your mother what you should do."

"Okay," said Red. "I'm really sorry, Dorrance. You *are* the best player. It shouldn't matter if you're a girl."

I went on to class. At morning recess the other boys on the basketball team told me they were sorry I couldn't play in the tournament. By dinnertime every boy in the upper grades seemed to have heard. Some of them caught up with me on my walk home for dinner. They all said it was unfair that I couldn't play.

I said, "Thank you." But I was thinking, "I hope these boys remember this when they grow up and vote for women's rights." I shared the problem with Gram and the girls over dinner. Gram said she would call Aunt Marilyn for advice. Becky was especially angry about my not being allowed to play. Cynthia was also angry. Sarah and Winifred didn't understand why everyone was so upset, saying, "It's only basketball."

Becky defended her anger saying, "It's not about basketball, Sarah. It's about girls having the same opportunities as boys, no matter what."

Then Winifred turned to me saying, "Why can't you just be satisfied with what you *can* do?"

"I could if I wanted to do those things, but I don't. And I don't think I should have limits put on my career, or my hobbies, or how I dress, or anything else as long as I'm a good citizen," I replied.

The discussion was becoming heated. Gram wasn't willing to let us argue until it cost us our friendship. So she said, "I see that you're struggling with the same issues grown-ups have been struggling with for years. I advise you all to keep open minds. Be careful not to cast aspersions on your friends while considering such important issues."

I could see all of us considering Gram's words. Slowly, one by one, we decided Gram was right. We would have to be careful not to let our political and social views ruin our friendships.

On Friday of this third week in January report cards were sent home with students. Becky approached me with her report card. She had tears in her voice as she asked me to look at it. Becky's grades had dropped a full letter grade in almost every subject. I read the teacher's comments: Rebecca is a good student. Her lower grades do not reflect her intellect nor her effort. Rather, I think Rebecca is having trouble seeing the blackboard. I suggest she probably needs spectacles. Sincerely, Miss Harris.

"I just can't get glasses," cried Becky. "Everyone will call me four-eyes." And then she burst into tears.

I hugged her and gently patted her back. Then I asked, "Do you have trouble seeing the board?"

"I do," replied Becky. "I moved to the front of the class, but I still can't see well. I get headaches from trying. Oh, what will I do?"

"You'll get spectacles and you'll ignore the teasing bullies," I told her. "You don't count them among your friends anyway. You'll always have the people who love you." I stopped short of saying *like me.*

Becky sniffed a final sniffle and nodded. Then she took her report card from me, gave me another hug, and headed home. I went to the playground for a basketball game. The tournament would begin Monday and I was wondering who my replacement would be.

"We're not playing in the tournament," Red told me. "You're part of our team and we've decided not to play without you."

The other boys assured me that it had been a group decision that they were all happy about. They all smiled at me and tossed me the ball. I made a half-court basket and the rest of the afternoon we had a great practice. Many of the boys from other teams took time out of their own practices to watch the team that wouldn't play in the tournament.

I presented Gram with my report card: "A"s in everything except music. I, quite frankly, didn't have much of a singing voice even though I loved to sing. But since Christmastime I had refused to sing *Dixie* in my usual lusty manner. Mr. Griffin must have noticed, since that was the only *music* we had learned all year. Gram listened to my explanation of the C grade and laughed out loud.

Then I told Gram about the boys' decision to not play in the tournament.

"My word," said Gram, "that was Aunt Marilyn's advice exactly. When I called her she said, 'Get the boys to boycott the tournament.' She said if there was more time we could go to the school board. Auntie said she would contact a school board member and have the issue added to the agenda for the spring Board Meeting. She also said that the school board is made up of a bunch of old geezers who will be horrified to think there are girls wanting to play sports. Anyway, I'm happy to hear your teammates are supporting a boycott."

Gram paused to think about what she had just said. "My word. I'm feeling more like my rebel self than I have in years. And you have been here only six months."

"I'm feeling a little guilty about the tournament," I said. "It's sad that my team won't have a chance to win the trophy."

"They made the decision to do the right thing," said Gram. "They undoubtedly feel good about their choice. Perhaps that victory feels better than a basketball trophy."

24

Saturday's library research, along with Sunday's deliveries and chores, made the weekend fly by. I brought my signed report card back to school and laid it on Mr. Griffin's desk with the others. Mr. Griffin talked up the noon basketball tournament, encouraging the girls to go and *cheer the boys on.* Red looked over at me and rolled his eyes. Several girls glanced at me and shook their heads, letting me know they would not be going. I was astonished that so many of the students had heard my plight and, evidently, supported a boycott of the tournament.

After morning recess, Mr. Owens the principal, brought the trophy to each classroom and encouraged every student to attend the tournament. Mr. Owens said a reporter from *The Bakersfield Californian* had been invited. He would take pictures of the winning team and the spectators for the daily newspaper.

My, my, I thought, the teachers and principal are certainly making it hard for the students to boycott. All they've forgotten is free food.

At dinnertime I headed for home. Then I heard Becky, Sarah, Winifred, and Cynthia running to catch up with me. I also noticed others walking home for dinner.

"There's a boys' team in the seventh grade that's decided not to play," said Becky. "Most of the girls decided to boycott, too."

"How did they know about it?" I asked.

"Well, I sort of asked Miss Harris if she thought a boycott could change things for girls' athletics," answered Becky. "She thought it was a good topic for class discussion. So all morning we discussed various ways to change societal rules and laws, *except when Mr. Owens came in.* I guess Miss Harris's students thought she had a better argument than the principal. Miss Harris said, 'As long as we participate in the status quo, nothing changes.'"

"Mr. Griffin sure made it hard *not* to attend," said Winifred, "with all his talk about cheering the boys on. But then it turned out the boys weren't going without you, Dorrance. So there would have been no one to cheer on anyway."

"I can hardly wait to get back to school to see what actually happened," said Cynthia.

We ate our dinner and played some music. We decided to go back to school a few minutes early to see how the first day of the tournament went. When we arrived at school, the basketball games had already ended. We proceeded to our classrooms. Red came running up to me in a state of excitement.

"Dorrance, the reporter has been waiting to meet you," he shouted, pulling my arm so I would follow him.

"Why?" I asked, as I ran along beside Red.

"*Why*? Because nobody played!"

"Nobody?"

"Nobody had a full team. The largest team was three people. And most of the spectators boycotted too. It's big news!"

"Here she is," shouted Red to a young reporter.

"So you're the infamous Dorrance, the one who wasn't allowed to play?" asked the reporter.

"Yes."

"I'm William Jones from *The Bakersfield Californian*. Tell me how you were able to stage this boycott."

"I didn't stage it. The students just heard about it and decided they didn't want to participate in supporting the status quo. In fact, Red and the other boys on my team were the leaders. They were the first ones to take a stand for justice."

"What do you mean *justice*?" challenged Jones. "Don't you know this is an act of insubordination and disrespect of your superiors?"

"The old ways are not always the best ways," I replied. "Slavery was accepted for centuries, but it wasn't right. Keeping women from equal opportunities is just another form of slavery. I'm immensely proud of Franklin School's students for being open-minded and courageous enough to stand up for their beliefs."

I decided to end this interview, so I said simply, "I need to go to class now."

On Tuesday morning Uncle Sabert pulled up in front of Gram's house driving his delivery truck. He had a paper tucked under his arm. I opened the front door and Uncle did a little two-step jig over the threshold.

"I brought the morning edition," he said, waving the paper in the air. Uncle unfolded the paper and laid it on the kitchen table. There on the front page was a story bi-lined: *Franklin Students Take Justice Stand.* The comprehensive article quoted people from both sides. But my words stood as truth. The article pointed out that the students had sought no publicity. They simply did what they individually thought was right. The Mr. Jones had quoted my interview in perfect context. The article concluded: "Equal rights for women is the future."

Uncle asked me, "Do you know what this means?"

I stood thinking until Uncle could stand it no longer.

"Dorrance," he answered his own question, "it means *The Bakersfield Californian* has taken a political stand to support women's rights in general — and the national right to vote in particular. You and your friends have done what the politicians have been unable to do with all their talk. You put your beliefs into action. And that action spoke the truth!"

Uncle gave me a huge hug and lifted me off my feet, swinging me around in mid-air until we were both overcome with laughter.

25

The last weekend in January marked the birthday anniversaries of Jack and Andrew. Because they were born on consecutive days, they traditionally celebrated together on the weekend nearest their birthdays. This year, however, the weekend fell precisely on Jack and Andrew's birthdays, January 24 and 25. Jack was to have a birthday dinner on Saturday night and Andrew would have a birthday breakfast on Sunday morning. This year Gram and I would spend the night, as we had on Christmas Eve.

I got up early on Saturday morning, ate breakfast, did my chores, played with Button, and gathered my research materials together. Then I took some of my tip money and the dollar Gram had given me and put them in the pocket of my blue gingham dress. I walked to Becky's house to pick her up for our weekly library trip.

"Becky, I need to shop for birthday gifts for my cousins today. I have to be home by three o'clock, so I won't be able to work on my paper as long as usual. Would you like to shop with me at about one o'clock?"

"Oh, yes. Can we get a hot dog from the vendor for dinner?"

"That would be fun."

So Becky begged a quarter from her mother and off we went to the library. At precisely twelve-thirty we began our dinner and shopping trip. Our first stop was at the hot dog vendor at 19th Street and Chester Avenue. We each bought a hot dog. Becky had hers topped with ketchup. I had mine with *the works* — ketchup, mustard, chopped onions, and relish. I passed only on the sauerkraut. We each ordered a hot cocoa. Then we sat on the cold sidewalk and leaned against the wall of the drug store to eat, drink, and chat.

The main topic of conversation was *The Bakersfield Californian* article from last Tuesday. We also talked about our reports. I told Becky about the Amazon women in Greek mythology. The women were the warriors and the men weren't needed at all. We laughed at the thought. Then we began to daydream about what life will be like when women have professions and are in charge of the government. We began calling each other Dr. Chegwidden and Judge Gaines. Then we got the giggles. Becky giggled so hard she choked on her cocoa and it came out her nose. Then we laughed even harder. It took us a full ten minutes to regain control of ourselves. The passers-by looked at us with expressions ranging from disgust to amusement. But Becky and I didn't care what anyone thought. We were having too much fun.

When the clock tower struck one, Becky and I threw our trash away, returned the cocoa mugs to the vendor, and headed to Kress. I had instructions from Gram to purchase a good-quality pocket knife for Andrew who was turning eleven. Jack had been begging for spats for two years. Now that he was turning sixteen, Gram thought he was old enough to *put on the dog* for the girls. Becky and I split up. I combed the main floor and Becky looked in the basement for knives and spats. When we found neither, I asked a clerk where we might find those products. The clerk directed us to the Mercantile on Chester Avenue for knives and to Sears for spats.

We went to Sears first, found some good white spats for eighty-five cents and I purchased them. The clerk gift wrapped them for an additional nickel. Then we walked up

Chester Avenue to the Mercantile. It was getting late, so I asked the clerk for help first thing. He lifted a large display case onto the counter. There was a plethora of pocket knives inside — so many I didn't know how to begin choosing.

"I want to spend about a dollar," I finally told the clerk.

He removed six pocket knives from the display and laid them on the counter. Becky and I began opening the blades. Then Becky pushed an exceptionally fancy knife to me for my inspection. The knife had not only whittling and carving blades, but a fork, scissors, and a screwdriver. I thought it was wonderful. And the handle was inlaid with leather.

"This is perfect," I told the clerk. "Do you wrap?"

"Maudie!" the clerk shouted.

Maudie materialized from the back of the store. She was a woman of fifty-something years.

"Wrap this up!" the young male clerk snapped, without so much as a *please*.

I handed over one dollar to the clerk. He put it in the cash box and walked away, obviously having more important things to do than say "Thank You" to a customer. Maudie carefully wrapped the knife in shiny paper with a small bow. She smiled shyly and asked me if the wrapping met with my approval.

I said, "It's perfect. You've been very courteous and helpful. Thank you so much." I took the small package and placed a five-cent tip in Maudie's hand.

Her eyes smiled as she dropped the nickel in her pocket.

"Please come back," she said.

Becky and I waved as we left the store. It was two-thirty now, so we briskly walked toward home. We talked very little as we walked, just enjoying being together.

Uncle Sabert arrived to pick up Gram, Button, and me at four o'clock. The ride to the cousins' was *so* enjoyable. Uncle was full of funny stories and he kept Gram and I laughing all the way to East Bakersfield and the home on Alta

Vista Drive. Button was ecstatic to see Jack and Andrew again. Andrew told Button not to worry, that the Christmas tree was gone. Andrew and I played catch in the yard until supper was called.

The celebration for Jack's birthday was already underway. Jack had invited some friends and they'd been dancing in the parlor. The long dining room table was set for twelve. Everyone found their own name card and took their seats. The family sat at one end of the table with Jack and his friends at the other. Everyone enjoyed a supper of fried chicken, mashed potatoes, and green beans prepared by Auntie and Gram. Jack and his friends kept things lively with their animated conversation and laughter. Then it was time for cake, ice cream, and gifts. Jack seemed a little embarrassed when he opened the spats. But I noticed them on his feet before he and his friends returned to the parlor for singing and more dancing.

Andrew and I played dominoes at the kitchen table once the supper mess was cleared up and the dishes were washed, dried, and put away. Gram began making bread for tomorrow's birthday breakfast for Andrew. At ten o'clock Uncle rounded up Jack's friends to drive them home in the back of the delivery truck. Andrew and I went to bed while Auntie and Gram waited for the bread to finish baking. We were fast asleep by the time Uncle and Jack returned.

Sunday morning began early. The excitement of the day woke Andrew before daylight. His loud clomping about on the oak floors soon had everyone else up as well. Auntie, Gram, and I worked on preparing breakfast. Uncle and Jack went to the grocery to load the truck for the afternoon deliveries and were back before breakfast was on the table. Andrew would not have a "friends party" until he was sixteen like Jack. So the family had a quiet and delicious breakfast — French toast with butter and maple syrup, eggs, country potatoes, sliced ham, biscuits, applesauce, and cocoa or coffee. Then gifts were opened while breakfast settled, making room for Andrew's favorite birthday dessert.

Andrew loved the pocket knife. He opened every blade and tried every tool. He spent some time smelling the leather handle. I could tell the knife was his favorite gift.

Gram carried in the birthday "cake." It was a huge strawberry shortcake. Uncle had ordered winter strawberries from the greenhouses in Watsonville near Salinas. They had been shipped by train to Paso Robles and brought by wagon from there to Bakersfield. A large dollop of sweet whipped cream topped each dish of shortcake. Andrew and I both wished we had eaten less breakfast, so we would have more room for dessert.

It was soon nearing one o'clock — time for Uncle and me to make deliveries. Gram decided to stay and visit with Auntie and the boys for the afternoon.

Uncle stopped first at Gram's house. I carried the boxes in and put the groceries away. Then I dashed upstairs to my bedroom and emptied the contents of my tithing box into my apron pocket. I collected the empty boxes and loaded them into the back of the truck.

Uncle and I continued our rounds, spending extra time visiting with Mr. Clark. As I put away groceries I washed up some dishes and tidied the kitchen. It was evident that Mrs. Clark's absence was being felt by both Mr. Clark and the once-tidy house.

When Uncle and I were on our way to make the last delivery, to Cynthia's house, I asked him to pull over for a chat. We stopped under a tall, bare tree on Oak Street.

"Uncle," I began, "I've been saving my tithes every week from my tips. I have $3.35. I've been thinking about how to use it. I've made a choice, but I'll need your help."

"I'll do what I can," he said.

"Well," I continued, "you know how Cynthia feels about accepting help."

I paused while Uncle nodded his head.

"I was wondering if I could put my tithe on Cynthia's account. I really can't tell you why because I've promised to keep her confidence."

"I understand," said Uncle. "Cynthia shared with me that her family will be moving to Los Angeles to live with her grandparents. I'm sure every extra dollar will help."

Uncle leaned over and gave me a hug.

"I do love you, Dorrance.". He gave me a warm smile and a wink.

"I love you, too, Uncle." And I gave him my tithes, a grin, and a wink.

26

During dinnertime for the two weeks before Valentine's Day, I brought out the scrap box and the girls and I worked on cards for our friends. First, I made an especially ornate card to send Mama. I even made a decorated envelope. I included a long letter telling her all about the basketball boycott. I mailed the card well in advance of Valentine's Day so it would arrive in Bishop by February 14th.

I had still not received a letter from Mama that mentioned her wedding plans. I began to wonder if Harry had gotten cold feet and decided not to propose after all. I started daydreaming about going home to Bishop for high school and living with just Mama. She did write that her health was still improving. She thought she would be able to leave the sanatorium by April or May. Mama said she had made some friends there and was not so lonely now.

I had written daily letters to Mama since August. It was getting harder to find things to write about now that I had exhausted information about the town, the school, and my friends. I decided in February to write only once a week, about the same number of letters Mama wrote.

The school announced there would be a Valentine's dance on Friday evening, since Valentine's Day fell on Saturday. Most of the talk around the scrap table was about the dance. Sarah and Winifred were very excited about it. Mrs. Gaines was making dresses for her girls that would be suitable for the dance and springtime wear. Winifred had been invited to the dance by a boy she didn't like. She was afraid to tell him no, so she said she already had a date. Now she was hoping Herbert would invite her. Sarah was hoping Tommy would ask her. She kept talking about how cute he was and that she would *simply die* if he asked someone else to the dance.

Cynthia said she was not planning to go due to previous commitments. I knew she would be working and watching her little sisters and brother. Becky could go to the dance because it was for the seventh and eighth grades, but her mother said she must go unaccompanied. I promised to go solo also, to keep Becky company. I so much wished I could dance with Becky.

In my daydreams I pictured myself in knickers and a white blouse with a string tie dancing with Becky who was wearing her new spring dress. We whirled around the floor in a polka, the envy of all the other couples. Becky was smiling up at me and I felt like her strong and loving protector as we moved to the rhythm of the music.

I was so afraid of Becky finding out how deep my feelings ran that I was especially careful whenever we were together. I had stopped holding Becky's hand. I was careful not to walk too close. I was also conscious of what I talked about, usually putting on my light-hearted and funny side. The only serious topic I discussed with Becky was women's justice issues. Becky seemed always to agree with me that there should be a Constitutional amendment allowing women to vote and that women should have equal job opportunities and equal pay.

I wished so much that I could hug Becky and tell her that I thought about her all the time and that I wanted to be with her when we grew up. But I was afraid I would scare her off. And Becky's friendship was more important to me than furthering the depth of our relationship.

As the dance grew nearer, Gram asked Auntie to accompany me to buy a new dress. I had never bought a ready-made dress. Auntie took me to Lu Ella's, a small shop in East Bakersfield on Baker Street. There she chose several dresses in my approximate size and I tried them all on in a small room off the main display floor. One of the dresses was "too girly" with lace that tickled my throat. One dress that I liked was too tight through the chest and arms. One dress was too short-waisted for my long torso. Then I tried on a "sailor dress." It was red, white, and blue with a wide, square collar and a drop waistline. And, best of all, it had a blue necktie. I thought it was perfect — except for the large blue bow in the back. Auntie promised to remove the bow and the belt loops that held the sash around the drop waist. So the purchase was made. Auntie and I drove to her house and made the changes I wanted.

On the way back to Gram's house, we stopped to buy new stockings and garters and new dressy shoes. I chose not to buy hair ribbons or costume jewelry, but consented to a small, navy blue shoulder bag to carry my hankie and money to the dance. And, of course, Auntie insisted Gram would not let me go without the requisite white gloves. I actually thought they were a good idea in case I was forced to dance with a boy.

On February 13th, I distributed the cards I had made to my friends at school, collecting several from other students in the process. Immediately after school, I went to Mr. Clark's house. I gave him his Valentine and had a cup of cocoa. Then I asked Mr. Clark if I might do up the dishes as we visited. I knew he was able physically to keep up with the household chores, but he was so emotionally depressed it was all he could do to keep clean and feed himself.

When I needed to leave, a tear came to Mr. Clark's eye. I looked away, not wanting to embarrass him. I began to walk to the door, but then I turned to give him a hug.

"I know it's too soon to ask," I whispered in his ear, "but when you're ready, I'd like to be your Valentine."

Then I kissed his cheek and ran all the way home, tears streaming down my face, as I felt the old man's pain and grief. Tomorrow would be Mr. Clark's first Valentine's Day since his wife's death.

At home I bathed, ate a quick supper, and dressed in my new clothes. At six o'clock I was at the school, meeting Becky for the dance.

The auditorium in the basement was decorated with red and white, hearts and snowflakes, roses and carnations. Benches stood along opposite walls. A refreshment table was set up at the end of the room. The boys monopolized the punch and cookies all evening. Miss Harris was responsible for playing music on the gramophone. We girls sat along one wall on the hard wooden benches, remembering to sit up straight, smile demurely with eyes cast downward, and keep our knees together.

Since the boys were stuffing themselves with cookies, and since it was bad manners for girls to serve themselves, we sat and quietly chatted, listening to the music. Winifred and Sarah sat side by side. Sarah had not been invited by anyone and was still alive to tell about it. The boy who had invited Winifred had spread the word to the boys, including Herbert, that she already had an escort. Not only did Herbert not ask Winifred to the dance, he did not attend at all. In fact, there were eight boys and twenty-three girls in attendance. And no one was dancing.

Sarah and Winifred began to be impatient with the boys. Even the chaperones could not pry those young gentlemen away from the refreshment table. Then Miss Harris played a familiar polka that we often danced to at dinnertime. Sarah grabbed Winifred's hand and they began to polka together. So Becky and I did the same. Other girls also began dancing the rollicking dance together. The chaperones didn't seem to care, so we danced the next several times together.

Then Miss Harris played a slow, romantic ballad. Becky and I stayed on the dance floor. I was enjoying

149

dancing close to Becky and she seemed to be enjoying the slow dance too.

Becky whispered to me, "I've wanted to be close to you like this for so long."

"I love you, Becky," I breathed into her ear.

And then we were yanked apart by a chaperone. All the boys stood around the refreshment table gaping at Becky and me. All the girls sat on the benches with their knees together and gawked at us. Horrified looks were on the faces of several chaperones. Miss Harris stopped the music and approached the chaperone who had pulled us apart.

"What seems to be the problem?" Miss Harris asked her.

"We can't have girls dancing like that!" the chaperone replied.

"The girls have been dancing together all evening," argued Miss Harris.

"But not like that! Not like sapphists!" spat the chaperone under her breath.

I looked at Becky who was red with embarrassment and had tears brimming in her eyes. I took Becky's hand and we ran from the dance. Miss Harris followed us outside.

Sarah later told me that the students left behind clustered in small groups trying to figure out what had just happened. A chaperone put a snappy tune on the gramophone. Frances took this opportunity to spin her nasty web of gossip, going from group to group saying, "I told you Dorrance was a sapphist." Most of the students looked at her with a blank stare, trying to figure out what she was talking about. The boys were feeling guilty, as if it was their fault Becky and I were dancing together. But Frances seemed to be the only one who understood and condoned the behavior of the chaperone. The boys drifted out the door to go home. The girls had no choice but to do the same, since they evidently couldn't dance together anymore.

Becky and I ran as fast as we could down 18th Street, avoiding Miss Harris and Sarah and Winifred. I wiped away Becky's tears and held her close as she sobbed out her fears of facing people at school again. I promised to always be there for her. I promised to stay away from her if that's what Becky wanted.

Inside my heart was broken, though. I was afraid Becky would choose to abandon me in order to save face at school. I was afraid to return to school, too, but I was more afraid of losing Becky as a friend. I didn't know what I would do without her. Now that she had told me how she felt about me, the prospect of losing her was even worse. Where would I ever again find someone with those feelings for me?

Then Becky asked, "What's a sapphist?"

"I don't know. I like dancing with you, Becky."

"Me, too. Does that mean we're sapphists?"

"I don't know," I whispered. "I'll walk you home now."

27

I was home from the dance before eight o'clock. I knew Gram was surprised by the early hour and concerned by my somber mood. But I was not willing to talk about what happened at the dance. I simply went upstairs and cried myself to sleep.

I woke up in the middle of the night and worried until dawn about the Valentine's Day disaster. I wondered how a person could survive such emotional highs and lows. I remembered my delight when I heard Becky say she loved dancing close. It had felt so right, holding Becky close and whispering in her ear as we slowly moved to the music. I knew Becky cared as much for me as I did for her. I remembered the warm and secure feeling. Then it was immediately spoiled by the hysterical chaperone. The violent touch and harsh words in front of all our friends brought my ecstasy to near despair. I remembered Becky's trembling body and heartbreaking tears. Anger had churned in my stomach as my fight-or-flight response engaged. I wanted to fight, but when I looked at Becky, I knew I had to protect her. Now as I lay awake I wondered what had happened after Becky and I ran from the dance. I knew Miss Harris was trying to defend our dancing. What I didn't know was how Becky and I would respond to questions and comments that were sure to arise on Monday. Every time I thought of Becky my eyes filled with tears and spilled over. What explanation did Becky give her parents and Sarah when she arrived home? On and on I thought and worried until it was time to get up.

I dragged my tired body from bed, washed and dressed, and did my most urgent chores. I didn't feel like eating or playing fetch with Button. I called to Gram that I was on my way to the library.

Becky met me on the corner of 18th and A Streets. Her eyes were swollen and she began to cry as soon as she saw me. I started to cry, as well. It was amazing to me that I so readily exposed my feelings to another person. But neither Becky nor I initiated a hug or any other form of comfort to the other. We were afraid of who might be watching.

"What happened when you got home?" I asked her.

"I was still crying so Mother and Daddy wanted to know what happened. Just then Sarah rushed in and hugged me. She said 'Oh, Becky, I'm so sorry. That Mrs. Connor was so mean. I can't believe she treated you and Dorrance so rudely.'"

"You mean that chaperone was Frances's mother?"

"I guess so," answered Becky.

"Then what happened?"

"Well, then Sarah told Mother and Daddy the whole story. When Sarah said 'sapphist,' Mother and Daddy gave each other a funny look. So I asked them what sapphist meant."

"What did they say?" I asked.

"Mother said, 'Never mind. It's just a nasty thing to say, especially to a young girl,'" answered Becky. "What did your Grandmother say?"

"Nothing. I went to bed. She didn't ask any questions. Becky, when we get to the library I'm going to find out what sapphist means. Do you want to know?"

"Yes, but nobody will talk about it. I looked it up in the dictionary last night. It said it means 'of the same kind.' That's no help."

"I'm going to ask the librarian," I said.

Becky's eyes got big. "Mother said it was a nasty word! You're going to ask the librarian about a nasty word?"

"I don't know who else to ask," I said. "I've been called sapphist all year. And before I moved here someone at home called some friends of mine sapphists. I want to know what it means. When I asked Gram months ago she told me to look it up in the dictionary, just like you did. It didn't make sense to me, either."

"My mother says she's going to talk to Mr. Owens on Monday about Mrs. Connor and Buttons calling names," offered Becky.

"I still want to know what those words mean. Instead of asking the librarian, maybe I'll just look at a lot of books to see what I can find."

"If you still can't find anything," said Becky, "I could ask Miss Harris about it on Monday. She was there. I think she'll answer me and I trust her."

"Okay, that sounds good. Then if we still can't find out, I'll ask Gram again."

At the library I looked up the word "sapphist" in the card catalogue. I couldn't find it. So, forgetting the plan Becky and I had just discussed, I went to the librarian, took a deep breath, and asked where I could find a book on sapphism. The librarian took a quick breath and gave me a long, sorrowful look. Then she jotted some Dewey decimals on a note pad, ripped off the paper, and handed it to me.

"These books are in the psychology and medical section," she said.

I began looking in the index of each book in the psychology section for the word sapphist. My research finally paid off when I found a psychology book with a short article on sapphism. The author said sapphism was "a deviant behavior." It was caused by distant mothers and uninvolved fathers, causing girls to identify with their fathers instead of their mothers. The "disorder" needed intensive psychotherapy to "cure." If the patient was not willing to spend years in therapy to correct the disorder, she could expect to live a life of being an "outcast of society" unless she ended up being committed to an "insane asylum," which was the best alternative.

My breathing became short and my palms were sweaty. I glanced around the library wondering if other patrons knew what I had been reading. Did they know I was a deviant that belonged in an insane asylum?

We must *never* let anyone know, I thought. We must always keep this a secret from everyone.

I needed to find Becky. I must be sure Becky didn't admit to being a sapphist to Miss Harris or her parents or her sisters or anyone. And then I thought of Gram's advice to remain true to myself.

How can I do that when I have to lie about who I am? I thought.

I slammed shut the book and replaced it on the shelf. I found Becky studying the encyclopedia.

"Come with me," I whispered. "I found it."

Becky packed up her papers and followed me out of the library.

"We need to go someplace private," I told her.

We walked west on Railroad Avenue until we found ourselves alone. I told Becky about all I had read.

"Well, there's nothing wrong with me," Becky stated emphatically. "And there's nothing wrong with you either. And there's nothing wrong with my parents. And you didn't even know your dad. So we can't be sapphists."

"But the book says if you love a person of the same sex, then you're insane," I said. "I know I've worried about not being interested in boys. Maybe I am insane if everybody thinks so. But I know I don't want to change and I don't want to go to an insane asylum either."

Becky considered this line of argument.

"I still think 'everyone' is wrong. What I feel for you is special and good. But I also agree that we have to keep this secret."

"It's like women's rights and slavery," I said, thinking more rationally. "Denying women their rights is wrong, but it still exists. Someday everyone will wonder why it took so long to give women their rights. Look how long it took to abolish slavery..."

"And people still treat negroes with disrespect," finished Becky.

"That's right. Maybe someday sapphists will have the right to love who they want..."

"And everyone will wonder why it took so long to let sapphists live in peace," finished Becky again.

"I love you, Becky."

"And I love you."

"But until things change we need to protect each other. We need to act like we're just friends. Okay?"

"Okay," said Becky.

"Remember, Becky, don't breathe a word to anyone."

28

I was emotionally exhausted when I arrived home. Gram was resting in her room, so I went straight to bed. My head felt heavy and my eyelids drooped. I dropped immediately into a deep, troubled sleep. Sometime during the afternoon Gram came up to the attic.

"Dorrance, are you up here?" she asked.

I found it difficult to pull myself from my disturbing dream state into an equally-disturbing reality. My hair was drenched with perspiration and my skin was cold and clammy. I opened my eyes to find Gram stooped over me and placing a soft, light hand on my forehead.

"I do believe you're ill," she said with concern in her voice. "Do you hurt anywhere?"

"My head. I'm just *so* tired," I answered listlessly.

"Put your gown on and get under the covers," ordered Gram. "I'll bring you some hot soup and lemon tea."

"Please don't bother, Gram. You shouldn't be climbing the stairs."

"You may be right about that. Put on a robe and come down to the parlor. You can sleep on the couch where I can keep an eye on you."

I did as I was told, mostly because I was too tired to argue. I tried to keep my mind from dwelling on the events of the past twenty-four hours.

Once I was settled on the couch, Gram brought me tea and soup. She plumped my pillow and tucked the blankets snugly around me. I sipped the hot tea as Gram talked.

"I called Uncle Sabert and asked him to find a substitute for your deliveries tomorrow. While I was on the telephone he asked Cynthia if she could do it. She said yes. So I want you to stay right here and get well in time for school on Monday."

I hoped I would die before school on Monday. I just did not feel strong enough to field questions and endure comments from students. I tuned back into Gram's monologue.

"Eat some of this soup now. I knew there was something wrong when you came home from the dance so early last night."

I thought, "I'll just let Gram think I was ill last night. She certainly can't find out that I'm insane. Where would I go if she turned me out? An insane asylum?"

After eating some of the warm soup, I scooched down further under the covers and shut my eyes. I heard Gram carry the dishes away. Again I slept fitfully. When I next awoke, the room was dark except for the light of the fireplace. Gram was rocking in her chair.

Then she was offering me another cup of tea. I drank it down quickly and dozed off again. The next time I woke up Gram's chair was empty, but the lamp was on. I dragged myself from the couch to the bathroom and back to the couch again. As I snuggled under the covers Gram returned with a glass of orange juice. I thanked her and drank half the juice. Then I turned on my side and slept again. When I woke up next, the room was light with rays of early morning sun. I could hear voices from the front hallway.

"Gram," I called.

Gram and a tall young man in a suit suddenly loomed above me.

"This is Dr. Fowler, Dorrance," said Gram. "I asked him to come and have a look at you."

Dr. Fowler set a black leather bag on the floor beside the couch. He shook down a thermometer, peered at it closely, and slipped it under my tongue.

"Keep that under your tongue with your mouth closed for five minutes," Dr. Fowler instructed.

Then he began asking me a whole series of questions about my symptoms, to which I responded "um hmm" and "hmm um." When the good doctor removed the thermometer, he frowned and asked Gram to follow him into the hallway. I tried to hear their conversation. Then I fell asleep again.

Gram returned some time later with a bowl of soup and a tall glass of water. She sat beside the couch while I ate some soup and drank most of the water. I vaguely remembered hearing Dr. Fowler say, "Someone has scared that child to death." But now, trying to remember back, I wasn't sure if that was a real conversation or just my dream.

Gram offered no information as to what the doctor thought this illness was. I was sure he had recognized my "deviant behavior" and was, at this very moment, arranging commitment papers to the asylum. Then Gram was wiping tears from my cheeks. But she asked no questions. She just waited and rocked and made small talk. Each time I awoke, Gram was there reading or dozing in her chair. It was comforting to me to know she cared enough to remain with me while I was feeling so alone.

Monday morning Gram asked me if I felt like going to school.

"No, I can't," I said. And I rolled over to stare at the back of the couch.

"I'm going to need to go out for awhile this morning," she said. "Will you be all right until I get back?"

I nodded as tears again sprang to my eyes. Gram leaned over and kissed my forehead.

"You'll feel better soon, Dorrance," said Gram. "I love you."

I lay there feeling emotionally weak and worthless. I was usually a scrapper. I couldn't understand my feelings of despair. But feeling too weak to analyze them, I went back to sleep. Gram was soon home again, sitting in her rocker beside the couch.

"Becky was by to see you," said Gram. "You were sleeping. Would you like me to wake you when she comes again?"

I nodded and a tiny smile struggled to free itself from my heart.

*   *   *

"Hi, Dorrance. Are you awake?" asked Becky.

"Becky," I said, trying to sit up and appear healthier than I felt.

Becky stepped forward and hugged me.

"Was it awful at school?" I asked.

"Not too bad. Miss Harris was really kind to me. She kept me in at morning recess to talk."

"You didn't tell her anything, did you?" I asked. "I mean about us?"

"I mostly listened. She said I could always count on her for support. She said she understood what we're going through. I think she really does. She said for us to be strong. She said not to make any permanent solutions to temporary problems."

"I'm sorry you had to face everything alone," I said.

"I'm not. I learned I was stronger than I thought."

We were both silent for a few minutes as Becky sat rocking in Gram's chair.

"Did your grandmother tell you she went to see Mr. Owens with my mom?" asked Becky.

"She did?"

"I don't think anyone will be calling names anymore. Mother demanded a letter of apology from Mrs. Connor and Buttons. But I doubt if that will ever happen."

"Did anyone tease you today?" I asked.

"Quite the opposite. But Buttons took a lot of teasing for ruining the dance. Are you coming to school tomorrow?"

"I guess."

"I'm glad," said Becky. "I missed you. We all came at dinnertime but you were sleeping. It's going to be okay, Dorrance, really." Then she kissed my forehead and was gone.

I got up, put on my robe and slippers, and went out to the kitchen. Gram was cooking a pot of chicken noodle soup. She heard my shuffling slippers and turned her head. I saw Gram's smiling face, but I sensed a deeper underlying concern. Gram poured two cups of tea and sat at the table beside me.

"I'm happy to see you up and around." She smiled warmly at me.

"I'm feeling a little better. I guess I'll go to school tomorrow."

"Dorrance," said Gram, "Mrs. Gaines told me what happened at the dance. I'd like to talk about it, if you don't mind."

I did mind, though. What would Gram do when she found out I was a deviant, an insane person?

Gram probably already knows anyway, I thought. Dr. Fowler probably told her. I might as well get this over with.

"We can talk if you want, Gram."

"Okay, then. I'm just going to say what I think needs to be said. If you see I'm way off track, just tell me so and I'll be quiet."

I nodded my agreement.

"First of all, do you remember asking me way back in September what a sapphist was?"

I nodded again.

"Well, it didn't occur to me at the time that someone was calling you that name. Do you know what a sapphist is?"

"I looked it up in the dictionary." And then I quoted the dictionary definition.

"That's technically correct," said Gram, "but there's another definition I think you should know about. A sapphist is a woman who prefers another woman as a life partner, instead of having a husband."

My eyebrows rose involuntarily as Gram frankly defined this word without any disparaging remarks or looks. I finally made eye-contact with her. I could see only the usual love and acceptance in her eyes.

"When I was still teaching high school in Los Angeles," continued Gram, "I knew several teachers who were sapphists. Of course, the school board didn't know. These teachers felt comfortable telling me because they knew they could trust me. The school board preferred to refer to these teachers as 'old maids.' And that's how these exceptionally fine teachers kept their jobs, by lying about their true identities."

I listened attentively but offered no information to Gram about my fears that I was a sapphist.

"Life was very hard for a particular couple I knew," Gram went on. "They bought a house with a great deal of difficulty. They were trying to buy a small farm outside of town. No one would lend them money, so they saved for years until they could pay cash. Even then people wouldn't sell to them. They wanted to sell to husbands with wives and children. Finally the couple moved to the inner city where people seemed a little more open-minded.

"They were able to buy a modest little house on a quiet street. They both continued to teach school. They took beautiful care of their home and yard. But in order to keep their personal lives secret, they told everyone they were cousins---old maids living together. They always maintained separate bedrooms with twin beds. That way they could safely invite people for dinner without raising suspicion.

"They never displayed pictures of themselves together. They never showed affection in public---not hand-holding, or hugging, or dancing, or even standing too close together. They always lived in fear that the wrong person would learn the truth about their relationship and their jobs and professional reputations would be lost."

I was now thoroughly absorbed in Gram's story.

"That sounds like a perfectly awful way to live," I said.

"That it was," continued Gram. "And the sad thing is that nothing has changed. I once asked my friends why they didn't just marry men and live a normal life like everyone else. When I think of that question now, I shudder at my ignorance. But my friends were patient with me and tried to explain. They said, 'if things were the opposite of what they are, if it was normal to be sapphist and abnormal to marry men, would you divorce your husband and marry a woman?'

"I thought of my own dear husband. I remembered all the good and bad times we had faced together. I thought about how long it took us to develop a solid, unconditional love for one another. And do you know what I realized?"

"No, what?"

"I realized," said Gram, "that sexuality has little to do with what happens in the bedroom. It has to do with whom your heart communes, be that person male or female.

"I'm almost through talking. Just one more thing: I want you to know that I love you unconditionally. I will always support your decisions in life as long as you remain true to yourself. Don't let other people's ignorance force you to be someone you're not. God created you and loves you just as you are."

Then she gave me a warm hug, just like the one she gave me on the day I arrived to live with her.

"Thanks, Gram," I said. "I feel much better. I was so afraid that you'd send me to an insane asylum."

Gram laughed out loud, then said, "Dorrance, you're probably the sanest person I know. You and Uncle Sabert."

29

Tuesday morning dawned clear and warmer than it had been in months. Gram called it "Indian Summer." She said the last two weeks of February were always warm and sunny with a promise of spring in the air. Then the weather would turn cold and wet until the end of March when spring "sprang" for real.

The sun and warmth gave me courage enough to face school. I left my coat behind and looked forward to playing recess games with the boys. I telephoned Becky to say I wanted to spend dinnertime at school instead of going home. Becky was also looking forward to eating on the grass in front of the school.

When I arrived at school, Becky was waiting on the steps for me. We stood outside and chatted for several minutes. I wanted so much to hug Becky, but I settled for a whispered "I love you" in her ear. Becky mouthed "Me too" and winked. No one approached us or even glanced our way. I felt secure as I walked to class.

As I made eye contact with her, Frances quickly turned to face the front of the class as if she were embarrassed.

Wow! I thought, maybe things really have changed.

The entire day progressed smoothly---no name calling, no teasing, and no mention of the Valentine's Dance.

When I arrived home after school there was a letter from Mama waiting on the kitchen table. Gram had made a pitcher of iced tea. I poured myself a glass and sat down to read the letter dated February 8th. Mama still mentioned nothing of a marriage proposal, but she did talk a lot about Harry, his business, and his impending move to Independence. She described Independence in great detail, as if she had often visited there. She even described the home Harry had purchased. Then she said she was allowed short absences from the sanatorium and was expecting to be released any time now. Mama told me she missed me and couldn't wait to see me again.

I wondered if she would feel the same if she knew I was a sapphist. Mama seemed almost a stranger now. Our lives had changed to such a degree that we would have to get completely reacquainted. I was feeling more and more like I would rather stay in Bakersfield than go back to the eastern Sierras. I was also suspicious about Mama's proposal. Surely Harry had proposed by now. I thought Mama must be keeping it secret. That annoyed me until I realized I had a secret from Mama, too.

I folded the letter and put it in the ribbon-tied bundle of her other letters. Then I did my homework and practiced the cello. I thought the cello was sounding good and I was proud of myself. I knew several songs now. I decided to tell Becky I would begin practicing with them soon.

Later, I was tossing the ball to Button in the front yard when Cynthia stopped by after work. She was angry and had been crying.

"What's wrong, Cynthia?" I was truly worried about my strong friend.

She sat on the front step with her head down for quite awhile. I was ready to ask her again when she looked up and said, "My mother's abandoning me and Gwen." Cynthia's fists were in trembling balls and her voice was strained and shaky.

165

"What?!" I was shocked. "She can't do that! Can she?"

"She's going to. She got a letter from Granna and Gramps. They said they don't have room for all five kids. So Mutter has decided to leave me and Gwen here. She says I'm old enough to survive and take care of Gwen."

"That's just crazy," I said. "You'd have to quit school. Where would you live?"

"Mutter just said she can't take all this responsibility anymore. I don't know why she's getting rid of me and Gwen. We've been doing most of the work---making money, cleaning, watching the little ones. It seems like we'd be more help to her than hindrance." Then Cynthia slapped her right fist into her left hand in anger.

"When is your mother going to leave?" I asked.

"I turned over all my earnings to her last night. After she had all my money she told me I wouldn't be going. When I went to work today I told Mr. Logan I'd need to keep my job. I asked him to put Mutter's account in my name. He offered to help, but I told him no."

"Cynthia, you might want to allow someone to help you. It would make your friends feel good. Asking for help doesn't mean you have to give up your independence. It just means you're open to people who have more experience and influence than you have."

"I just feel so alone and desperate," Cynthia replied. "And I feel so betrayed. Mutter and I haven't agreed on much since Patter left, but I never thought *she* would leave me, too. I must be a really terrible person for everyone to abandon me."

"Gram says sometimes we have to choose our family when the family we're born into doesn't work out so well. *I'd* like to be part of your chosen family."

Cynthia sniffled and cried as I sat beside her patting her back.

"Cynthia," I said, "I haven't told you this but Mr. Logan is my uncle. My mother's brother, actually. He's a really good person and he gets a great deal of joy out of helping people. Please, let's ask for his help."

Cynthia sat silently while I waited for her decision. Then I noticed Cynthia slowly nod her head. I wasn't about to let this opportunity slip away. I grabbed Cynthia's hand and pulled her into the house. I picked up the telephone receiver and placed a call to Uncle Sabert. I quickly explained Cynthia's situation and asked his help.

He said, "I knew she was in some kind of trouble. Keep her there and Aunt Marilyn and I will come over after we close the store."

I pulled Cynthia into the kitchen where Gram was frying chicken and putting the finishing touches on a large potato salad. Gram invited Cynthia for supper. I told Gram that I had invited Uncle and Auntie to come over to discuss a problem. Gram glanced from me to Cynthia and back with a look of curiosity on her face.

All at once, Cynthia opened up to Gram. She told her the whole story, spilling her anger and hurt into Gram's warm embrace.

"Don't you worry, Sweetie," said Gram. "We'll figure out a suitable solution."

Cynthia said she wasn't hungry as Gram dished out supper. But Gram filled her plate anyway. Cynthia must have gotten her appetite back because she ate two chicken legs, one thigh, two helpings of potato salad, and a dish of warm applesauce with two cookies.

At a few minutes past six, Uncle Sabert and Aunt Marilyn arrived. Everyone sat around the kitchen table with glasses of iced tea. Uncle Sabert began the discussion.

"Marilyn and I have been discussing your situation, Cynthia. We know from watching you work at the store that you're dependable and honest. We also know that you're a good student, capable of going far in life. But we know that everyone needs some support and encouragement along the way."

Uncle paused while everyone waited for him to collect his thoughts. Auntie became impatient and continued for him.

"It will be hard for you to continue on without your mother and sisters and brother. It will be an aloneness that you'll have to grieve. But it will be easier to bear with supportive friends around."

"Yes, well," said Uncle, "in light of all that, we have a couple of options to offer you. First of all, Mr. Clark (you know him) is in need of someone to help him clean and cook and to just keep him company. We thought you might like to help him in exchange for room and board. You could attend school and work at the store for spending money."

When Uncle paused again, Cynthia tentatively asked, "What about Gwen?" Then tears spilled from Cynthia's eyes as she thought of tiny 7-year-old Gwen with a mother who loved her too little.

Auntie began, "It seems as if little Gwen has had far too much responsibility for her years. Sabert and I would like to offer Gwen a home with us. Of course, there are drawbacks to this plan. Gwen would have to change schools and she wouldn't see you on a daily basis. But you could visit on weekends."

Auntie paused to try to read Cynthia's thoughts. Cynthia had stopped crying and was listening carefully.

"On the positive side," continued Auntie, "Gwen would be able to lead a more carefree life, without the responsibilities of younger siblings. She could concentrate on her school work. When she gets older she can work at the store if she chooses. Sabert and I will provide all her necessities and a loving home."

Everyone was silent for a few minutes. Then Uncle Sabert said, "Marilyn and I had first talked of inviting both you and Gwen to live with us. And that option is still open as well. But knowing you as we do, Cynthia, we thought we might be asking you to give up too much by living with us. We know you have good friends at Franklin School. We know you're already quite independent and self-sufficient. We thought we might be stifling your growth, asking you to take a step backward. Of course, the decision is up to you."

"And if neither of these options is something you can live with," said Auntie, "we can explore other solutions."

I again saw tears leaking from the corners of Cynthia's eyes. But, somehow, these tears seemed different. Then Cynthia's wavering voice said, "No one has ever been this kind to me. I feel like a load of logs has been lifted off my back."

Cynthia smiled through her tears. "I would like to live with Mr. Clark and stay at Franklin School, at least for now. I think Gwen would like to live with you. She needs a lot of attention that I can't give her while I'm hurting so badly myself."

"If it's all right with you, we'd like to speak to your mother about this arrangement," said Auntie. "I'm sure she's worried about your and Gwen's well being."

Cynthia let go with a sound like, "Hrumph!"

"I know it doesn't seem like she cares," said Uncle, "but deep inside I'm sure she's worried. She was planning to take you both to Los Angeles with her until your grandparents said *no*. Your mother probably thinks she has no choice in the matter."

Cynthia sighed and said, "I guess you're right."

"Would you like to come with us to see your mother?" asked Auntie. "We can go now if you'd like. We'd like these arrangements to be made legal before your mother leaves town. We'd like to have legal guardianship of both you and Gwen."

"I'll go with you now," said Cynthia. "I'm kind of excited about this plan. But why are you doing this?"

"Because we love you," answered Uncle. "You and Gwen are perfect children. You need every opportunity to live a life that is happy, joyous, and free."

Then Uncle, Auntie, and Cynthia left to see Cynthia's mother.

At about nine-thirty there was a knock at the front door. Gram and I were already in bed. I pulled on my robe and slippers and ran to open the door. There stood Uncle and Cynthia.

"May Cynthia spend the night?" asked Uncle Sabert. "Tomorrow I'll come and move her things to Mr. Clark's."

"Yes! Yes! Yes!" I shouted. I was so glad Cynthia was staying close by and going to Franklin School. I looked past Uncle to the carriage in front of the house.

"Gwen is going home with us tonight," Uncle said. Then he turned to Cynthia and said, "We'll get you girls together on Saturday." And he gave her a quick hug.

Cynthia carried her school clothes to my attic room. We snuggled into bed together. We began to chat but were soon fast asleep, recovering from the stress of the past few days.

30

Wednesday was a busy day for Cynthia. Uncle Sabert picked her up first thing after breakfast. They drove in the delivery truck to Mr. Clark's house, so Cynthia could move in and learn her duties. Then Uncle brought Cynthia to school in time for morning recess. I had never seen her so relaxed and smiling.

"I have my very own room with a soft twin bed," she told me. "And Mr. Clark seems really happy to have me living there."

"I'm so glad you're not moving to Los Angeles," I said.

"It's all because of you and Mr. Logan. You've been a loyal and trustworthy friend. Thank you for helping me and Gwen."

"I wonder how Gwen is doing."

"Mr. Logan says she fell asleep in the carriage on the way home last night. She ate a big breakfast this morning. Mrs. Logan is keeping her home from school today to take her shopping for new clothes. She'll be so excited. She's always had to wear my hand-me-downs."

"I know it's all quite exciting now, but soon you'll both be feeling homesick," I warned. "That's what happened when I moved here, but it goes away in time — mostly."

"I'll remember the good things and remind Gwen to do the same," said Cynthia.

Then it was time to go back to the classroom.

That afternoon Mr. Owens went to the sixth, seventh, and eighth grades to announce track and field season. The competitions would not take place until April, but practice would begin right away. All the students were encouraged to exercise and run laps during dinnertime and after school, weather permitting. Events would include the 50-and 100-yard dashes, the 400-yard relay, the running broad jump, the standing broad jump, and the softball throws for distance and accuracy. I began to rearrange my schedule in my head to make time for practices.

At the end of Mr. Owens' explanation, Red's hand went up.

"Yes, Red," said Mr. Griffin.

"Mr. Owens, will the girls be allowed to compete?"

"I believe so," answered Mr. Owens. "The matter of girls' athletics is currently before the school board."

"Excuse me, sir, but when will the board rule on the matter?"

"Sometime this spring, I suspect. Are there any *other* questions?"

"Excuse me again, sir," said Red. "With all due respect, sir, I don't think anyone will be practicing until the students know for sure that the girls will be allowed to participate."

"Are you threatening me, young man?" challenged Mr. Owens.

"No, sir. Just stating a fact, sir."

"Young man, er, Red," said Mr. Owens, struggling to control his temper, "the school has been given a substantial sum of money by a private benefactor to be spent on a track and field program. It is imperative that students participate in order for us to keep that money."

"Excuse me, sir, Mr. Owens, sir," Red said, his mouth beginning to go dry, "did the source of the funding say the program should serve students or boys?"

"Well," said Mr. Owens, turning red in the face, "I believe it said 'a program for students.'"

"Then don't you think, sir, it would be dishonest to use that money for a program that benefits only boys, sir?"

By this time most of the students were sliding down in their seats trying to disappear. None of us had ever seen a student so openly defy authority. And Red was doing it so respectfully. And with so many witnesses.

Cynthia and I exchanged glances. I looked at Red with new respect. He was toying with Mr. Griffin's ruler as well as expulsion for insubordination.

Mr. Owens glared at Red and raised his voice to just below a shout. "Young man, I'm sure the school board will decide the matter in a fair and legal manner."

I could keep my hand down no longer. Mr. Griffin, relieved to have a diversion from the confrontation with Red, called on me.

I tried to control the tremor in my voice. "Mr. Owens, sir, I believe the school board meets the last Thursday of April, well after the competition is to occur."

"Your point is, young lady?" he spluttered.

"Well, sir, it seems this decision will be up to you since it's impossible for the board to take action in time. Of course, sir, we know you are not only honest, but fair. Surely you would not divert money meant for all students and use it for boys only."

Mr. Owens stood silent for a moment. Then he looked Mr. Griffin square in the eyes. Mr. Griffin raised his eyebrows in a humorous manner and I saw that sparkle in his eyes that I remembered from the first day of school. Mr. Griffin was definitely amused at this turn of events. I could almost see Mr. Owens imagining *The Bakersfield Californian* headlines: *Principal Misuses Funds* or *Owens Spurns Rights of Girls* or *Principal Fired Under Accusations of Misappropriation.*

"Practices for Track and Field will begin tomorrow at noon. Coach Wells will be here," said Mr. Owens, ignoring the issue at hand. Then he abruptly left the classroom.

At noon on Thursday we girls settled on the front lawn for dinner. We could see Coach Wells on the playground with a whistle in his mouth. He slowly perused the students eating their dinners. Then he looked at his pocket watch. He paced back and forth, kicking up dirt with the toe of his shoe. At twelve-ten he finally blew a shrill blast on his whistle. He threw his arms in the air beaconing students to join him. A lone student rose and walked slowly to the coach. Red spoke briefly with Coach Wells. All the students watched. Then they saw the coach shrug his shoulders and shake his head. Red made one final comment to the coach and returned to the grass where he sat with his friends eating a cookie. Coach Wells again tweeted his whistle and gesticulated half-heartedly for students to join him. He looked at all the various groups of students sitting about on the lawn in the fourth day of "Indian Summer." No one moved. Coach left the field with a puzzled look on his face and headed for the office.

Red rubbed his hand nervously on his pants. I wondered if he was anticipating Mr. Griffin's ruler. Certainly any harm caused to Red would initiate a mutiny among students, not just a boycott.

On Friday, Coach Wells and Mr. Owens stood on the playground. Students ate on the lawn in their usual small groups. Promptly at noon Coach Wells blew three short, loud blasts on his whistle. No one moved. Mr. Owens snatched the whistle and blew it long and shrill. Then he yelled, "Come over here now, everyone!"

One student rose and walked slowly to the center of the field, his red curls shining and blowing in a light breeze. The students watched in silence. They saw Coach Wells take a step back and Mr. Owens take a step forward. Red was about as tall as Mr. Owens' armpit. He looked up into Mr. Owens eyes and said something. Then Mr. Owens shook his head. Red turned to leave.

In anger, Mr. Owens stamped his foot, shouting, "Come back here!" before he groaned and sat down, plunk, on his butt in the middle of the field, holding his ankle.

Then Coach Wells was on his knees beside Mr. Owens. Red said something to the coach and ran to the office. Soon the coach and Mr. Griffin carried Mr. Owens into the building.

On Saturday morning I met Becky for our walk to the library.

"I can't believe Mr. Owens broke his ankle stamping at Red," said Becky.

"Reminds me a little of THE FALL," I said.

31

Becky and I were at the library until one o'clock, writing the rough drafts of our research papers. When I got home I spent several hours turning over the garden to mix in the fall and winter ashes. Gram sat on a stool with the seed catalog in her lap. As Gram watched me work, we discussed what should be planted this spring. Gram said Bakersfield had short springs and long, hot summers. So we decided against "winter crops" such as lettuce, broccoli, and cauliflower. Instead we would plant five rows of corn, so that it would pollinate correctly. We would also grow tomatoes. Gram already had the seeds started in the kitchen window. Still to be ordered were seeds for radishes, zucchini, carrots, turnips, summer squash, pumpkins, cantaloupe, pole beans, cucumbers, and peppers. Gram slowly and carefully made the list to send to the Burpee Seed Company.

I had my heart set on growing a prize-winning pumpkin for the Kern County Fair. Pumpkins could grow to several hundred pounds. I daydreamed about next Halloween. I would carve my prize-winning pumpkin into Bakersfield's largest jack-o-lantern.
I would sit on the front porch with Gram. She would hand out treats and I would accept the plethora of compliments on my Halloween work-of-art.

At the end of the afternoon, I was ready to call it quits on the garden. My back and arms ached from so much physical labor after the largely-sedentary winter. All the ashes were at least turned over and much of the garden was well-mixed.

Button lay in the shade exhausted from digging with me. Small clumps of dirt hung from his long ears. I brushed the clods away and cleaned his paws. Then I put the shovel in the carriage house and followed Gram to the back door. I removed my dirty boots, dungarees, and socks before going in for a refreshing soak in the claw foot tub. Once I was clean, I popped Button into the tub for a good scrub. I rinsed him well and set him on the floor on a large towel. As I tried to dry him off, he shook water everywhere and trotted out of the bathroom nice and fluffy. I spent five minutes wiping up all the water droplets from the floor, walls, and fixtures.

Gram had a light supper on the table when I came out of the bathroom. Button lay in front of the stove hoping for a bit of warmth. But the stove had not been lit today. I went upstairs and pulled an old blanket from the linen closet, brought it down to the kitchen, and wrapped Button up. He stayed where he was for the remainder of the evening, snuggled in the soft, warm blanket. Gram and I sat eating macaroni salad, sandwiches, and applesauce. Button ignored the opportunity to beg for supper scraps.

"Gram," I said, "Some of the girls were talking religion at school. Frances interrupted and said that Jesus hates sapphists. I've been reading the New Testament all week. I've read all the words of Jesus. I can't find anything mentioned about sapphists."

"What *have* you read that Jesus was concerned about?" asked Gram.

"Well," I hesitated as I thought back over the many teachings. "Mostly Jesus spoke about love and forgiveness."

Grandmother smiled. "Yes, He did. Above all else Jesus taught love and forgiveness. That's what we need to practice. Forgiveness is sometimes difficult, but without it resentment, and even hatred, can make our lives miserable. Being unforgiving hurts *us*, not the one who is unforgiven."

"Is it true that God forgives everyone?" I asked.

"That's been my experience," answered Gram. "Sometimes we are our own worst enemy. We have trouble forgiving ourselves most of all. Why do we expect such perfection from ourselves when we don't expect it of anyone else?"

"Maybe because we think if we're perfect no one will judge us."

"But how do we know what's perfect in God's eyes? We can really only guess. We will probably *all* get a big surprise on Resurrection Day," answered Gram.

"Then I guess all we can really do is try our best," I said.

"It's kind of like getting an A in effort on a report card that shows mostly 'C's. I certainly wouldn't fault a child who's trying her best," replied Gram.

Then both Gram and I had a glass of iced tea and chatted about school and Cynthia's new home and plans for Sunday. I cleaned up the dishes. When the sun went down, I practiced the cello and then sat at the kitchen table working on the draft of my research paper until bedtime.

Sunday was again clear, sunny, and warm. Trees all over the neighborhood had burst forth with white and pink blossoms. I found it hard to believe winter had not been completely left behind. I begged Gram to put away winter coats and hats and to put spring coverlets on the beds, storing away the heavy quilts and comforters until next year.

"It's only Indian Summer," said Gram. "In another week we'll be back in the throes of winter."

We had our customary Sunday breakfast with Uncle, Auntie, and the cousins, including Gwen. Then I dressed for deliveries. When I finished dressing and went out to the truck, there was Gwen sitting in my place in the front seat. So I climbed into the back with the groceries. I felt myself becoming jealous as our rounds continued. At each stop the customers made a big to-do over little Gwen. As I put groceries away, Gwen sat at kitchen tables eating cookies and sipping punch.

Between stops Uncle chatted with Gwen while I bumped along in the back of the truck. Gwen honked the horn at each house. Two customers forgot to give me my now-anticipated nickel tip. By the time we arrived at Mr. Clark's house, I was angry and sullen. Then Mr. Clark came rushing down the steps with a broad smile on his face. And I felt myself caught up in his warm hug.

"How are you feeling, young lady?" he asked with a smile. "I was worried when you missed your delivery last week."

"I'm fine now, Mr. Clark," I said. It was hard for me to believe only a week had passed since I was so depressed. Mr. Clark put his arm around me and pulled me into the house before I could collect his order. He sat with me at the kitchen table as Cynthia fetched the groceries and put them away. Cynthia poured iced tea for everyone. Then she and Gwen went to Cynthia's room to visit while Mr. Clark pampered me.

I noticed the house was spotless. Everything had been cleaned and polished. The kitchen had been rearranged to suit Cynthia's cooking style. The rugs hung on the clotheslines where Cynthia had beaten them yesterday. Laundry was in the tub waiting to be scrubbed and wrung out. Mr. Clark said he liked having Cynthia's help and company.

"But you'll always be my best girl," he said to me.

My mood lifted. Mr. Clark had known just what to say to remind me that I was still loved. I had a tour of Cynthia's room. Then I helped her carry in the rugs and re-lay them. When Uncle, Gwen, and I re-boarded the delivery truck, Gwen took a seat in the back. Uncle chatted with me all the way home.

"Uncle," I said when we arrived at Gram's house, "will you forgive me for doubting your love? I thought Gwen had taken my place."

Then, turning to Gwen, I said, "Please forgive me for being jealous of you."

Both Uncle and Gwen stared at me in surprise.

"I didn't know you were jealous," said Gwen.

"Nor I," said Uncle. "Of course, you're forgiven. Please forgive me for anything I did to make you feel less loved."

"And I forgive you, too," said Gwen. "I'm sorry about taking your attention today."

"That's okay," I said. Then we hugged all around and said our goodbyes.

While lying in bed that night, I thought about what Gram said about forgiveness. If I hadn't forgiven Uncle and Gwen and asked their forgiveness, I'd be the only one hurting. They didn't even know I was hurt until I told them. And I was the one who needed forgiveness because I had unfairly judged them, thinking they had hurt me on purpose. It's like Gram says — the one who can't forgive is the one who suffers and the one who judges is most in need of forgiveness.

32

On Monday when I arrived at school, a group of students was standing around Mr. Jones from *The Bakersfield Californian*. Several students were talking at once, trying to explain how Mr. Owens had broken his ankle. The reporter saw me approaching and extricated himself from the cluster of children in order to speak to me.

"Hi, Dorrance," he said, "Remember me?"

"Yes, how are you?" I asked cordially, as I recalled the story in the newspaper about the basketball boycott.

"May I speak with you?" he asked. "IN PRIVATE," he shouted at the group following him.

Jones and I walked toward the street.

"Are you staging another boycott?" he asked abruptly.

I stood silently, feeling a sense of deja vu.

"I'm sorry," said Jones, "I guess that question may be a little off-putting without some preliminary explanation. *The Bakersfield Californian* has been contacted by a reputable source that another boycott is in progress here---this time over girls not being allowed in the track and field program. Can you confirm this?"

"First of all, we don't know if girls will be allowed in the competition. Mr. Owens has refused to say. So the students have refused to practice until they know for sure.

Second, this is not a 'staged boycott.' It's just students exercising their freedom of choice. We choose not to participate in activities where all students are not welcome."

"I heard Mr. Owens broke his ankle in a fracas on the playground Friday," Jones said.

"Mr. Owens broke his ankle because he lost his temper. Red told him the students would not participate until he decided if girls could compete. Mr. Owens stamped his foot in anger. He had to be carried off the field by Coach Wells and Mr. Griffin." Then I snickered a little when I remembered how hard Becky and I had laughed about it on Saturday.

"That's the funniest thing I've ever heard!" said Jones with a laugh. "Carry on," he called as he walked to his horse-and-buggy.

At noontime Coach Wells was on the playground, as usual. At twelve-thirty he blew his whistle. When no one came forward, he walked to his carriage and left.

I stayed after school to toss a ball around with the boys and to speculate about Jone's visit. None of the boys owned up to notifying the newspaper. Someone thought Mr. Owens had called them to gain sympathy for his broken ankle. Red thought Coach Wells had called and told them he was afraid of being injured by out-of-control students. Tommy thought Mr. Griffin had called. He visualized a whole line of students standing before Mr. Griffin with their hands held out awaiting his dreaded ruler.

"I guess we'll know soon enough," said Red. "I hope it's not as bad as I'm imagining."

"Me, too," was the consensus of the others.

When I arrived home a letter from Mama was waiting on the kitchen table. Gram handed me a glass of iced tea and two oatmeal cookies. Wanting to forewarn her about possible trouble, I told her about the reporter at school. She laughed about Mr. Owens' ankle.

"Honestly, Gram," I said, "You have become a regular rebel since I came to live here!"

"Oh, Dorrance, I've always been a rebel."

Then Gram left me alone to read my letter.

Well, I thought as I read, he finally got up the gumption to propose to Mama — on Valentine's Day — how romantic. Mama had accepted. They planned to get married during the summer so I could be there. Mama was to be released from the sanatorium on May first. She would go to Fish Lake Valley to stay with Uncle Leonard while she continued recuperating. Harry still wanted to adopt me, so we would all have the same last name. Big deal, I thought. Harry had promised to pay for my higher education all the way through college. I'll believe that when I see it, I thought. At the end of the letter I crumpled it into a ball and threw it at the stove.

"Dag nab it! I can't even burn it on such a warm day," I fumed. Then I grabbed my school books and ran upstairs. Button nuzzled my hand as I lay on the bed crying. Gram came upstairs with the rumpled letter in her hand. She sat on my bed and watched my emotional outpouring. When my crying began to subside, Gram told me to sit up and wipe my eyes.

"We need to talk," she said. "I found this on the kitchen floor," handing the paper ball to me. "I don't know what has you so hurt and angry."

I told her the entire contents of the letter.

"Why are you angry?" asked Gram. "You've known all this for weeks. Your mama and Harry have kept you informed every step of the way. You gave your blessing to the wedding."

"I know I did!" I raged. "Why did I do that? I'm just so confused."

"Sometimes knowing something *may* happen and finding out it really is going to happen are two different things. I think you probably were hoping Harry and your mama would change their minds about marriage," offered Gram.

"I did. I just want things to be like they used to be."

"Dorrance," said Gram, "life *is* change. Life is a journey. Sometimes the journey moves faster than we would like. But we need to enjoy the journey."

"Well, I don't like change and the only journey I want is one back to Fish Lake Valley without Harry," I sobbed.

"Eight months ago," said Gram, "I thought my journey was over. I was comfortable with that. Every day was exactly the same. Eat, sleep, read. See Sabert and Marilyn and the boys on Sundays. My life had been so for several years."

I stopped sniffling and thought what a boring life Gram had had. As if in answer to my thought Gram said, "I had to think long and hard about allowing you to live with me. I thought of every negative I could: what if she's noisy? ill-mannered? violent? too prissy? and on and on. I thought of every possible way my life would be disrupted. And I almost said no. But my sense of responsibility got the better of me.

"I tell you, the first day you were here and came home after a fight with boys, I thought I had made a huge mistake. Many days and nights I lectured myself about looking for the good in you and in our situation together. Now I can hardly remember what my fears were. When I think back over the last seven months I laugh. My journey is still going. I have relived the days of my own skinny-dipping and boycotts, girls athletics and growing up. And I now know what a perfect great-granddaughter you are in every way."

Gram pulled me into her arms. "Supper will be ready soon. I love you."

"I love you, too, Gram."

After supper I thought about forgiveness. I thought about life as a journey. Then I got out a piece of paper and sat at the table making a list of all the good things in my journey the last seven months. The more I wrote the more I remembered to write until I ran out of paper.

"Look at all I would have missed if I had stayed on the ranch with Uncle Leonard," I said to myself.

Then I got another piece of paper and wrote a letter to Mama asking her forgiveness for being angry. I told Mama I had discovered how valuable my journey had been. I wished Mama a safe and happy journey with Harry in Independence.

On Tuesday morning Uncle Sabert came running up the steps waving the morning edition.

"Wait 'til you see," he said, spreading the paper on the table.

"What's all the excitement?" asked Gram, entering the kitchen.

"Just look at this!" exclaimed Uncle. "Our little trouble-maker has a following." And he winked at me. All three of us carefully read the article bi-lined "Victory for Girls Athletics."

It seems Miss Harris made a sizeable donation as the result of the basketball boycott. The donation was to be used for an all-student track and field program at Franklin School. Miss Harris asked *The Bakersfield Californian* to administer the grant.

The *Californian* hired Coach Wells from Bakersfield College to coach the noontime program. When students refused to participate, the coach became suspicious. He did some investigating and found out that Principal Owens intended to provide a program in which girls would be allowed to practice but not to compete in the meet. It seems Principal Owens was hanging on the coattails of a couple of the school board members in hopes of advancing to Superintendent of Schools.

Anyway, Coach Wells notified Miss Harris and *The Bakersfield Californian*. Miss Harris graciously agreed to let the donation stand provided a girls' track and field program be launched immediately. The final line of the article read, "Hurray for Franklin students for recognizing the equal worth and talent of all students."

Underneath this article was a small box which read: Principal Owens of Franklin School reported having had his ankle broken by students in a playground fracas on Friday. After interviewing both students and Coach Wells, *The Bakersfield Californian* has determined his injuries were the result of his own bad temper and political aspirations.

"What a difference you've made in our community, little girl," said Uncle, swinging me around the kitchen.

33

On Saturday, February 28th, winter was again upon us. Rain pelted the windows of my room, awakening me before dawn. I pulled the comforter up under my chin to try to chase away the cold. I was glad Gram had insisted on leaving the winter linens on the beds. I lay there wondering if the rain would stop in time for my walk to the library. Just then a powerful wind gust drove rain inside around a loose window sash.

"I guess not."

At six-thirty I tiptoed to Gram's room and knocked lightly.

"I'm awake. Come in," said Gram.

"Good morning, Gram. You were right about the weather. May I invite Becky to come home with me for dinner?"

"Of course."

"Thank you. About one o'clock?"

"I'll have something hot ready for you," Gram promised.

On my way to meet Becky, bundled in my coat, hat, muffler, and gloves, I saw the fruit trees, bare of yesterday's blossoms. The wind had stripped the branches clean. Wet blossoms covered the street. By the time I reached A Street I was soaked through. Becky was not there to meet me, so I walked on to the Gaines house. Mrs. Gaines opened the door and pulled me inside.

"Surely you don't intend to go to the library in this storm," Mrs. Gaines chastised. "Take those wet things off and I'll hang them by the fire to dry."

"I didn't think it rained this hard in Bakersfield," I replied.

"Only about five inches a year, but sometimes all at once," Mrs. Gaines said. "My, I hope it lets up soon so we don't have another flood."

Becky came running in from the back yard where she had gone to feed the chickens. She carried three eggs in her hands which she put in a bowl on the kitchen counter.

"Dorrance," she said, giggling, "you look like you've been skinny-dipping. Do you have your report done?"

"I'm just recopying the draft," I said. "It'll be ready to turn in on Monday."

Mrs. Gaines brought me a robe to wear while my coat, dress, and shoes dried by the fire.

"Come sit at the table with me," said Becky. "We can finish up our reports and then play in my room."

"Gram said we could have dinner at my house," I said.

"Please call her and tell her not to bother," said Mrs. Gaines. "I have a casserole planned and already half prepared. You can eat here."

So I called Gram to say I'd be at Becky's until suppertime. By eleven o'clock we had finished our reports and admired each other's papers. We ate a hearty goulash for dinner. Mrs. Gaines made hot cocoa for us to take to Becky's room. Julia and Sarah had gone to their grandparents' house for the weekend. So the huge room that was shared by the three Gaines girls was a rainy-day refuge for Becky and me. Becky set the Chinese checker game by the windows in Julia's part of the room and shut the French doors between the large room and this porch of Julia's. The rain pounded down and sounded like hail when it hit the tin roof of the tiny room. Becky pulled back the curtains so we had an unobstructed view of the storm. The plum tree outside Julia's window would probably not have much fruit this year. All that remained of its blossoms were a few pink petals blowing along the ground.

Becky sat on Julia's bed and I sat in a soft-seated wooden chair opposite. Soon the marbles had been divided and the game was in progress. Becky and I talked about Miss Harris's donation and the new track and field program. Mr. Owens was still out with his broken ankle. Wouldn't he be surprised when he returned to school to find the track and field program in full swing? The competition date was set for the third Saturday in April. Becky said she would compete in the standing and running broad jumps. I planned to compete in everything except the relay. I wanted to be on the relay team with Red, Tommy, and Herbert. But girls would be competing separately from boys, so I gave my spot to Jesse.

After school-talk was exhausted, I shared my mother's wedding plans with Becky. I said I would need to go to Bishop for a month in July and August, but that I would come back to Bakersfield right after the wedding. Becky wanted to know why I wasn't going to stay longer. I said Uncle needed me on Sundays for deliveries. I also told Becky that Gram's garden would need attention. Soon I found myself sharing my feelings of abandonment and began to cry. Becky caught my hand and pulled me over to the bed. She held me and comforted me, then pulled me down into a lying position on the bed. But I popped up again, telling Becky I was afraid her mother would catch us and ban Becky from seeing me. She conceded it was probably a good idea to be upright if her mother came in. Then she leaned forward and kissed me full on the lips. And I kissed her back. The kiss, the first for both of us, was soft and sweet and innocent.

I could have felt very safe with Becky. But I was afraid to let my guard down. Afraid of losing someone else I loved. And afraid society would condemn our love and publicly humiliate us both. I gave Becky a final kiss and said I had to go home. Her eyes filled with tears.

"Becky," I said, "we're thirteen. Well, you're almost thirteen. We have years to live before we can be together. I want to be with you forever. But until then we have to be careful."

I kissed Becky on the forehead, collected my papers, bundled up, and walked home. The rain pelted me in the face. I was glad because it disguised my tears. I was thinking of our first kiss. It was so sweet and welcome. Then I thought I would like to share the story of it with my friends at school, just as they had shared the stories of their first loves. But I knew I couldn't ever share stories of my love. It was forbidden. I could never tell anyone how much I loved Becky, how much she meant to me. Even after we were grown, we would have to live this secret. It was just too much to bear—this secret we must keep. I was terrified that I would forget and blurt it out to the wrong person. Somehow the secret tainted our perfect love. I was so incredibly sad I didn't know if I could stand it.

By the time I arrived back at Gram's I was in a deep depression. I didn't want to do anything but sleep. But I knew I couldn't continue to worry Gram about this whole sapphist thing. So I went about my chores and spent the rest of my time in the library trying to read, but mostly wiping tears from my cheeks.

On Sunday I dragged myself from bed and pretended to be happy to see Uncle, Auntie, Jack, Andrew, and Gwen. Then I acted as if I wanted to make deliveries. I was respectful to my customers, but my heart was not in it. I wondered how many of them would still be friendly if they knew about my sapphism and my new girlfriend. I felt as if I could trust no one with matters of my heart. When we were riding home, Uncle commented on how quiet I was. I just made an excuse about being tired and not liking the rain. But when I got home I spent the afternoon sleeping.

By Monday the only thing left of the rain storm were puddles in the street. I walked to school with my head down, deep in a thoughtful depression. I stepped off a curb into a puddle and was splashed by a passing wagon.

The driver hollered out to me, "Be careful there, little girl!"

I looked down at my muddy dress, coat, and stockings and my soaking shoes. Better if he had run me down and put me out of my misery, I said to myself. Then I became frightened. I had never before wished to die. I did not remember being so sad with no thought of my mood ever lifting. I wondered if I would be brave enough to kill myself. I decided I didn't want to find out the depth of my courage. I needed to get some help.

I thought of going home to Gram but decided against it. I wanted the opinion of a "disinterested third party." I walked to the school office and asked if I could talk to the nurse. Miss Scott noticed my muddy clothes and gave me a pass to the nurse in room 13.

Room 13, I thought, didn't sound too promising. As I walked to the stairs several students spoke to me, but I answered none of them. I walked doggedly on as if in a trance. I turned the knob on the door marked 13. As I pushed the door open, I hesitated.

"Please come in," said a woman's voice. "My, what happened to you?"

I looked down at my clothes but said nothing.

"Sit down here," said the voice, indicating a chair.

I sat trying to think of something to say to get help without mentioning the real problem, my sapphism. Finally I said in a soft, strained voice, "I've been sad for a very long time."

"How did you get so muddy?" the voice wanted to know.

"A wagon splashed me," I answered, "but that's not why I'm here. I've been so terribly sad."

"Would you like to go home and change your clothes?" asked the voice. "I'm sure that will make you feel better."

"Listen to me," I implored. "I don't want to live anymore!"

"Oh, dear, you mustn't say that," said the voice. "Now here's a note so you can go home and change."

Then I found myself in the hallway, a note in my hand. I walked out of the school and turned toward home. Gram was still in bed when I came in the back door.

"Dorrance, is that you?" she called.

"It's me. I got splashed and came home to change clothes."

I went upstairs and dropped my wet, muddy dress on the floor and pulled on my dungarees, shirt, and boots. Then I put my red coat back on, in spite of the mud, hoping for the comfort I always felt when I wore it. I called to Button who sleepily followed me down the stairs.

"I'm going now," I called to Gram.

We walked down 18th Street to Oak and across the field to the river. I collapsed under a live oak tree near the water with Button at my side. This was the first time I had seen the raging power of the Kern River. The heavy rain of the past two days had swelled the river to its banks. The yellow-brown current carried branches as large as tree trunks. It was scary to watch. I hugged Button close to me.

For what must have been an hour, I weighed the pros and cons of throwing myself into the certain death of this turbulence. I held my coat close around me. Button must have sensed my despair because he licked and licked, my hands, my face, every visible part of me. And he whined pitifully.

Then I moved further from the water into a sunny spot. I lay down with Button by my side and spread my coat over us. I didn't know what to do except pray. "Dear God, I need help. My heart is broken. My mind is blank. I'm afraid to be myself. God, if you love me, please send me help." I immediately found myself worrying about the term paper that would be turned in late because I missed school today. At that point I realized I had made my decision. I would continue to live. The anxiety lifted from me and Button and I fell asleep in the grass.

When I woke up I didn't know what time it was. I knew it was late, though, because the sun was low in the western sky. I got up and told Button we had better go home now. Gram would surely be upset that I had skipped school. I trudged across the field and up the street toward home.

When I neared the house I saw Uncle's truck parked out front. I wondered why he was here before the store closed. Button's paws were muddy so we walked around back. As soon as the door opened I was snatched into Gram's arms in the warmest, hugest hug I ever remembered. Then Uncle hugged us both from the other side. It felt like I was peanut butter between two slabs of fresh-baked bread.

When Gram finally released her hold on me, I saw tears rolling down her cheeks.

"I was so worried about you," she said, wiping her tears with her palms. "Where in the world have you been?"

Before I could answer Uncle interrupted. "I've been all over town for hours looking for you and Button."

"I'm sorry," I said. "I didn't think…"

"Well you need to think," said Gram. "Me, Uncle, Rebecca, Sarah, all of us worried sick. Let's sit down and have some tea and talk about it."

So we sat down at the table and Gram told me what had happened at home while I was sleeping by the river. Gram had got up shortly after I left and noticed that Button was missing. She'd gone outside, calling and calling, all the way to the corner and back. When Button didn't come home she called Uncle Sabert to go looking for him. At dinner time Rebecca and Sarah came to the door wondering where I was. That's the first Gram and Uncle knew that I had skipped school. Uncle went out again in the truck, driving up and down every street and checking with my customers and friends. He even drove by the river and noticed the raging torrents. He became terrified that I'd fallen into the water and drowned.

The more Gram shared, the worse I felt. I had been so wrapped up in my own pain I'd thought nothing of her and Uncle. I hadn't thought of Becky either.

"Did Becky go back to school after dinner?" I asked.

"Yes, poor thing. She was in tears, simply beside herself with worry," said Gram. "She'll be so relieved to know you're safe."

"I'm so sorry, Gram, Uncle. Please forgive me," I said.

"Of course, you're forgiven," they both replied.

"But there is more to this than an apology and forgiveness. We're concerned this may happen again," said Uncle. "What can we do to help? Exactly what *is* bothering you? You really need to trust us to help you through this."

Before I could reply there was a knock at the front door. Uncle waved his hand indicating that I should answer it. I pulled the door open and there stood Becky, eyes swollen red and tears still wet on her cheeks. She threw herself into my arms.

"I was so worried," she cried. "No one knew where you were."

"I was at the river. I'm so sorry I worried everyone."

"I just knew you were dead somewhere. That's the only reason you would miss turning in your term paper... at least that's what I thought," said Becky.

"I was just really sad. I couldn't face school today, so I skipped it. I took Button and went to the river."

"Dorrance," said Becky, "I broke the promise I made. I told Miss Harris about us."

"You what?" I asked in disbelief.

"I was so scared and I had to talk to someone. I knew I could trust her, so I told her everything."

"What do you mean by *everything*?" I asked.

"About us being in love. About us being sapphists." And then Becky hung her head.

Uncle called from the kitchen summoning me to return. So Becky and I went and sat at the table. Gram poured Becky some tea and sat down. We started to talk again, but there was another knock on the door.

"I'll get it," said Becky.

A moment later, Becky led Miss Harris and another woman into the kitchen. Miss Harris introduced herself to Gram and Uncle and then introduced the other lady as Miss Burke. Gram suggested we all move into the dining room where we could sit around the big table. She put another pot of water on the stove for more tea. Soon we were all settled and everyone was looking at me for some kind of explanation. It was odd that I felt so comfortable. But I did, so I started to tell my story.

I told them about my terrible sadness and about the nurse at school. I pulled the note from my pocket and passed it to Gram who passed it around the table. Miss Burke seemed upset about the lack of help I received at school. Then I told about coming home to change clothes and going to the river with Button. I told them that I had considered jumping into the water, then prayed, falling asleep in the grass. Then I again apologized for causing so much trouble for everyone.

There was a long pause after I'd finished. Gram and Becky were wiping their eyes. Uncle was sitting beside me and put his arm around my shoulders.

"I'm so sorry you're that sad," he said, "but I understand it. Everyone wants to be accepted for who they are."

Then Miss Burke turned to me. It seemed her warm brown eyes looked right inside me.

"Dorrance," she began, "Miss Harris and I are life companions."

I glanced across the table at Becky who looked back at me in surprise.

"Companions?"

"Em and I like that word. We are life companions," said Miss Burke.

"You mean roommates? Old maids?" I asked.

"No," she said. "We live together as a couple because we love each other."

"Then you're sapphists," I whispered.

Miss Harris and Miss Burke smiled.

"But you're so normal. And you're happy, right?" I asked.

"Very!" replied Miss Harris.

"Oh, Miss Harris, Miss Burke, I'm so glad Becky found you. I'm so glad we're not the only sapphists."

Then the conversation got serious.

"Dorrance, Rebecca," said Miss Harris, "it's important that you understand. Although we are very happy, we are also very private. Bakersfield is too small a town to allow even idle gossip. An accusation from anyone could end everything Mae and I have worked so hard to build. But we felt you were worth the risk.

"It's very hard to grow up feeling different. When I was fourteen, I thought seriously about suicide. But I met a nurse who sensed my situation and took me under her wing. Even in Bakersfield there are many of us sapphists. We are decent, hard-working people. Having strong role models made it easier to grow up sapphist. But it will always be hard, too.

"It's still hard to watch my pronouns. Saying 'she' instead of 'he' can be disastrous. I live one life at home and another at school. Someday it may not be necessary, but for now it is. But you'll get used to it."

Miss Burke interrupted. "You'll scare the child to death," she admonished.

"I've already been scared to death," I replied. "Nothing can be worse than what I was feeling this morning. Gram already told me what it was like for her sapphist friends, so what you just told me is no surprise. I can't tell you how awful I've been feeling the last couple of days. I'm so glad we found you both."

Then Miss Harris and Miss Burke talked further about what Gram and Uncle could do to support me and Becky. They talked about the importance of loving, supportive friends and family. She talked about the importance of recognizing differences in others so our difference would not seem so large. She talked about listening to God, not those who claim to be God's messengers. When they left, Miss Harris handed me a slip of paper with her address on it.

When I lay quietly in bed that night, a warm, safe feeling enveloped me. Not only was I certain of the love of Gram and Uncle, I was sure I could trust Miss Harris and Miss Burke. I was glad to have the secret out in the open to these few people, so glad Becky had told someone we could trust. Most of all, I was certain of God's love for me just as I am.

34

I met Becky on the school steps early Tuesday. We spent a few minutes talking about yesterday's events, especially the dining room meeting.

Suddenly she leaned forward and whispered in my ear, "I was so scared when you were missing."

"Becky, I'm sorry. I didn't mean to hurt you. I was so sad I couldn't think of anything but ending my pain."

"Please don't leave me, Dorrance," whispered Becky.

"Becky, I won't. Not ever."

Then we both went to our classes. Frances snickered at me when I turned in my term paper and Mr. Griffin said, "I will have to lower your grade a full letter for a late paper."

All the rest of the day I tried to notice differences in others, as Miss Harris had suggested. I noticed that I seldom paid much attention to appearances of others. I paid little more attention to behaviors, unless it was a caustic problem like Frances's name-calling or Mr. Griffin's method of discipline. Today I studied several people carefully.

Red not only had red hair, but pale skin and blotchy freckles. His ears stuck out on either side of his head like hollowed orange peel halves. Red's expression was usually serious. His dark brown eyes hid his pupils and his feelings. But he also had a ready sense of humor. His wide grin and hearty laugh cheered everyone. I recognized that without his winning personality he could easily have been teased into being a lonely shell of a boy.

Frances, on the other hand, had a perfect appearance. A clear, pink complexion, gorgeous naturally-wavy hair, bright blue eyes, and long lashes, like the ones with which boys are usually blessed. Her clothing was up-to-date and expensive. Unfortunately, her appearance didn't upstage her dark personality. I'd seen her laugh only at the expense of someone else. So the joy usually evident in a laugh was replaced in Frances by a sinister shriek.

I understood why Red was so well-liked in spite of his goofy appearance and why Frances was so despised in spite of her outward beauty.

Cynthia sat behind me in class, so I closed my eyes picturing how she had looked on Sunday. She was wearing an old work dress with no shape to it. Her hair was up under a scarf as she cleaned house. Her eyes were deep brown, but they glistened with interest. She looked straight at you when she listened, like she genuinely cared about you. Her mouth was in a perpetual upward curve since she'd begun living with Mr. Clark. He doted on everything she said and did. He talked to her at length each day as she did the household chores. He told her how much he loved her.

I thought about Cynthia at the beginning of the school year. I realized I hadn't even noticed her until the day of the spelling bee. She was so quiet she had become invisible. Isolated as she was at home and at school had made her seem no more than a doormat, there to do the bidding of others, never to act or think in behalf of herself. Her drab only dress had made her even more unnoticeable.

What a difference Uncle and Mr. Clark had made in Cynthia's life. They built her spirit up so that it could finally shine forth. All the qualities of work ethic, caring for others, and caring about her own future, now shown on Cynthia's face and in her actions.

That positive energy had begun to attract others' attention at school. Cynthia was making friends. On the other hand, I found my own friends drifting away lately. The more I showed my fear and worry, the more others avoided me. I remembered myself last summer, before I knew the accursed label of *sapphist*. I was happy-go-lucky, at ease in my boy's clothes, at ease with my boy's activities, at ease holding Becky's hand. Times were more joyous. I had lots of interests and lots of friends. The whole school had stood with me in the basketball boycott. I remembered what it felt like to laugh. It felt so much better than crying. I wondered if I would ever again be my real self.

I'll pretend to be my old self, I thought, even if it seems like a lie. If I do that, maybe it will become a habit again. I would so like to love myself again.

At noontime I went to the playground to participate in the track and field practice. It felt good to be physically active after so much worry yesterday. The running and jumping put a higher level of energy into my body and mind. I found myself effortlessly smiling the rest of the afternoon. I felt as if I were on the mend.

35

Wednesday morning Becky was waiting on the school steps wearing her new spectacles.

"Becky, you look positively intellectual," I teased.

"Oh, Dorrance, I can see the individual twigs on the tree branches and the blades of grass! I don't care how many names I'm called, it's worth it."

"It took a long time for the spectacles to get here, didn't it? I almost forgot you were getting them."

"All the way from Los Angeles," said Becky. "I had almost forgotten them myself."

"Well, your spectacles are spectacular! Your eyes are bigger and bluer than ever. And your lashes are *so* long."

As soon as I entered the classroom, Sarah ran up to me.

"Dorrance, I've been trying to talk to you without Rebecca around."

"Oooh! Secrets?" I asked.

"As a matter of fact, yes. Rebecca's birthday is on the fifth. She's not expecting a party because her spectacles were so expensive. So we're trying to plan a surprise party, but we need your help."

"You want me to keep her out of the house so you can decorate?"

"Not exactly. Something more creative than that. Actually, Mother and I want to borrow *your* house. It will be easier to hide the decorations and guests."

"How will you get her there for the party? You want me to keep her busy and then take her home for supper?" I asked.

"That's the best part!" Sarah laughed out loud. "We want you to do something outrageous. Then Mother will hear about it and pretend to be angry. She'll take Rebecca with her to your house to speak to your grandmother about your behavior. Rebecca will be so nervous and worried. But when your gram opens the door, everyone will yell SURPRISE!"

"That sounds almost cruel," I said. I knew my eyes were twinkling with anticipation. "But it also sounds hysterically funny. What am I supposed to do?"

"Mother says you'll come up with something. She says your behavior has been way too normal lately. She thinks you must be absolutely ready to explode with pent-up outrageousness."

The thought of doing something outrageous with no fear of repercussions cheered me to no end. Several ideas sprang to mind right away. But I needed to remember that this was a birthday gift for Becky. What would please her most? Then I knew!

I conspired in my mind all day long while sitting at my desk pretending to study. I needed help to execute my plan. There were several people I could ask, but who could I trust to keep my secret?

That evening after supper I made my decision. I went to the telephone in the front hall and called Uncle's house.

"Hello." It was Jack.

"Hi. Is Andrew home?"

"Just a minute. He's washing dishes."

A couple of minutes went by before I heard, "Dorrance?"

"Hi, Andrew. Sorry to interrupt your dishes," I said.

"I'm not sorry," he said.

"Are you alone or is somebody listening to what you say?" I asked.

"I'm alone. What's going on?"

"Can you keep a secret, Andrew? It's really important. I need your help but you can't tell a soul."

"I guess so," he replied. "People don't usually ask me that. They usually keep secrets from ME."

"Well, here's your chance to retaliate then."

"Okay. What's the secret?" he asked.

"It's not that kind of secret. I need you to do something for me and not tell anyone or raise suspicion."

"Okay. What?"

"I need a set of boy's clothes. Nice ones. Ones that'll fit me.

"What for?" he asked.

"That's not part of the secret. Can you get me the clothes and bring them to the store? Tomorrow?"

"You're not gonna tell me why?" he asked.

"No."

"I don't see why you can't tell me. I said I'd keep the secret."

"That part is a surprise. I just can't tell you now. Do you want to help me or not?"

There was a long pause.

"I'll do it," he said. "But you owe me."

"I promise to work at the store for you some Saturday when you want a day off. And I won't charge you for it."

That tipped the balance in my favor.

"All right," he said. "I know where Ma keeps Jack's hand-me-downs. I'll find something a little too big for me. That should fit you."

"Nice clothes, Andrew. Pants, dress shirt, tie, and jacket."

"I get it. I'm not stupid," he snapped.

"Thanks, Andrew. I'll pick them up at the store tomorrow."

"I get to work at three-thirty. They'll be in a bag in the alley. Don't be late or someone might steal them."

I heard Gram's footsteps coming my way. So I said, "Gotta go," and hung up.

The next afternoon I crouched behind some bushes in the alley behind Logan Grocery. Auntie's buggy soon pulled to a stop. Jack jumped out and tied the horses. Auntie went inside.

Jack shouted to Andrew, "C'mon, Slow Poke!"

"I'll be right there," Andrew shouted back.

When Jack disappeared inside, I came out of my hiding place and ran to the buggy. Andrew pulled a package from under his coat and flung it at me.

"You have no idea how much trouble this was!" he said, as he ran inside.

No matter how much trouble it was, I knew it would be worth it.

I rushed home and hid the clothes in the carriage house. I ask Gram's permission to go downtown. I told her I wanted to make a banner for Becky's party and needed supplies. Gram said I could have an old sheet from the linen closet and that she had a brush I could use. Then she said not to be too late getting home.

I walked fast to get to Kress before closing time. At four-fifty I walked into the store and asked the clerk for paints. She directed me to an area of art supplies. I looked at the colors carefully before choosing red, blue, and yellow. I knew I could mix all the colors I needed from those primary colors. Then I went to the men's fashion accessories where I purchased a pair of fake spectacles and a fake mustache. I paid a dollar and five cents of my tip money and walked home.

Every evening after supper, Gram and I worked at the big dining table painting the sheet into a banner. When it was finished I laced it with rope, rolled it up, and took it to my room for some secret finishing touches.

On Monday evening I carried a pack to the school and hid it in the bushes. The pack contained a hammer, some nails, the banner, and my boy clothes.

Tuesday morning I arose before daylight. I sneaked into the carriage house for the six foot ladder. It was made of wood and was so heavy I had to drag it to the school. Halfway there I stopped and wondered if there wasn't an easier way to hang the banner. Nothing came to mind, so I again dragged the ladder along on the grass of people's front lawns so the noise would awaken no one. When I finally reached the school, I leaned the ladder against the front wall and retrieved the pack from the bushes.

I carefully, quickly, and expertly (if I do say so myself) hung the banner over the front entrance to the school. Then I stashed the pack in the bushes and dragged the ladder back to the carriage house. I was snuggly back in bed before daylight.

An hour before school I entered the lobby with the pack I had again pulled from the bushes. I went to the girls' restroom, removed my school clothes, and dressed in Jack's old clothing. I put my braided hair up under a snappy black cap, put on the spectacles, and admired myself in the mirror. I decided against the mustache, thinking it was overkill.

Then the bathroom door squeaked open.

"Young man, I think you're in the wrong toilet," said an outraged first grade teacher.

"Oh, I'm sorry, ma'am." I grabbed my pack stuffed with my school clothes and left.

I glanced at the clock on the wall. It was still thirty-five minutes until school would start. I hid in the bushes where I had an unobstructed view of children walking to school from the east, the way Becky would come. My heart fluttered with excitement.

Several students and teachers stopped to read the banner on their way into the building. Some students commented that they would be embarrassed to have their birthday announced like that. But, to me, they sounded a little jealous. None of the teachers questioned the display. Surely they thought it had been approved by someone in authority.

When I saw Sarah and Becky coming up the street, I took my place on the steps, slouching against the railing and looking like any other boy in school. I blended in like all the other 'invisibles' at school. Then Becky was looking up at the sign reading: Happy Birthday, Rebecca. Her eyes slowly lowered to read the smaller note in the right-hand corner of the banner: I love you, Becky. D.

At that moment I strode forward and took Becky in my arms for a long kiss.

"Who's that boy kissing Rebecca?" everyone was asking. "I didn't know she had a boyfriend."

Then, out of the corner of my eye, I saw Mr. Griffin step onto the porch from inside the building. I whispered, "I love you" in Becky's ear and jumped over the railing before Mr. Griffin could grab me. I ducked behind a bush for my pack and ran up the street.

In fifteen minutes I was back at school in my blue gingham dress. The classroom was all atwitter with the story of the birthday banner and, especially, the forbidden kiss. Shows of affection were absolutely forbidden under the rules of common decency and decorum. The banner had been removed and was being held as 'evidence', Frances said.

Evidence of what? I thought. If they only knew it was evidence of sapphist love.

Mr. Griffin entered the classroom. He had a peculiar look on his face as he scanned the pupils before him. I hung my head and pulled a pencil from my pocket, attempting to act nonchalant. Then the glasses from my disguise hit the floor with a soft clunk. I quickly put them away before anyone saw (I thought). As I looked up at Mr. Griffin I noticed his lips trembling as he tried to control his emotions. He suddenly turned his back on the class and walked into the hallway. His steps quickened into a run as he hurried to escape the building. Red jumped up and ran to the window.

"What's he doing?" asked several students.

"He's laughing!"

The desired effect of the outrageous incident was successful. Mrs. Gaines spent so much time at school that day, in conference with Mr. Owens, that she barely had time to decorate for the party. I was nervous all day thinking I would be called to account for my abhorrent display of loose morals. But soon the day was over.

As I left the classroom Mr. Griffin said to me in a soft voice: "Don't worry. I'll keep your secret."

When I arrived at home, party preparations were in full swing. Julia, who had gone home early, was hanging paper chains. Gram was frosting a three-layer birthday cake.

I pitched in by setting a buffet table. First, I spread the white table protector and covered it with a hand-crocheted table cloth. I made thin rolls of the napkins and inserted them into napkin rings. Gram and Mrs. Gaines had prepared several platters of light supper foods. There was a platter of delicate sandwiches, another of winter vegetables and dipping sauce, a potato salad, coleslaw, a relish plate with pickles and olives, dinner rolls, butter, and an assortment of jams. I attractively arranged all these items on the table. I then placed a stack of plates and a selection of silverware at one end of the table. At the other I set the punch bowl and several crystal cups.

"The table looks lovely, Dorrance. Why don't you hang the banner now?" asked Gram.

"Uhhh…" I stammered, gazing everywhere to avoid looking at Gram.

"Right there, I think, above the mantel," she pointed.

"Well, Gram, I took it to school today and it's still there, I think."

"Why on earth. . ." began Gram. Then I interrupted and told the whole story.

Gram sat down halfway through with a soft smile of amazement on her face.

"Should I expect a call from the school then?" she asked.

"No. Mr. Griffin is the only one who knows it was me and he said he'd keep my secret. But I have no idea what poor Becky has been through today."

"We'll know soon enough, I expect. I guess Mrs. Gaines will think twice before asking you to be outrageous in the future."

At five-forty-five the guests began to arrive. All the lights in the front of the house were turned off as everyone found hiding places.

At exactly six o'clock a perturbed knock rang out. I opened the door, stepping behind it and peeking through the curtain. Mrs. Gaines had an outraged look on her face. Becky positively cowered behind her mother, her face ashen and terror showing in her eyes.

Mrs. Gaines pulled Becky through the doorway saying to me, "I need to speak to your grandmother at once, young lady."

Becky made eye contact with me and quickly hung her head.

At that moment the lights flashed on and everyone jumped up shouting "Happy Birthday" and "Surprise!"

Becky, overcome with relief and shock, fell into her mother's arms and cried and laughed simultaneously.

Mrs. Gaines turned to me and said, "Most outrageous! And it looks as if it worked. She's truly surprised."

Mrs. Gaines pulled me into her embrace with Becky.

"I love you both," she whispered.

Then she released us and the party began in earnest. Everyone ate heartily. I played Happy Birthday on the cello while we all sang to Becky. The thirteen candles were extinguished in one mighty breath from the birthday girl. We all ate cake and strawberry ice cream. Mrs. Gaines made the ice cream and flavored it with strawberry preserves from last summer.

Becky opened gifts from her friends, parents, Uncle Sabert, and Gram. But she told me later her favorite present was the long kiss on the school steps from the strange boy in the funny glasses.

36

I kept a low profile at school and at home for the next few weeks. By the end of March spring was here to stay. The sky was clear and bright. The Tehachapi Mountains to the east still had patchy snow. The tops of the Breckenridge Mountains also had white caps. But the valley floor was warm and dry. An occasional breeze dried the perspiration on the faces of residents at work in their yards and gardens. The only thing lacking was the scent of blossoming trees — Indian summer and the following storm had seen to that.

One day at the end of March Gram announced that the seeds had been delivered. She handed me a box with *Burpee Seed Company* printed in the upper left corner.

"I saved them for you to open," said Gram.

I eagerly cut the twine and tore the paper from the box. Inside this small package lay the entire summer garden, enough vegetables and fruit for me and Gram for a whole year.

"What an efficient way to ship a garden," I said. "Just add water and sunshine."

In the box were paper packets of seeds marked radish, carrot, turnip, string bean, corn, green pepper, cantaloupe, pumpkin, zucchini, cucumber, watermelon, and summer squash. Also in the box were starts for rhubarb and *strawberries*! Strawberries were a bonus. Burpee Seed Company had sent them to "try" in Bakersfield. The company asked for a report on how they grew and produced in the hot, dry climate. The tiny strawberry plants seemed almost dead, limp and wilted as they were.

Gram suggested planting them in a container of some sort. Then they could be moved into the shade when the afternoon sun became too hot. I went out back to survey the garden space. I looked for a location that would get morning sun only. Because of the location of the carriage house and the mulberry tree, the garden would all receive the hot afternoon sun. So I went into the carriage house to look for a container. In the corner was a small barrel full of old salvaged nails and other miscellaneous hardware. I immediately had a vision of my strawberry container when I looked at the barrel. I emptied the nails into a wooden crate I lined with some paper. Then I cleaned the barrel and bore two-inch holes in the sides above the halfway point with the hand drill. Once that was done I went into the kitchen to run cold water on my blistered hands. Then I carried the barrel to the garden to fill it with soil. I realized just how heavy it would be when filled and decided I had made a mistake with this plan.

I walked up the block to Becky's to ask a favor. The girls had an old wagon in the back yard. I had never seen anyone use it. So I asked Mrs. Gaines if I could borrow it to pull my strawberry barrel. She said, "Of course," and I brought it home.

I set the barrel in the wagon and shoveled soil into it, occasionally sprinkling it with the watering can so it would be moist all the way through. Then I gently removed each delicate strawberry plant from its shipping package, watered it well, and inserted it into one of the two-inch holes and patted the soil firmly around its roots. When all eight holes were filled, I placed the remaining four plants in the soil on top of the barrel. Then I wheeled the wagon to a spot in the side yard that would get morning sun.

As long as the days were cool, I would leave the barrel to enjoy the sun all day. But as summer neared, I would pull the wagon a few feet into the protection of the house at dinner time. There the delicate leaves and fruit would not burn.

Gram came out to admire the finished project.

"My," she said, "you must feel like a mother who has just completed the nursery for her babies. Nothing to do now but water them and watch them grow." Then, after careful inspection of the tiny, shriveled plants, she added, "if they're not already dead."

"They'll grow," I announced. "They'll be the only strawberries at the fair. Maybe Andrew will eat our strawberries for his birthday this year. Uncle won't have to send to Watsonville for them."

"If not this year, then next," Gram said and laughed, "with your tender loving care."

Then Gram and I went to the garden to discuss placement of the other crops. The tall crops like corn and pole beans would need to be planted where they would not shade the rest of the garden. Some crops like radishes, which grow to be table-ready in three weeks, could be planted again and again. Gram and I sat at the kitchen table late into the evening planning and re-planning.

Finally, locations for every crop were put on a map. Tomorrow I would start planting the crops that were slowest maturing and could tolerate the cool spring nights. I took the garden very seriously. Gram had always kept her own garden. She had given it over to me with great reluctance and much necessity. She was simply too old to dig and weed and cultivate and harvest. I was eager to see what kind of a harvest I would have this first year of being solely in charge of a garden.

I had been practicing for the track and field competition every day after school. But now that it was spring I would practice only at noontime and work in the garden after school. Becky, Sarah, Winifred, Cynthia, and I had planned to meet at school on Saturday mornings to practice and eat dinner together. But then the students in my class had their graded term papers returned. I got a B because my paper had been turned in late. Sarah got a B- because she used no Latin in her footnotes and she had some grammatical errors. Winifred got a C- because she had no footnotes and several grammatical and spelling errors. When Mr. Griffin announced a second term paper for those scoring below a B, I was glad I had spent those Saturdays at the library trying to do an excellent job.

Sarah and Winifred had to drop out of Saturday practice in order to write another research paper. Cynthia had somehow found time in her chaotic life to write an A paper about Mount Etna. But she decided to spend Saturdays visiting Gwen instead of practicing. So Becky and I spent Saturday mornings at the school running and jumping and then eating a bag dinner.

One Saturday, two weeks before the scheduled competition, as Becky and I sat talking on the grass over dinner, Miss Harris and Miss Burke stopped their carriage beside the school. Miss Harris waved and went into the school and Miss Burke came to chat with Becky and me. When Miss Harris emerged from the building, she jogged over waving a stop watch and said, "Let's see what you can do."

I jumped up and asked, "Will you call ready, set, go?"

"Certainly," replied Miss Harris.

"Would you like me to jot down your times and distances?" asked Miss Burke.

"Oh, yes!" we chimed.

"Okay. Fifty yards. Becky goes first. Give me a minute to get to the finish line," said Miss Burke.

She held up her right arm from the 50-yard mark. When she said "GO" and dropped her arm, she also started the stop watch. Becky ran as fast as she could and crossed the finish line in 8.1 seconds. Miss Burke congratulated her. Becky walked back to the starting line as I took my mark. Miss Burke's arm came down and I ran my fastest. 7.5 seconds.

When we were all back together, Miss Harris asked how much coaching the girls had received from Coach Wells.

"Well, he pretty much just supervises us," I replied. "Sometimes we overhear instructions he gives the boys. One time he showed the boys how to get in starting position with their hands on the ground, heads up, and feet staggered for a fast start. Some of us girls tried it and I think it helped. But then Coach said the next day that girls weren't allowed to start that way because it was undignified and indecent to stand with our petticoats all up in the air."

"So the girls haven't been given their running suits yet?" asked Miss Harris.

Becky and I looked at each other in confusion. "We just run in our school clothes," said Becky, "but so do the boys."

"Boys' school attire is better-suited to running," said Miss Harris. "Beginning Monday I will be here after school to coach the girls in their running suits."

Now that we had a girls' coach I decided to stay after school for practice every day until after the competition. After all, I had planted all the crops and I could water and weed just before supper. Becky said she would be at Monday's practice, too. Sarah and Winifred were allowed also, in spite of their still-incomplete second research papers. Cynthia said she could stay for an hour only and for only two weeks. Her responsibilities at work and home would not allow more time.

So Monday after school we girls reported to the playground and lined up behind the boys, as usual. Coach Wells began leading the group in exercises. Before we finished the fifteen-minute warm-up, Miss Harris came running onto the field wearing a blue cotton one-piece outfit, similar to a swimsuit but with a bit more fabric all over. In one hand she carried a cloth duffle bag. Miss Harris stopped next to Coach Wells and dropped the bag on the ground.

"Take your boys now, Coach," she said. "We girls have work to do."

Coach blew a short blast on his whistle and the boys took off running laps around the field.

Miss Harris opened the duffle and began pulling running suits out one at a time. She looked inside the neck of each garment for the size. Then she scanned the group of girls and called someone forward who would fit into that suit. Soon all sixteen girls had an outfit and there were some still left in the bag.

Miss Harris handed the duffle to me and sent all us girls running into the building to change in her classroom. When the first girls began to arrive outside, Miss Harris began coaching them in the starting position for the dash. She gave them pointers for cutting their time, such as "don't slow down until you cross the finish line."

Miss Burke stood at the finish line with her stop watch and a clip board. She wrote down the base time for each girl on the team. Then Miss Harris said she wanted each girl to shave a full second from her time by the competition. Miss Harris would teach us how to do that.

Then the group went to the jumping area, a long pit filled with sand. Each girl did the standing broad jump and Miss Burke wrote down the distance between the jumping board and the heel of the girl's backmost shoe. Miss Harris told the girls she wanted them to jump six inches farther by the competition. She said she would teach us how.

The next event we practiced was the running broad jump. Miss Harris showed us how to pace our approach so that we hit the board exactly right. Then she asked each girl to jump and Miss Burke recorded her base distance. Miss Harris would show us how to increase our distance by up to three feet.

Last of all we practiced the softball throw. Most of the girls threw like girls, of course. Miss Harris demonstrated how to get more distance from our throws. Then each girl made her best effort and Miss Burke measured the distance and wrote it on the clipboard.

It was now close to five o'clock and the boys had already gone home. We girls wanted to keep practicing but it was time to go. Miss Harris sent us into the building to change our clothes. We were to leave our running suits in our desks for practice tomorrow.

Miss Harris, Miss Burke, Becky, a couple of other girls, and I were still talking on the playground when one of the sixth-graders came running out of the building crying.

"Someone's taken all our clothes! My mother will be so angry! My dress was nearly new. And what will we wear home? Oh, who would do such a thing?"

Becky and I looked at each other and said, "The boys." We all went inside and searched the school. The clothing was nowhere. The duffle with the extra uniforms was also missing. Miss Harris sent all the girls home in their running suits and called the police.

37

Gram received a phone call from Miss Harris at about seven o'clock that evening. She was calling all the girls who had telephones to let their parents know what had happened. Miss Harris told Gram that the police had taken the names and addresses of all the boys on the track team. They would go to each home in search of the missing duffle, four running suits, and sixteen dresses with petticoats. The police also wanted the names of anyone who might have a grudge against someone on the team. Miss Harris left Officer Franklin's telephone number with Gram in case she needed it.

Gram and I sat at the kitchen table over dessert. We speculated about who could have had both opportunity and motive. I said I had immediately accused the boys. But now that I thought more about it, I doubted it was any of them. First, they had supported the girls' athletic program all along. Second, I considered most of them my personal friends. Third, the boys on the track team were also good students and of high moral character, like me. I could think of no motive among any of them.

I began to think about opportunity. All the boys had been busy on the field until just before the girls went home. I had seen the boys scatter and leave and had not noticed anyone going into the building. The culprit had to have a grudge or some other motive like sale of the stolen property. The thief had to be able to gather all the items, stuff them into the duffle, and carry it away without anyone noticing. The duffle must have been quite heavy. So it had to be an adult or upper-grader or more than one student. Of course, everyone on the team was absorbed in their practice on the playground and paying no attention to the comings and goings around the building.

"I hate to say this," I said, "but Frances has had a grudge against me since the beginning of the year. Since she was embarrassed about her and her mother's behavior at the Valentine dance, she has become brooding and distant with everyone. Even her friends don't spend time with her anymore. But she has stopped taunting the other students. She's the only student I can think of who is hateful enough to do something like this. But I don't want to accuse her without some evidence. I didn't see her anywhere around school this afternoon."

"Well, this is a terrible crime," said Gram. "Some of those girls lost their only school clothes. I think I will report Frances as a suspect anyway. Let the police render her guiltless." And Gram called Officer Franklin with the name Frances Conner.

I worried the whole rest of the evening and into the night about accusing Frances. What if she was innocent and this drove her more into herself? What if she found out that I named her? Would she call me names again? Would she add other words like snitch-baby and liar? I felt my stomach churning.

I wished I had not said anything. I wished I had let the others speculate about the thief and kept my own thoughts to myself.

On Tuesday there was much talk about the theft. All the students who hadn't yet heard about it, soon had their ideas about who had motive and opportunity. Ideas ranged from Coach Wells and Principal Owens to Mr. Griffin and the custodian. No one mentioned Frances. I again wished I hadn't been so eager to point a finger.

I had first suspected the boys and said so. So I had to apologize to each of them. Then I had accused Frances and would need to apologize to her. I worried and worried all morning during class. But then I decided I must face up to my snap judgment of Frances and ask her forgiveness.

At dinnertime, before sitting down to eat, I sought her out. She was sitting on the lawn alone looking terribly dejected.

"Frances," I said, "I was looking for you."

"Well," she said, "you found me."

"I want to apologize."

"What for?"

"It just seems like we got off on the wrong foot. And ever since then I've been quick to judge you and jump to conclusions," I said. "I just want to apologize for anything I've done to hurt you."

Frances stared a cold, hard look off into the distance. She made no eye-contact with me.

"Thanks," she said. And she took another bite of her sandwich.

I stood there a moment waiting for something more, but not knowing what.

"What *do* you want *now*," snapped Frances.

"Nothing," I said sadly. "Goodbye."

I walked a short distance away and turned to look at her again. She was dressed in a pretty lavender dress with tiny sprigs of leaves embroidered all over it. Her hair ribbon nearly matched. I wondered where she had found such a color of ribbon embroidered so intricately with small buds and leaves. Certainly there were none like it at Kress. I wished she were that beautiful on the inside. Her heart must be shriveled and black. What could have caused her such pain and distrust?

The girls and I ate our dinner and practiced running and jumping on the playground. When classes resumed, everyone was in his or her seat except Frances. I worried and fretted that I had somehow hurt her to the point that she had gone home.

After school we girls changed into our track suits and bundled our clothing, carrying them with us to the field. We lined up behind the boys and did our warm-up exercises. Miss Harris came walking across the field with a duffle bag. She stood next to Coach Wells and had him dismiss his boys. Then she held up one item at a time from the bag and the owner went forward to claim it.

Finally, someone asked, "Who took our things and how did you get them back?"

"The police recovered them this afternoon," Miss Harris said. "It isn't important who took them. However, it is important that two of the girls in this group had the courage to give the police information that led to the recovery of your property."

"What will happen to the thief?" asked Becky.

"The thief is getting the help he or she needs," said Miss Harris.

We girls were unusually subdued for the rest of the day, thankful to have running on which to focus.

Tuesday evening Becky came to the front door. Gram answered her knock and sent her around back to the garden. I was sprinkling the plants and examining the tender shoots that were reaching for the sunlight.

"Dorrance," said Becky, "I know who it was. I know who took our clothes."

"Really," I said, keeping my head down and acting as if I didn't care.

"It was Buttons. Abigail in my class saw her wearing a ribbon Abigail's grandmother had sent from back East. The police went to Buttons' house at dinnertime and found everything hidden in her closet. I still can't figure out who else told the police about her, though."

"I guess it doesn't really matter, does it?" I asked.

"No, I guess not. I heard something else."

"What?" I asked, but not really wanting to hear more gossip.

"Buttons turned herself in at dinnertime, before the police got back to the school. She said to tell the girls she was sorry for anything she did to hurt them."

I got up from the ground and held Becky tight.

"Thanks," I said.

"You're welcome," said Becky, "I knew that would cheer you up."

School seemed emptier now that Frances wasn't sitting in the front seat. I had become accustomed to her taunts and realized that the negative attention had also been appreciated. I often thought of her after that, imagining her sitting alone in a jail cell. I felt kind of sorry that she was no longer among us.

38

The last week before the track and field tournament was a busy one for me. I went to practices after school and played softball at recess. At home I practiced the cello, took care of Button, weeded and watered the garden, did my household chores and laundry, wrote to Mama, and gave my homework only cursory attention. I wished I could settle down in a chair with a good book. I remembered when I first entered Gram's library in August. My goal had been to read every book. But as my life filled with school, job, friends, and other activities, my reading time had become less and less.

I had spent some time studying the Gospels, trying to find out how Jesus felt about sapphism. I also read many magazine articles and geography accounts of the Amazon Valley when I was writing my research report. But when I counted the literature from Gram's library, I realized I had read fewer than a dozen books.

"Oh, well," I sighed. "School will soon be out for the summer. I'll have lots of time then. I'd better get a good night's sleep tonight so I'll be rested for the track meet tomorrow."

Then I remembered I hadn't told Gram about the change in tomorrow's event. I found her in the parlor reading.

"Gram, there's been a change of location for the track meet tomorrow. Are you still planning to go?"

"Well, that depends where it's going to be," she answered. "Los Angeles is definitely out of the question."

"Not that far," I said and laughed. "It's going to be at the field that Bakersfield College shares with Kern County High School on California Avenue."

"It's a good thing Aunt Marilyn is coming," said Gram. "She can drive us in her carriage."

"I'll ride over with the Gaines girls," I said, "because the athletes have to be there early."

"I must say I'm surprised at this last minute change," said Gram. "The school spent quite a bit of money to put in the jumping pits and to be sure the running surfaces were smooth and well-marked. It also is sure to create a hardship on some of the participants. Just think how much farther people like Cynthia will have to walk."

"It was a sort of last resort, you might say. I might as well tell you the whole story, although it's kind of an unsavory tale to go to sleep on," I teased with a smile.

"That's all right. You know I like to hear all the scuttlebutt from school," replied Gram.

"Okay, then," I began. "First of all, Mr. Owens came back to school today, the day before the competition, and a Friday at that. Someone said he took the splint off his leg early just so he could be there to put a stop to the girls' participation. Anyway, at dinner recess he limped out to the field and talked to Coach Wells and Miss Harris.

"He told Miss Harris thank you for working with the girls. And then he said she wouldn't be needed any more. He said this was the last day of the girls' program.

"Then he turned to Coach Wells to ask about the plans for the boys' competition tomorrow. Coach told him, 'There are no plans for a boys' competition tomorrow. There are plans only for a school competition for boys and girls.'

"Then Mr. Owens said, 'I just told you the girls will not participate.'

"Then Coach Wells said, 'Then neither will the boys.'

222

"Then Mr. Owens said, 'You're fired. I'll run the competition myself!' And he limped off toward the building."

"Oh, my," said Gram. "Why didn't you tell me this sooner? When you first came home from school, for instance?"

"Well, because it all worked out okay, in the end," I said.

"Tell me the rest, then!" exclaimed Gram.

"After Mr. Owens went inside, all the boys and girls made hysterical and angry threats against the principal. The students weren't willing to simply boycott this time. Some of the boys wanted to soap the windows of Mr. Owens' house. Some of the students wanted to call him on the telephone all night so he couldn't sleep. Red wanted to call the reporter from *The Bakersfield Californian*.

"Coach Wells and Miss Harris stepped aside and talked for awhile. Coach Wells went into the school to make a phone call. When he returned to the field Coach called everyone to attention and said, 'I work at Bakersfield College. We have an excellent track and field area with a spectator section. It's not being used tomorrow. I just signed our group up to have the competition there. However, it needs to be an independent competition. Otherwise it could be viewed as insubordination to defy Principal Owens' decision. You boys may compete here tomorrow, under Principal Owens' leadership if you wish. Everyone is invited to participate at the college. Athletes should be there by nine o'clock so you will have time to register. The competition will begin at ten o'clock. The number of events will depend on how many sign up for each.'

"Then Miss Harris stepped forward and asked for suggestions on what the competition should be called. There were lots of suggestions but we finally decided on the Children's Co-Educational Track and Field Meet. Then Coach Wells said interested students should come to the sidewalk across from the school after dismissal today. He would be able to confirm by then if the Meet would really happen. We all went to class and Coach Wells left. Miss Harris went to the office and made a phone call."

"Do tell me what happened after school," pleaded Gram.

I laughed at Gram's look of anticipation and then continued.

"After school *everyone* on the team met across the street. Coach Wells and Miss Burke were there. She had filed for a business license to conduct athletic programs for boys and girls. Coach Wells had reserved the field in the name of the business. Miss Harris had guaranteed the rental fee. Miss Burke ordered ribbons and trophies. They are to be delivered to the field by ten o'clock tomorrow. Miss Burke called Logan's Grocery who promised to deliver concessions by nine o'clock. The money cleared from concession sales will go to pay for the rental and awards.

"And this is maybe the best part — there is to be a story in tomorrow's paper with a follow-up on Sunday."

"I still can't believe you waited until bedtime to tell me all this," reprimanded Gram.

"I'm sorry, Gram," I said. "I guess I didn't realize how much you liked hearing the school news."

"Of course, I like hearing about it. I worked for years for women's rights. It's wonderful to see you continuing the work," said Gram.

At nine o'clock Saturday morning the college field was crowded with all sixteen girl athletes and 31 of the 33 boy athletes. Many parents were on hand to help with concessions, organize events, and register athletes. Miss Burke was giving the athletes cloth numbers to be pinned to the backs of their shirts when they registered. The athletes roamed around the field looking at the track, the jumping pits, and the softball-throw area. The spectator stands began to fill as early as nine-fifteen. The athletes chatted about how this setting made them feel the competition was being taken seriously. Someone joked about Mr. Owens' track meet that morning with only two boys.

Just before nine-thirty Uncle Sabert tapped me on the shoulder. When I spun around, he caught me in his arms and swung me around. Then he whispered in my ear, "I have the morning edition in the truck." Then, seeing all my friends around me, he said, "Tomorrow I'll have the Sunday edition. We'll look at them both at breakfast. I'd better take my seat now."

I hugged Uncle and said, "I'm *so* happy Andrew and Jack are watching the store so you can be here. Tell them thanks a million times."

We athletes began to warm up. At precisely ten o'clock the first event was called. For the next three hours we showed off our best efforts. The fans cheered. The concessions disappeared. The parents assigned to janitorial duty pulled gunny sacks behind them, picking up candy wrappers, popcorn sacks, and soda bottles.

At two o'clock awards were announced. Event records were established by the winners of each event. Those records would stand until someone in a future competition of the Children's Co-Educational Sports Foundation broke the record.

Of the girls' events, I set records in the 50-yard dash at 6.9 seconds, the 100-yard dash at 11.3 seconds, and the softball-throw at 218 feet. Becky set the standing broad jump record at 5'2". Cynthia set the running broad jump record of 13'7".

The boys' records were all slightly faster in running and slightly longer in jumping. But my softball throw beat the closest boy competitor by 27 feet. It stood as an all-city record until it was broken in 1923 by a 15-year-old boy.

Everyone who competed earned a ribbon of honorable mention. Second and third place winners won large ribbons in either red or white. First place winners in each event received a small trophy. The athlete with the most overall points won a large trophy. Red carried that away by taking first in boys' standing and running broad jumps, the 100-yard dash, and the 400-yard relay.

When Gram and I sat down to supper that night, talking about the events of the day, Gram said, "You know, the Children's Co-Educational Track and Field Meet was a true miracle. In just twenty-four hours the whole event was planned and executed. It's amazing what can be accomplished by a community committed to a single purpose."

39

April 19 was the Sunday after the track meet and before the School Board Meeting. When Uncle Sabert, Auntie, Gwen, and the boys arrived for breakfast, we all sat down to discuss *The Bakersfield Californian* stories. Saturday's story highlighted the Franklin students and their continuing struggle for equality in athletics. The story was very supportive of Coach Wells, Miss Harris, and Miss Burke in their actions to allow girls to compete.

Sunday's paper listed all the event winners and participants. It named Red as overall athlete. A small paragraph at the bottom stated that all athletes from Franklin School had chosen to participate in the Co-Ed Meet. It also said, "Two boys did not participate on Saturday due to chicken pox."

"Wow!" I said. "That's the first time every student stood together."

"Yes, and look at all the parents who were there in support," said Uncle.

"The School Board Meeting on Thursday night should be very interesting," added Auntie.

Uncle Sabert and I began our Sunday rounds. Some of the customers had seen my name in the paper as winner of three events. They praised me and teased me about my

227

strength and speed "likely developed on your Sunday delivery route." I had not laughed so much in a long time. I felt encouraged about life and loved by these once-a-week friends.

At Mr. Clark's, he and Cynthia had prepared a celebration party. Mr. Clark was so proud of "his girls" that he wanted to do something special. He had frozen ice cream and Cynthia had baked a chocolate cake. The cake had "Hurray for Girls' Athletics" written in white icing. The ice cream was vanilla with shredded chocolate.

The four of us ate and talked for more than an hour. I invited Mr. Clark to attend the School Board Meeting, as I had all my customers. I didn't expect anyone to go because of transportation difficulties, but I hoped they might write letters in support of girls' athletics.

Cynthia and I hugged each other goodbye. She told me again how happy she was to be living with Mr. Clark.

"It's like having a loving grandfather," she said. "Now I understand how you must feel about living with your great-grandmother. It's simply grand, isn't it?"

I thought about Cynthia's words all the way home. Again I really appreciated my life in Bakersfield. I had love and security. I had opportunities that would never have been available to me in Fish Lake Valley or Bishop. I had support in my activism for women's rights. I was accepted as a sapphist by those who knew, with the exception of Frances. I had a plethora of loyal friends. The more I counted my blessings, the better I felt.

Uncle Sabert saw the smile on my face and said, "After the rain, the rainbow. It's God's promise."

I came home immediately after school on Monday, running the last half-block when I noticed Uncle Sabert's carriage out front. Aunt Marilyn and Gram were in the parlor chatting.

"There she is," said Auntie. "I have something exciting to show you." Auntie produced a stack of papers an inch thick. She handed them to me and waited while I read the top sheet.

"These are letters addressed to the School Board," I said.

"Yes," said Auntie. "People have been giving them to me since the basketball boycott. They want me to present them at the School Board Meeting. They're all in favor of girls' athletics."

I read through the letters quickly, looking at each signature. Some signatures I recognized as parents of students at Franklin School. Some I didn't recognize at all, but were obviously known to Uncle and Auntie. Here was one from Mr. Griffin and one from Miss Scott in the office. There were others from long-time citizens of Bakersfield.

I looked at Auntie in awe. "All these people want girls' athletics. We can't possibly lose the support of the School Board now," I said.

"Hopefully the Board will listen to the people," said Aunt Marilyn. "But there is one problem. The Board has a five-minute rule. Since these letters will take much longer than that to read into the record, we need readers — people who are willing to stand before the Board for five minutes and read letters. I think we'll need at least ten. Sabert will give people rides in the delivery truck. We thought the athletes would be the perfect readers. What do you think, Dorrance?"

"I know Red will read. He's planning to go anyway, and he's not at all shy about speaking in front of people. The rest of the athletes I'll have to ask. Will we be allowed to say our own message to the Board as well?"

"Of course," said Auntie. "Everyone is encouraged to speak to the Board on their own behalf, too. I intend to alert the Board that it will need to be a long session, since many citizens will want to be heard."

At school the next day, I asked the athletes to be readers at the School Board Meeting. I was overwhelmed by the response. The first ten people I asked committed to attend. Even those afraid to speak before the class said they would read letters if they could practice ahead of time. I divided the letters among the athletes and told them to meet at the school at six o'clock Thursday evening. I invited the rest of the athletes to go also, to make a strong showing for the Board. Everyone was encouraged to speak to the Board about why girls' athletics should be supported.

On Wednesday I reminded everyone of the meeting. I did the same on Thursday. One athlete reader was absent from school on Thursday. But later in the day his mother delivered the letters to me. I was able to find a last-minute replacement.

Uncle Sabert and I were at the school at five-forty-five. Uncle had filled the back of the truck with hay bales, so everyone could sit down without mussing their good clothes. Everyone was on time and in good spirits. Uncle spoke to parents as the students were dropped off. He encouraged them to attend the meeting at seven o'clock. Then, with everyone on board, Uncle Sabert drove downtown to the courthouse. The meeting location had been changed so there would be ample seating.

The athletes entered the courtroom with hushed voices and took seats up front. We were the only ones there at six-forty and even Uncle Sabert wondered if we were in the right place. Then a page came in and placed nameplates of the School Board members on the judge's bench. Five chairs were carried in for the Board members. The page set pitchers of water and glasses out on the judge's bench and at the speaker's podium. While this setting-up took place, citizens quietly filed in and took seats behind the students.

I saw Aunt Marilyn and Gram, Mr. Clark, Miss Harris, Miss Burke, Coach Wells, parents of several athletes, Mr. Griffin, the school custodian, Miss Scott, and many others. At precisely seven o'clock the School Board members took their seats. Last of all, Mr. Owens limped in and took a seat near the door.

The Chairman of the School Board rapped his gavel and called the meeting to order. As the secretary read the minutes of the last meeting, I tried to read the faces of the Board members. I decided Aunt Marilyn was right. They were a bunch of "old geezers" — all bearded, gray-haired men in black suits. There was not a smile among them. I noticed they all had worry-lines between their eyes, but none had laugh-lines at the corners. They made me nervous. I turned in my seat to look at Aunt Marilyn. Auntie smiled and held up her right thumb. That eased my nerves some.

Once the minutes were approved, the roll called, and the agenda read, the meeting began in earnest. Aunt Marilyn approached the speaker's podium.

"My name is Marilyn Logan. I respectfully request a change in the order of the agenda. As you can see, there are several school children here to address the Board. As it is a school night, I request the matter of girls' athletics be moved to the first order of business, so the children can get a good night's sleep."

Chairman Barker denied the request saying, "If the children need to leave before their topic is called, it will be continued to the fall meeting."

Aunt Marilyn said, "I request the change in agenda order be put to a vote of those present."

"Madam, do you intend to continue to waste the time of this Board? Or will you be seated so we can conduct business?"

"Mr. Barker, I intend to continue to waste the time of the Board until this matter is put to a vote," said Aunt Marilyn in a well-modulated and calm voice.

"Madam, there are very few here who have the right to vote at a School Board meeting," said Mr. Barker as if talking to a kindergartner, "namely the Board members. Now please take a seat or I will have you removed from the room."

Aunt Marilyn quietly walked to her seat, head held high, as Mr. Griffin took her place at the podium.

"My name is Jim Bob Griffin. I'm a teacher at Franklin School. And I have the right to vote you out of office in the fall. I believe you, Mr. Barker, and Mr. Smith, and Mr. Nevell are all up for re-election. Please put the agenda matter to a vote of the eligible voters present at this meeting."

"Mr. Griffin is it? I don't know where you come from," said Mr. Barker imitating Mr. Griffin's southern drawl, "but in the West we don't threaten elected officials." Mr. Barker was obviously amused with himself because he snickered and looked at his fellow Board members for support.

"Mr. Barker, I am from the great State of Mississippi. And in the South we know how to treat women with respect. In addition, the School Board is charged with serving children. It appears all you gentlemen are interested in serving is your own self-aggrandizement."

Until this moment the audience had been quiet and respectful. But when Mr. Griffin said the words "self-aggrandizement" the crowd erupted in loud applause. Mr Jones from *The Bakersfield Californian* snapped pictures of the Board members, Mr. Griffin, and the crowd. I saw the tiny tablet peeking out of his shirt pocket. I knew he had taken down every word and that the morning edition would be ever so entertaining.

Mr. Barker and the others had evidently seen the reporter, too. Soon the five Board members huddled together whispering and glancing at the audience.

Then Mr. Barker responded, "Very well, we'll put it to a vote of anyone over the age of twenty-one."

Mr. Smith asked, "All those in favor of hearing the girls' athletics question first, please say aye."

"Excuse me, Mr. Smith," interrupted Mr. Griffin. "I respectfully request a hand count so as to be absolutely certain of who is voting and what the final count is."

Mr. Smith sighed audibly and looked to Mr. Barker for direction. Mr. Barker threw his hands in the air in defeat and said, "A show of hands, Mr. Smith."

Mr. Smith again called for the vote saying, "All those in favor of hearing the girls' athletics question first, please raise your hands."

Mr. Nevell and Mr. Griffin, in addition to Mr. Smith counted hands. The consensus was that there were 14 votes in favor.

"All those against, raise your hands," said Mr. Smith. The five Board members and Mr. Owens made six votes against. So at seven-twenty-five the meeting finally began. Mr. Barker called the first speaker to the podium.

I took a deep breath to steady my nerves and walked confidently to the podium.

"My name is Dorrance Chegwidden. I'm an eighth-grade student at Franklin School and an athlete with the Children's Co-Educational Sports Foundation. I wish to say that I'm in favor of allotting a budget amount for girls' athletics equal to the amount allotted for boys' athletics. I also have letters from citizens in the community and addressed to the School Board which I will now read into the record." I articulately read five letters including one from the mayor.

"Thank you," I said and took my seat.

Each of the ten readers followed my lead and spoke at the podium. Some, such as Becky, were perspiring and pale with fright. But they, nevertheless, presented their letters well. Then the grown-ups began to speak one at a time.

Mr. Griffin spoke about how participation in extra-curricular activities in general, and athletics in particular, helps children excel in academics. He cited particular improvements in scores of students who took part in track and field.

Miss Harris spoke about the students' desires to see everyone treated equally, as called for in the Constitution of the United States.

Mr. Clark spoke about the improved attitude and work ethic of those who participate in athletics. He specifically named Cynthia and me and told the Board what our accomplishments included.

On and on, the speakers came forward with reasons for girls and boys to participate in athletics. At nine-forty the speakers in favor of athletics finished speaking.

Mr. Owens approached the podium.

"Athletics make girls aggressive," he shouted. "Why, my ankle was broken in a playground fracas over girls' athletics! As for athletics being responsible for better grades, how can students improve grades by taking them away from their studies? And why would girls need a better work ethic to stay home and care for their husbands and children? Quite the contrary. Athletics will encourage women to compete with men in the work place. Just think what would happen if women took all the good jobs. Men wouldn't be able to support their families!"

Then from the back of the room someone shouted, "It sounds like you're afraid you can't compete with a woman, Mr. Owens. Are you afraid you'll lose your job to Miss Harris?"

The crowd laughed until the rafters shook as Mr. Barker pounded his gavel and called for order.

Mr. Owens shook his finger at the speaker and yelled, "You just wait! You'll see! It'll be just like when the slaves got free and took up all the best western lands. If women get the national vote, they'll be running everything!"

The crowd again erupted in laughter. At that point, Mr. Barker completely lost control of the meeting and adjourned with no action taken.

Friday morning Uncle Sabert came running up the walk waving the paper. "I've got the morning edition," he called.

Gram and Uncle and I gathered around the kitchen table reading over one another's shoulders. Jones had done some investigative reporting and found out some incriminating evidence. An unnamed source said "Girls' Athletics" was put last on the agenda on purpose. The Board had planned to drag out other matters so long that the "athletics supporters" would leave, or else the Board would continue the matter to the fall meeting.

Then the article rehashed the arguments on both sides. It concluded it was only a matter of time before girls' athletics *and* women's suffrage were approved by the public: "The fact that the School Board adjourned without action is only a postponement of the inevitable."

40

School on Friday was full of talk about the School Board Meeting. The students who spoke were glad they had their say, even though the Board took no action. I felt a particular closeness to Mr. Griffin. He had changed over the year to being less of a pompous disciplinarian. I especially liked the fact that he took the time to analyze athletes' academic performance. Although it wasn't sophisticated research, it meant he had kept an open mind. It also took courage for him to speak at the Board meeting. As a new teacher this year, it could cost him his job.

I recognized that I had some strong allies at Franklin School — and in a month I would graduate to high school. There, I would have to meet students from all over Kern County. I would have to establish my place in a whole new community of students and teachers. One thing I was sure of was that I would live with Gram until I was out of high school.

I knew that I was obligated to go to Independence this summer. I was scheming to see just how short I could make the visit. Given my druthers, I would rather not go at all. But I was sure a railroad ticket would arrive before long, sealing my fate. I also knew that I longed to see Mama and that my reluctance to reconnect was simply my fear of change. As long as I stayed with Gram, I could imagine life in Fish Lake Valley just as I remembered it — just me and Mama together.

My studies had gone well all year. I was self-disciplined now and managed to participate in all the activities I chose, still making time for chores, school work, and job. I was counting the days until summer vacation so I could enjoy some leisure time. Then the school books would not cover the desktop, always calling me away from thoughts of reading for pleasure.

I yearned to spend more time with the cello, too. I had never once gone to practice with the Gaines girls. Uncle had recently begun paying me an hourly wage of 15 cents in lieu of further lessons. It was now my responsibility to build on what Uncle had taught me about the cello. Improvement would only be accomplished through practice.

I wanted to spend time alone with Becky. I wanted to go for walks, attend concerts in the park, picnic, skinny-dip, shoot my slingshot, go fishing — do anything unrelated to school, work, chores, and crowds of other kids. I could hardly wait until June.

But first there was May to get through. I must perform well on final examinations. Then there was the eighth-grade graduation ceremony, followed by high school orientation. While preparing for these grand events, I must be sure the garden didn't die and Button was properly nourished and nurtured. My time with Becky was confined to school dinners and Saturday mornings.

I thought, "What will we do next year? We'll be attending separate schools. Saturdays will just not be enough."

Each night I marked another day in May off my calendar. After school I did homework and household chores. In the evening I weeded and watered the garden. Then I walked Button and played fetch with him. I saw Gram at supper and sometimes at breakfast. Saturday morning Becky read to me as I worked in the garden. Afternoons were beginning to be hot. So at noon Becky and I took a picnic dinner to the park or the river. Saturday evenings I practiced the cello, wrote to Mama, and studied. Sundays were filled with Gram's delicious breakfasts and afternoon deliveries. And then another week was over and summer vacation was that much closer.

Finally the last week of school arrived. I had one final exam each day, beginning with math on Monday. Tuesday was history and geography. Wednesday was grammar and spelling. Thursday was devoted to creative writing and handwriting. Friday was a kind of trivia contest in which each student was graded on items answered correctly. Questions included math problems, parsing sentences, identifying locations on a variety of maps, as well as questions relating to health, history, and current events. The exams were challenging and a couple of students confided to me that they feared they would not graduate.

On Monday, June 1, 1914, the results of the final exams were posted on the classroom door for all to see. Those who did poorly suffered the humiliation of everyone knowing. I scored 100 in math, 96 in history and geography, 98 in grammar and spelling, 95 in writing, and 99 in trivia. Cynthia, Red, and I tied with an overall score of 97.6 percent. We would wear special stoles around our necks at Thursday's graduation ceremony.

The lower grades finished classes on May 27th, so Becky was able to attend graduation ceremonies on Thursday morning at ten o'clock at the school auditorium.

Only two students from Mr. Griffin's class were held back — the two who had confided to me that they feared failing. I felt badly for them, but also acknowledged that they had not applied themselves all year. It was simply a matter of logical consequences. One must master self-discipline in order to survive higher education.

By nine-thirty Thursday morning, the auditorium was filled with proud parents and friends of the twenty-eight graduates. Red, Cynthia, and I stood in the rear of the auditorium, ready to lead the procession of students to their seats in the first two rows.

When *Pomp and Circumstance* was played on the piano, we sedately marched to our seats. The Reverend of the Presbyterian Church led the audience in prayer. Mr. Owens gave a long, boring speech about "bright futures for all those who persevered." Then the pianist played *Eine Kleine Nacktmusik* (an unusual selection, I thought) and each student was called forward to receive the grammar school diploma, as Mr. Griffin read the accomplishments of each.

I admired Mr. Griffin again for his resourcefulness in making each student feel valued and important. After all the diplomas had been awarded, another Reverend gave the benediction. The pianist played another inappropriate piece and we students filed out.

Outside in the sunshine we all greeted our families and received hugs, handshakes, and pats on the back. And we finalized plans to meet that evening at high school orientation. I removed my gold stole and handed it to Mr. Griffin. It would be used again next year by the top graduate.

"It's been a pleasure, Dorrance, to have you in my class," said Mr. Griffin. "You know, they say the teacher always learns more than the pupil. That was certainly true for me this year, largely because of you."

I was stunned to be so praised. What could I say?

"Thank you, Mr. Griffin. I learned a great deal from you also," I finally managed to say. But my eyes sparkled with gratitude in response to Mr. Griffin's approval.

"I wish you success and happiness in your life," he said. "I know you're capable of much. One person can sometimes influence great transformation. You're a leader who inspires others to be extraordinary."

Then Mr. Griffin patted my shoulder gently and walked toward the building, speaking to no one else.

I was ready and waiting on the front porch when Uncle Sabert arrived to escort me to orientation. As I walked toward the carriage, Uncle jumped down and asked me to come into the house with him. Then he and Gram made a big to-do about presenting me with a graduation gift. *THE* cello was now *MY* cello. I smiled and cried and thanked Gram and

Uncle over and over. Gram handed me a clean hankie to take along and wipe my tears and nose. I was so surprised and moved that I cried most of the way to orientation. I remembered the hankie Uncle and I shared on my first day in Bakersfield. It made me smile.

As the carriage pulled up in front of the school, I saw Sarah, Winifred, and Red entering the building. There were also dozens of students I didn't recognize.

"I'll pick you up at nine o'clock," said Uncle. "Have a good time."

Inside the large meeting room, there were five long tables with paper nameplates for each school. All students would sit with their grammar school classmates tonight. I took a seat between Cynthia and Sarah. We chatted excitedly with the others at our table. Then I began watching students at the other tables. I thought I recognized someone at the end of the third table. There were still a few minutes until orientation started, so I excused myself and walked over. As I drew near I realized I did, in fact, know this girl. But I also noticed a change in her. This girl was smiling and chatting. She was dressed in a simple calico dress. Her hair was in a long braid down her back, just as I wore my own hair.

I approached slowly, drinking in the positive energy emanating from that end of the table. Then the girl turned and looked into my eyes.

"Dorrance!" said Frances, "I was hoping I'd see you here tonight."

"Frances, it's good to see you so well and happy."

Frances excused herself from the table and we stepped to the back of the room where there was more privacy.

"Dorrance, I want to ask your forgiveness for all the hurt I caused you with my silly name-calling and for refusing your attempts to be friends."

"Of course, I forgive you," I said. "What's happened to make you so much happier? If it's not too personal, that is."

"You're the only one I'll tell because I know I can trust you to keep my confidence."

But before Frances could go on, the orientation was called to order.

"Meet me after," she said as she walked to her table.

I quickly took my seat, also.

The orientation was interesting enough, but I had trouble focusing as my curiosity about Frances grew. I took notes on what all the speakers said so I could review them before school began in the fall. The biggest difference between grammar school and high school was the number of teachers, one for each subject. I was also allowed to choose one of my classes, called an elective. As I filled in my schedule card, with *intramural sports* as my elective, I knew I would again be embroiled in controversy when school started. Only boys were allowed to enroll in *intramural sports*. At about eight-forty-five the meeting was adjourned and the attendees invited to enjoy refreshments.

I ignored the refreshment table when I saw Frances hurry out the door. I was afraid she would "escape" and I would never find out her story. As I rushed to catch up with her, I almost knocked her down.

"Oh, I'm sorry," I apologized. "I was afraid I'd miss talking with you when I saw you leaving."

Without bothering to accept my apology, Frances launched into her story.

"I owe you so much, Dorrance. When I stole those clothes from the athletes, I began to realize how sick I was. People had told me for months how mean I had become, but I had never done anything illegal before. Every time I did something mean I would lose another friend. I kept telling myself I didn't need anyone. But when you came to me to ask forgiveness, my heart just broke. I had to get the old Frances back. I hated who I had become. So I turned myself in.

"The police took me to a home for kids in trouble. I was able to talk to other kids and some grown-ups about how I was feeling. And I started to get better. After a few weeks I went to stay with a family across town and I went back to school."

"What about your mother?" I asked. "You don't live with her now?"

"Not now. She was a big part of the problems, always criticizing me and other people. I began to think that was how I should act."

"Will you go home eventually?" I asked. "Won't your mother get well, too?"

"I don't know yet. You see, Mother wasn't always the way she is now. I remember when she and Papa used to laugh and play. Times were so good then. But one day Papa left her. She got very angry and depressed. The truth is, Papa rejected her for someone else."

"Oh, my, that's very sad."

"Yes, but instead of forgiving him and looking for happiness again, Mother let her anger take over her life. The anger turned into hatred, against everyone, and she became very abusive with her tongue. She drove all her friends away.

"Mr. Griffin tried to help when he saw my behavior. He talked to Mother a couple of times over dinner. Mother got the idea that Mr. Griffin was trying to court her. He set her straight on his second visit. After he left that night, Mother broke everything in the kitchen. The next day I told Mr. Griffin, but there wasn't much he could do about it. I was so isolated by then that all I could think to do was seek revenge.

Since I couldn't hurt Mother, I stole the athletes' clothing and hid it in my room."

"Oh, Frances, I'm so sorry for all that happened to you." I hugged her as tears sprang from her eyes. "I wish I'd known. We could have shared our sadness and been friends all this time."

"I hope we can be friends from now on," she said.

"I do, too. I want you to know that I'm loyal and won't breathe a word to anyone about what you've told me. I hope you'll do the same with what I'm about to tell you."

"You have my word," said Frances. "I, too, can be loyal."

"I think you should know that I *am* a sapphist," I said.

241

A wide smile spread across Frances's face.

"Of course you are. Why do think I targeted you for my taunts? You were everything I longed to be and couldn't. I acted like I did to hide the real me. I knew my mother would stop loving me if she knew that I'm a sapphist, too."

My mouth dropped open but not a sound emerged as I thought to myself, *My goodness, we are everywhere. And less than a year ago I thought I was the only one.*

"I'm glad we're finally friends, Frances. I'll see you at school in the fall." And I gave her another small hug.

"See you then. I signed up for *intramural sports*." Then she grinned and winked.

The End

Afterword

The events in this story are 100% fiction.

However, certain characters are inspired by my ancestors and life experiences. If you think you recognize yourself within these pages, you are *probably* wrong.

If you actually have inspired me, I hope you find my reflections enlightening.

Dona McAfee Glasscock

November 13, 2014

A Heartfelt Thank You To

All the folks who read or listened to the original manuscript or one
of its many revisions, offering criticism and encouragement,
including: Michelle Pellersels, Jerry Ellis, Donna Bell Sanders,
Janet Peacey, & Janet Dalby.

Don Green for ultimately convincing me to self-publish.

Frances Dayee, my editor, for her discerning eye and constant
encouragement.

Janice Lind, proofreader and typesetter, and her dog, Pugzilla, for
allowing her mistress to devote her time and lap to my final
manuscript.

Steven Layne Grice, fine artist extraordinaire, for taking time out of
his own work to design the cover.

www.ingramcontent.com/pod-product-compliance
Lightning Source LLC
Chambersburg PA
CBHW022108240626
47153CB00007B/2279